"Are you proposing to me? Isn't that unconventional in white society?"

"Where is it written that a woman can't propose?" Josie challenged quietly.

"Nowhere I know. It's what I'd e̶ ̶ ̶ ̶ ̶ ̶ ̶ ̶ ̶ sfit like you…. So I accept."

He draped his arm famil̶ ̶ ̶ ̶ ̶ ̶ ̶ ̶ ̶ ̶ ̶ ̶awing her closer. Ordinarily ̶ ̶ ̶ ̶ ̶ ̶ ̶ ̶ ̶ ̶ ̶away when a man crowded her s̶ ̶ ̶ ̶ ̶ ̶ ̶ ̶ ̶ ̶ver, she didn't object to Tremai̶ ̶ ̶ ̶ ̶ ̶ ̶ ̶ ̶ction.

"You know this is̶ ̶ ̶ ̶ ̶ ̶ ̶ ̶on't you?" Tremain whispered devilishly̶ ̶ ̶ ̶ ̶

"*How much*, Tremain?" s̶ ̶ ̶sked when she saw the wicked gleam in his sea-green eyes and noticed the ornery grin twitching his lips. "I'm saving my funds for improvements on my homestead, *if* I manage to stake one."

"We'll work something out, trust me."

"Just so you know, I don't trust any man's intentions…."

Her voice trailed off when his raven head came slowly and deliberately toward hers. Then he kissed her, satisfying her curiosity—and stirring something wild and hungry deep inside her.

* * *

Oklahoma Wedding Bells
Harlequin® Historical #1115—December 2012

CAROL FINCH

OKLAHOMA WEDDING BELLS

HARLEQUIN®

entertain, enrich, inspire™

ISBN-13: 978-0-373-29715-3

OKLAHOMA WEDDING BELLS

Copyright © 2012 by Connie Feddersen

www.Harlequin.com

Printed in U.S.A.

**Did you know that these novels are also
available as ebooks? Visit www.Harlequin.com.**

This book is dedicated to my husband, Ed, and our children, Jill, Jon, Christie, Durk, Shawnna and Kurt. And to our grandchildren, Livia, Blake, Kennedy and Brooklynn. And to Kurt and Shawnna's children whenever they may be. With much love.

Chapter One

~~~~~~~~~~~~~~~~~~~~

El Reno, Oklahoma Territory
April 1892

Josephine Malloy sat on a rickety wooden bench in the tent city near the river. With practiced strokes, she replaced a button on a worn shirt that would have served better as a rag. Beside her, Muriel Wilson stitched a patch on a tattered jacket for one of their many male customers.

"Brace yourself, Josie," Muriel murmured confidentially when Orson Barnes approached.

Josie inwardly groaned when the big, burly cowboy lumbered toward her. Orson claimed to be twenty-nine, but with a woolly brown beard and mustache covering his face, and a frizzy crop of dark hair surrounding his broad head, it was hard to tell his age. She took his word for it.

Muriel nudged her discreetly. "Why don't you put the poor man out of his misery before he spends all his money ripping buttons off his shirts so you can sew them back on?"

"I'm hoping he'll run out of extra spending money before he works up the nerve to pop the question," she mumbled.

Orson was one of the self-appointed leaders in the tent community—a former soldier who was well respected by the hopeful settlers. Yet he was exceptionally bashful around women. Josie had listened to Orson stammer and hint that a man needed a wife, and that he would be a protective provider and landowner after the run. Maybe today would be the day he proposed and she rejected him....

Her thoughts trailed off when Orson halted in front of her, casting his broad shadow over her. "Mornin', Miz Malloy. You, too, Miz Wilson." His wide smile exposed the noticeable gap between his two front teeth.

Orson chitchatted about the weather and the upcoming race to stake free land in the area that had once belonged to the Cheyenne and Arapaho tribes. Then he inhaled an enormous breath that made his barrel chest double in size. "Miz Malloy, as you've likely noticed, I've become quite fond of you while you've done mending for me."

Here it comes, Josie thought with an inward wince.

"If you'll do me the honor of being my wife after the run, we can stake our one-hundred-sixty-acre claims side by side and have twice as much land to start our new ranch."

Same proposal, one hundredth verse. No, she silently

corrected, one hundred *two*. Muriel was at ninety-nine. With literally thousands of single men swarming the area to chase dreams of building ranches on free land, Josie and Muriel were constantly bombarded with marriage proposals.

It was nothing new, however, Josie reminded herself. She had rejected several hundred proposals before participating in the race for land to help her brother and sister-in-law in the Run of '89....

She was jolted back to the present when Muriel elbowed her in the ribs. Josie raised her gaze to meet Orson's expectant eyes.

"You are too kind to offer for me, Orson. But I don't consider myself good wife material and neither should you," she replied, repeating the practiced rejection speech she'd given literally hundreds of times before. "If you knew me better you would realize I'm much too independent, outspoken and contrary to be a dutiful wife. In addition, it's my dream to have a ranch all my own."

Beside her, Muriel muffled a chuckle with a cough. Josie wasn't sure which quality—her independence, frank speech or contrariness—amused her friend more. She had witnessed examples of each since they had become acquainted and formed their sewing partnership three weeks earlier. At twenty-one, Muriel was well on her way to perfecting those characteristics herself.

As Josie's older brother was fond of saying, a man who tangled with an independent, free-spirited woman had no idea what he was getting himself into. Nevertheless, Noah had married Celia, who was no shrinking violet.

Orson's buffalo-size shoulders slumped dejectedly as he curled and uncurled the brim of his sweat-stained hat in his meaty fists. "Maybe if we spent a little more private time together—"

Josie thrust his mended shirt at him. "No, Orson," she said as gently—but firmly—as possible. "I'll accept payment for repairing this garment, but I can't accept your proposal. It wouldn't be fair to you. I'm very sure that you'll be much happier with someone else."

As had happened often in the past three weeks, her rejected suitor turned to the brunette beside her and flashed his best smile. If Josie or Muriel rejected a man's proposal, he'd immediately transfer his attention to the other woman, as if they were interchangeable. Which served to prove that a man wasn't very particular about whom he acquired for his wife. One female was as good as the next, and Josie refused to let herself forget that.

There were a few exceptions, she conceded. Her brother actually loved Celia.

At twenty-three, Josie had become exceptionally cynical because of several unpleasant experiences with overeager single men who had hounded her before—and immediately after—land runs.

"How 'bout you, Miz Wilson?" Orson asked hopefully. "We would suit well, too, I believe."

"Thank you kindly, but no, Orson," Muriel replied politely. "Like Josie, I fancy being on my own, and I've learned to take care of myself. I'm chasing my own rainbows and I'm not ready to settle down."

"But you can double the amount of land—"

"No, thank you," Josie and Muriel said in unison. "Good luck staking your land claim."

After Orson glumly paid the fee, crammed his mended shirt under his arm and walked off, Josie came to her feet to work the kinks from her back. "I think I'll hike into town for lunch. Want to come along?"

Muriel tucked the patched jacket in the knapsack where they kept their sewing supplies, then tossed the bundle into the tent she and Josie shared for their protection. "One hundred proposals and counting," Muriel muttered. "And not one that interests me."

"Maybe we're too particular. Or shrewish," Josie remarked as she walked alongside her friend. "Getting to know one another doesn't appear to be a prerequisite for marriage in this territory. But I wish men would wait *at least a week* after making our acquaintance before proposing."

"That didn't bother Rachel Winters or Annabelle Mason." Muriel smirked, her golden-brown eyes sparkling with humor. "They paraded up and down the streets in fine fashion to snag husbands. Neither of them knew their new grooms for more than a *day* before getting hitched. Though I wonder why they didn't want to wait until *after* the run to wed. They could have staked their own claims and combined them with their husbands' to double the size of their property."

"There are opportunists galore milling about," Josie

insisted as she led the way up the tree-choked riverbank to reach the bustling community. "But I don't blame the former saloon girls for trying to improve their situations, even if they hurried along their weddings. Extra land was the least of their concerns. They are in their late twenties, from the looks of them, and likely have endured a hard life. *They* were searching for an escape, while *we* are chasing our dreams of claiming homesteads of our own."

"Mercy me," Muriel muttered when they reached the edge of town. "There is that infuriating Captain Holbrook again. He's always bossing folks around and running off the Sooners that sneak in to claim prime land before the day of the race."

"I'm all in favor of routing those greedy settlers who are trying to cheat their way into acquiring the best property!" Josie insisted emphatically.

"So am I," Muriel agreed. "But Holbrook's domineering attitude riles me. He snapped at *me,* just because I wandered over the borderline while trying to avoid a clump of men tossing proposals left and right. The captain is too much the authoritarian and too full of himself, if you ask me."

Josie glanced back and forth between her friend and the commander of Fort Reno, who was in charge of maintaining control of thousands of people who filled the town to overflowing, and was obliged to protect the Indians on the soon-to-be-opened land. "Has the captain insulted you or made improper advances?" she asked worriedly.

Muriel thrust out her chin, causing tendrils of dark

hair to ripple around her face. Her thick-lashed eyes threw sparks. "He accused me of leading men on, is what he did!" she huffed irritably. "You know perfectly well that I can't help it if ten cowboys decide to follow at my heels and toss out proposals simultaneously. The same holds true for you."

That had become the story of their lives the past three weeks, Josie acknowledged.

"I'm trying to *avoid* men, not attract them." Muriel snorted, and added spitefully, "I'd like to see that stuffed shirt of a soldier down on bended knee. I would smack him on the head with a skillet to punctuate my rejection."

Muriel's burst of temper befuddled Josie. She was also curious why the handsome captain cast Muriel the evil eye as he reined his horse toward her. With his shiny brown hair, brown eyes and muscular physique, Grant Holbrook was not unpleasant to look at. At age thirty or thereabout, he held a position of authority, and was highly regarded by his men. Why Muriel and the army officer provoked each other so easily was beyond Josie.

Captain Holbrook halted his roan gelding beside them and looked down from his advantageous position. He nodded politely to Josie, then focused a hard stare on Muriel. "What? No string of men trailing behind you today, Miz Wilson?" he said, and smirked. "Off day, is it?"

Muriel tossed him a caustic smile. "I sent them away because I've decided the only proposal I'll accept is from *you,* Captain. I don't want you to have to compete with the others, since it's obvious you are so short on charm. Of course, my answer would still be *no.*"

"I wouldn't ask," he assured her crossly.

Muriel hitched her thumb toward Josie. "Then maybe you prefer blue-eyed blondes."

"Don't drag me into whatever personal feud you two have going," Josie protested. "I, for one, will be relieved when the day of the run arrives so all these unattached men will have something better to do with their time than make a last-minute grab for a wife.

"I even passed out mail-order-bride magazines and matrimonial newspapers last week to divert attention from us, for all the good it did," she added. She stared earnestly at Captain Holbrook. "Can't you do something about the constant harassment? Muriel and I are tired of wading through would-be husbands to reach our destinations."

He jerked up his head and frowned. "Has someone attacked you? Give me his name and I will deal with him severely."

Josie noticed the captain directed his question and vow to Muriel. Hmmm… Wasn't that interesting?

"I carry a knife as a deterrent," Muriel replied. "I've managed to defend my own honor when the occasion arises."

"Don't stab anyone without provocation," he warned. "I'd have to toss you in the stockade, and you might miss the run altogether. And why, may I ask, are you two racing off to claim property that you can't possibly work by yourselves?"

Both of them puffed up with indignation. Apparently, this wasn't the first time the captain had posed the question to Muriel, because she took extreme offense, even more so than Josie.

"Do I look incapable of fending for myself or setting up a temporary tent until I can hire someone to build my house?" Muriel challenged sharply. "I'll have you know that I managed to work tirelessly as a seamstress and care for my ailing mother after my father died. We had to sell our farm and move into a run-down boardinghouse in town, but I did what had to be done until Mother passed on last winter. I long for what I had as a child. To that end I have saved every spare cent to make the run and to pay for farm improvements after I stake my claim!" Her voice rose indignantly. "I assure you, Captain High-and-Mighty Holbrook, this is not a whim!"

She dragged in a deep breath, crossed her arms over her chest and stared him down. "I doubt you know what it's like to scratch and claw, Captain, but *I* do. Necessity demanded it. I'm chasing my long-held dream and it doesn't include taking a husband who sees me as his cook, housekeeper, seamstress and personal harlot—"

Muriel clamped both hands over her mouth to halt her runaway tongue. The captain's eyes nearly popped from their sockets. Josie burst out laughing.

Holbrook was first to regain his composure. He shifted on his horse, then looked down his patrician nose at Muriel. "Are you quite finished spouting comments that are considered improper in mixed company? If you had any manners you would know that."

Josie's gaze bounced from Muriel to the captain while the two exchanged blistering glares. They were so sensitive to what the other one said and did that they set off intense reactions in each other.

Ordinarily, Muriel took life in stride, as Josie did. A determined woman, she dealt efficiently with the throng of men hounding her with proposals. But poof! The captain arrived on the scene and Muriel bristled with hostility.

Josie had never been interested enough in a man to react to his words and glances the way Muriel did with Grant Holbrook. To Josie, the bothersome male masses were one more difficult obstacle to overcome on her way to establishing her own home and ranch in the soon-to-be-opened territory.

When Muriel wheeled around and stamped off, the captain scowled sourly, Josie saw. She hurried to catch up with her friend. "Feel better, now that you've put the commander in his place?"

"Much, thank you," Muriel insisted, then dragged in a restorative breath. "Do you see why that arrogant soldier annoys me so much?"

"No, I don't," she said honestly.

Her friend stopped in her tracks to gape at her. "You don't think he's irritating beyond belief?"

"If you say so…" Josie's voice trailed off when four men on the boardwalk spotted them. All smiles and eager anticipation, they surged forward like an ocean wave. But then she grinned, as a brilliant idea struck her. "Maybe we're going about this the wrong way. Maybe we should *accept* a marriage proposal."

Muriel stared at her as if she had vines sprouting from her ears. "Are you out of your mind?"

"Think about it." Josie eyed the gaggle of men scurrying toward them. "If we *accept* a proposal we will be off the marriage market."

A slow smile curved Muriel's lips. "You're right...." Then she frowned disconcertedly. "But how do we discard our unwanted fiancés after they serve their purpose? Surely we aren't actually going to *marry* them."

"No, of course not. We'll just get a bad case of cold feet the morning of the run...while emotions are running high," Josie suggested, warming to her bright idea.

"We can claim it is too much to deal with, too rapidly," Muriel suggested enthusiastically.

"Other prospective suitors won't hear that we called off the betrothals until *after* we claim our land," Josie continued. "By then, the men will be too busy setting up housekeeping to bother us. For a while at least."

Muriel stared speculatively at the approaching group. "Maybe I'll agree to the first proposal tossed at me before lunch. Someone other than the infuriating, uppity captain, who was likely born with a silver spoon in his mouth and descended from a long line of self-important military martinets."

Josie studied her friend for a thoughtful moment. "The way you're carrying on, I'm beginning to think the captain's proposal is the one you secretly want to accept."

She gasped in outrage. "Holbrook is the last man on earth I'd want to marry!"

Josie smiled impishly. "Well, then, propose to *him,* since you have no intention of keeping him. If he accepts, then you will have the wicked satisfaction of jilting him before you leave him choking in your dust on the day of the run."

Muriel snickered wryly. "Now I know why I befriended you. You are clever and intelligent. That's an interesting notion—"

It was all she had time to say before the four cowboys descended, spewing the same nauseating flattery Josie and Muriel had heard for three continuous weeks.

Solomon Tremain led a string of a dozen prize horses into town—and drew an immediate crowd, as usual. Would-be settlers were eager to purchase swift, powerful steeds to outrun the other hopeful contestants and reach their promised land. This was Sol's third trip to the town sitting on the eastern border of Cheyenne-Arapaho territory—which was about to be overrun by land-hungry whites.

Sol gnashed his teeth when the ever-constant conflict of his half white, half Cheyenne heritage rose within him. Although his physical appearance was more like his father's than his Indian mother's, Sol was Cheyenne at heart. He resented the white intrusion on the tribe's hunting grounds and sacred sites.

Unfortunately, restraining the greedy white settlers was like holding back floodwaters. At least Sol was in a position to help his people—as much as they could be helped when the fickle government approved another land run in Indian Territory. The *Twin* Territories—Oklahoma and Indian—he silently corrected, and scowled.

From the time Sol became a member of the elite, highly trained fighting force known as the Wolf Warriors, within the special clan called the Bowstring Society, he had been involved in law enforcement and held positions of authority. He'd gone on to join the Lighthorse Police of the Cheyenne Nation, and then was hand-picked as one of Judge Isaac Parker's Deputy U.S. Marshals. Sol dealt with outlaws, Indian haters, greedy ranchers and pesky squatters that encroached on tribal property.

This assignment demanded that he pose as a horse trader, to gain the confidence of shysters and gather incriminating evidence to ensure convictions. Land runs were breeding grounds for trouble, and Sol was well aware of the underhanded tactics often employed in acquiring property, such as the schemes used during the Runs of '89 and '91.

If Sol had his way, all offenders would be watching this upcoming run from the stockade at Fort Reno. Then again, there wouldn't *be* a run if he had his druthers. Which he didn't.

Sol focused his attention on the men congregating around him, and promptly sold a half-dozen horses.

When the group dispersed, he looked up to see his local contact, Captain Grant Holbrook, sitting atop his horse, staring off into space.

Sol followed the captain's gaze to two women surrounded by four cowboys. Then three more men joined the crowd and another two. The scene reminded Sol of honeybees buzzing around a hive.

"Must be nice to attract so much attention," he said with a chuckle. "If women flocked to me the way men flock to those two ladies, I'd be a happy man."

"What?" Holbrook jerked to attention, then glanced sideways at Sol.

"I said those women must be something special."

"Those two?" Grant snorted. "They can fend off their hordes of admirers by themselves for all I care."

Sol raised a brow, then scrutinized his friend, who was two years his junior. "Am I missing something here?"

"Not unless you like sharp-tongued shrews who delight in the attention they receive from men anxious to acquire a fiancée before the run," he muttered sourly. "One is a mite worse than the other, however."

Sol assessed the two women. "Which one? The blonde or brunette?"

"Brunette. I've met more agreeable rattlesnakes." He shook himself loose from his meandering thoughts, then noticed the fine quality of horseflesh Sol had brought with him to town. "Where do you keep gathering such good stock for your cover, Tremain? Last week you arrived with a dozen exceptional mares and geldings to sell, and you left with a pocketful of money."

"My Cheyenne cousins trained these horses," he confided. "I make sure they receive top dollar for these animals, which are well adapted to this terrain. I'm making double damn sure the tribe profits from this offensive encroachment on their property."

Grant nodded somberly. "Another treaty discarded for the sake of white expansion. Sometimes I'm ashamed to be white." He glanced curiously at Sol. "How many acres did the Cheyenne and Arapaho lose this time?"

"Over six hundred thousand." Sol scowled resentfully when he thought of how the tribes had been forced to take their land allotments and relinquish the rest of their reservation to the government for settlement. "Not counting their land in Colorado and Kansas the government confiscated years ago."

"And I'm stuck in the middle of this, just like you are," Grant mumbled in frustration. "It's hell trying to protect the tribes and their allotments before the white mob descends to claim the surplus land."

The captain expelled an agitated breath. "I'm holding more than a dozen Sooners in the stockade because they sneaked in to set up camps along the creeks on the wrong side of the starting line, and refused to leave. With your help, I've flushed out nearly a hundred early birds, but I don't have enough soldiers to patrol the area to keep those blasted Sooners honest." He snorted and said, "Now there's a contradiction in terms if I ever heard one."

"I'll continue to do what I can to help," Sol promised. "I carry my special trader's license to prove I can cross the territory as I please. If I see more illegal squatters, I'll contact you. I can also question my tribe about the location of other whites illegally encroaching on their land."

"Good," Grant said. "I'll run off as many as I can, and you do the same."

"If I flash my marshal's badge it won't be easy to gain trust and gather evidence of fraud among these would-be settlers," Sol reminded him. "But I can alert you to their location so you can take a patrol of soldiers to rout the squatters out."

"I appreciate whatever help you can give, Marsh— I mean *Tremain*."

Sol eyed him warningly. "The last thing I need is a careless slip of the tongue alerting folks that I'm in law enforcement."

When half a dozen men leaning negligently against the supporting posts of the porch outside the Saddle Burr Saloon noticed their conversation, Sol reached into his vest pocket to retrieve his special trader's license.

"We're drawing attention," he told the military commander quietly. "Look over my license thoroughly, then nod your head. I want those men to think you're checking the authenticity of my credentials."

Grant took the license and studied it closely. "They look like hired guns to me," he murmured, his head bent in supposed concentration. "Is that what you're thinking?"

"That'd be my guess," Sol agreed. "I want to know what scheme is about to play out, who the gunmen are working for and why they chose *this* particular area to make the run."

"We'll have to confine our future conversations to out-of-the-way sites to avoid suspicion," Grant said, returning the license with a clipped nod.

Sol tucked away the paper. "We'll meet tonight at seven o'clock at Shallow Springs, south of the garrison. Find out what you can about those men without contacting them directly."

Grant inclined his head in an authoritative manner for the benefit of the suspicious-looking group watching. Then he flicked his hand to shoo Sol on his way.

With a mock salute, Sol led his string of horses down the middle of the street—and drew the attention of the other crowd of men, who were fawning over the two women Grant had pointed out earlier.

From the corner of his eye, Sol surveyed the group outside the saloon, while pretending to assess the two women. Until the shapely blonde turned her head toward him, and sunlight gleamed on her thick, curly hair. The lustrous strands seemed a fascinating combination of sunbeams and moonbeams, and when she tilted her face up to him, Sol forgot all about the hired guns outside the saloon. Luminous eyes the color of forget-me-nots locked with his, and the jolt of awareness that sizzled through his body shocked the hell out of him.

According to Grant, this alluring blonde was the more tolerable companion. Holbrook insisted the stun-

ning brunette was the devil's sister, or at the very *least* a
first cousin. Sol spared the fetching dark-haired woman
a cursory glance, then his gaze settled on the blonde
again as he halted his string of horses in the middle of
the street.

"Anyone interested in prize horseflesh to make the
land run?" he called loudly. "Only a half-dozen left
today. Get one while you can!"

Four of the fawning admirers hurried over to exam-
ine the horses at close range. The other men continued
to hover around the women like puppies on the trail of
fresh milk—until the objects of their rapt attention pivoted toward Eugene's Café of Fine Foods. Sol smiled
appreciatively as he studied both women's backsides,
encased in formfitting breeches and shirts that accentuated their curvaceous physiques to advantage. As if
they didn't already stand out in a crowd because of their
bewitching facial features, he mused.

Sol didn't consider himself a connoisseur of women,
and he had no time for lasting attachments. Still, he
could easily understand why men salivated over the
brunette and blonde—who looked to be about twenty-
three, give or take a year. The brunette, he guessed,
was a year or two younger.

"Keep my proposal in mind," a tall, gangly sod
buster called to the women before they disappeared
inside the café.

Sol focused on the crowd gathering around him.
Within five minutes, he had sold two horses. Then he
continued on his way, and by the time he reached the

opposite end of town, had made the last of his sales.
The closer to the day of the run, the faster he depleted
his supply of well-trained horses.

After stopping at the Silver Dollar Saloon to wet his
whistle, he decided to return to the property where his
cousin Red Hawk lived, so he could replace the horses
he'd sold. When Sol reversed direction on the street,
he noticed the two women emerging from the café. He
decided that if he was in the market for a bride—which
he doubted he'd ever be, since his duties left him roam-
ing around as if he had wanderlust—he could flip a
coin and be satisfied spending time with either of the
attractive females.

Of course, he predicted both ladies were holding out
for the best offer, to ensure the best financial security.
He'd seen it happen before—and after—the other two
land runs. Women were as opportunistic as men were,
he reflected cynically. Everyone, good and bad alike,
had a hidden agenda.

Damn, Tremain, he mused. *You've spent too many years
associating with murderers, swindlers and thieves*. He
needed to socialize with a better class of people before
his skepticism swallowed him alive.

Unfortunately, he wasn't well received by new acquaintances after he mentioned his mixed heritage, so
he didn't bring it up often these days. He wondered if
the blonde and brunette would consider him poor marriage material if he disclosed his background to them.

Not that he cared what they thought. He had more
important things to do besides ogling attractive females

wearing trim-fitting clothing that defined the lush shape of their hips and the enticing curves of their legs. He'd be in the area only long enough to complete his assignment, before moving on to the next one in Indian Territory.

His thoughts disintegrated when a fresh batch of would-be suitors gathered around the two women. Sol did his best to ignore his fierce physical attraction to the blonde. He turned away, refusing to be lumped in the same category with every witless, hot-blooded male in town.

Chapter Two

Josie gnashed her teeth as she led her contrary sorrel, with his striking flaxen mane and tail, away from the camp after supper that evening. The stallion was not the horse she had originally planned to ride in the high-speed race during the run.

Unfortunately, the gelding she had trained had stepped in a prairie dog hole while she was exercising him, and had injured his leg. She'd been forced to re-sort to the high-strung animal that had bucked off her brother a few weeks earlier. Noah was still hobbling around with an injured back.

"Behave, Rooster," she cooed to the flighty stallion. "You'll get your chance to run at breakneck speed this evening, so have patience."

"I agree with your brother," Muriel said as she brought her docile dapple-gray mare, Bess, alongside. "That horse is cantankerous."

"He's also all I have," Josie muttered, pulling herself into the saddle while Rooster pranced in a tight circle and tossed his head. "He runs like the wind...once I get him pointed in the right direction."

"You think Rooster won't come unglued when the soldiers fire off the cannons and shoot their rifles to signal the beginning of the race?" Muriel scoffed. "You should have bartered with that horse trader we saw in town today. You could have selected a mount with a better disposition."

Josie recalled the green-eyed, raven-haired man whose five o'clock shadow was about three days old. He'd seemed nine foot tall sitting astride his horse—and was likely well over six foot when he wasn't. She couldn't figure out why the powerful-looking horseman had captured her attention immediately. After all, she was fed up with men and their constant badgering.

"There's no guarantee the horse trader's stock would be better behaved than Rooster," Josie contended as she pulled on the reins to bring the stallion under control—if that was possible.

"If you don't watch out, you'll end up like your brother, or worse," Muriel warned. "You will be *forced* to accept a marriage proposal, because you won't be in any condition to make the race for a homestead by yourself."

"Thank you, Miz Gloom and Doom," Josie muttered caustically. "And let me point out that if *you* don't brush up on your riding skills, you won't stay on your horse long enough to claim any property."

Muriel expelled an audible sigh. "You're right. I didn't get to ride as much as I wanted while working such long hours and tending Mother." She got that determined look on her face that Josie had seen often. It was like staring into a mirror. "But I'll die trying to stake a place of my own," she declared.

Josie winced. "Let's hope it doesn't come to that for either of us. As for tonight, let's ride along the—"

Pistol shots rang out in a copse of nearby trees, cutting her off midsentence and spooking her flighty stallion. Her head snapped back when Rooster reared, then plunged forward, galloping headlong across the rolling hills—*inside* the boundary to territory that was off-limits until the day of the run.

"Josie!" Muriel shrieked, as her own horse jumped sideways, then shot toward the sandy creek bank.

Josie yanked back on the reins as hard as she could, but Rooster lowered his head and raced across the prairie, where belly-high grass waved in the evening breeze. Glancing over her shoulder, she noted that Muriel hadn't been bucked off, thank goodness. Josie decided to quit trying to control Rooster and let him have his head.

Wasn't this what she expected of the stallion during the race? She *wanted* him to run in a high-speed gallop so she could outdistance the other settlers and locate the best land. Then she'd place her stake in the ground to claim her one hundred sixty acres. The trials and frustrations she had dealt with the past three weeks would be worth it.

Keeping that in mind, Josie nudged Rooster in the flanks and held on to him for dear life. She'd always thought she had a way with horses, but had to admit that not all her whispers of encouragement and tempting treats affected Rooster's unpredictable temperament. The horse lived to run, like the untamed mustangs— and she'd better clamp herself to him like a barnacle to a ship or she'd end up in worse condition than her brother!

Sol glanced up sharply when he heard the unmistakable thunder of hooves. His mount, a sleek buckskin stallion named Outlaw, pricked his ears and shifted beneath him. The string of fifteen horses Sol had picked up at Red Hawk's cabin milled around, tugging restlessly on the lead rope he held.

To Sol's amazement, he saw the same blonde he'd encountered in El Reno flying over the hill on a powerful sorrel stallion. With its contrasting flaxen mane and tail, which matched the woman's long, shiny hair, the twosome would capture any man's attention. The horse equaled Outlaw in strength, speed and stamina, but was running out of control, and the blonde was in danger.

Sol hurriedly tethered the lead rope to the extra horses around the nearest tree. He gouged Outlaw in the ribs and raced off to intercept the woman at the mercy of the runaway stallion.

He held his breath when the flashy-colored sorrel leaped a creek. Sol expected the rider to go flying, kerplunk, into the water. Miraculously, with her arms wrapped around the horse's neck, she stayed on board— this time at least.

Scowling at the blonde's idiocy in mounting such a spirited horse, Sol slapped Outlaw on the rump, demanding his fastest gait. Their path intercepted the rogue stallion on a steep downhill slope. Sol snaked out his hand and grabbed the reins in an attempt to stop the animal.

Wild-eyed, the sorrel reared up, jerking Sol off his horse and unseating the woman. She fell backward with a thud and groan—and Sol landed directly on top of her, forcing out her breath in a whoosh. His thigh wedged intimately between her legs and his chest slammed against her breasts.

She shrieked, panicked and shoved him aside. But their arms and legs were in a hopeless tangle, so they were knotted together as they rolled pell-mell down the hill. When they finally came to a dizzying stop on level ground, Sol was sprawled on top of her—a position he admitted held provocative appeal for him.

The same didn't appear to hold true for her.

She struggled again to push him off her, but suddenly her eyes rolled back in her head and she wilted. Sol watched her flushed face turn an interesting shade of blue, then pasty-white.

"You okay, miss?" he asked as he rose onto his hands and knees above her.

Her ample breasts heaved while she struggled to draw breath—and couldn't. Sol grabbed her arm and jerked her over his knee, to whack her between the shoulder blades until she began breathing again.

"Stop—*whack*—doing—*whack*—that!" she wheezed, then squirmed away from him to fall back on the ground.

Sol watched her inhale several shuddering gulps of air. But his attention kept dropping to the top button of her blouse, which had come undone during their downhill tumble, exposing her enticing cleavage.

"You okay now?" He tried to focus on her rattled condition, not her enticing physique. It wasn't easy. She had sensuous curves in all the right places. And he had been *trained* to be exceptionally observant. Now that talent was working against him.

Forget-me-not-blue eyes zeroed in on him, narrowing into an accusing glare. "I was *okay* before you jerked me off my horse and threw yourself on top of me!" she huffed indignantly.

"I didn't unseat you," he contradicted. "Your devil horse did that when he reared up. Then he yanked *me* off *my* horse."

"It's what you deserve for roughing me up," she muttered as she twisted gingerly from side to side to assess her condition. "You're that horse trader I saw in town today, aren't you?"

He nodded. "And you're that blonde with wedding proposals galore. Find one to your liking yet?"

"No." She rose unsteadily to her feet, rejecting his offer of support. She brushed grass off her breeches and glared at him some more.

"Not to worry, there are several single, *wealthy* shopkeepers and hotel owners in town, in case your slew of cowpunchers and plowboys don't meet your high expectations," he assured her, then smirked.

She jerked up her head, causing the coil of shiny,

spring-loaded, silver-blond curls to dangle above her left ear like a lopsided fountain. She took a challenging step toward him. He noticed she was tall for a woman—five foot five inches of feminine defiance, to be specific. Since he was six-two, he held the height advantage. Nonetheless, that didn't stop her from standing toe to toe with him, refusing to be the slightest bit intimidated.

"And what is that supposed to imply, Mr. Horse Trader?"

The woman was bristling with indignation and bad temper—all directed at him. And Grant swore the brunette had a worse disposition? Ha! She had nothing on this sassy blonde, who hadn't even bothered to thank him for risking *his* neck to save *her* gorgeous hide.

"You're welcome, by the way," he said sarcastically.

Her chilling glare could have formed icicles. "For what?"

Sol did a double take. "For saving you from disaster, of course. That devil sorrel didn't look like he planned to slow down until his legs gave out or he launched you off his back. Whichever came first."

"Which is the whole point of the exercise," she insisted in a scathing tone.

"What exercise?" he scoffed caustically. "Catapulting off his back to see how many bones you can break at once?"

"No, I have to be able to hold on while Rooster runs hell-for-leather if I want to stake my claim in the run."

"Lady, the only claim you'll stake is a cemetery plot if you ride this animal." Sol flashed her a stern glance.

"You need to buy one of my horses. They are trained for riding, not green broke like this unruly stallion."

She tilted her chin and scoffed at him. "How convenient that you *just happen* to have a string of mounts for sale. And *you* call *me* an opportunist? Ha! That's a laugh."

To his surprise, she became huffier by the second. She nearly stood on top of him, despite the fact that she was a head shorter and at least one hundred pounds lighter than he was. "I will have you know, Mr. Horse Trader, that I am not trolling for a husband in this sea of would-be settlers. I'm here to claim land for a ranch of my own, so I can raise horses and cattle. I don't need a man lording over me and getting in my way. I do not need to be saved from the sire of my future horse herd... and you stay *off* me!" she shouted as she stabbed her forefinger into his chest.

Sol tried to pay attention to her lecture while she was yelling at him, he really did. Nevertheless, his betraying gaze zeroed in on her lush, tempting mouth. She had plump pink lips that he hungered to taste. The thought prompted him to lick his own lips in anticipation.

Apparently, he'd been too long without a woman, if this firebrand aroused him and sent his thoughts skittering off in the wrong direction. She was all sharp claws, biting teeth and prickly criticism, as spirited and contrary as her stallion. Not to mention wildly attractive— if a man could convince her to use that sassy mouth for something besides delivering scornful lectures.

When she lifted a questioning brow, Sol blinked and

scrambled to find his place in the one-sided conversation. He finally gave up and said, *"What?"*

She cast him a withering glance. "Never mind. You men are all alike. You can't get past outward appearances to pay attention to anything as inconsequential as intelligent conversation."

She pivoted around to hobble toward her horse, which was trying to pick a fight with Outlaw. The two stallions laid back their ears, snorted and pawed the ground.

It reminded Sol of his confrontation with the blonde.

"I suppose I don't need to know you by name." She tossed the comment over her shoulder flippantly. "I can think of plenty to call you, even if you refuse to provide the one you were given at birth."

Which was not the name he used now, he reminded himself. He had been born in a Cheyenne camp, not in white society.

Why did she want to know his name, anyway? So she could tattle to the El Reno city marshal that he had attacked her? Which he most certainly had not…but he was thinking about it now.

Before she could walk between the two stallions and get trampled, Sol let out a sharp whistle, startling Rooster and bringing Outlaw obediently to him.

"The name is Solomon Tremain," he said as he grabbed Rooster's trailing reins, then handed them to her. "And you are?"

She climbed slowly onto the horse and grimaced.

Obviously, she had sustained some sort of injury during her fall and his subsequent collapse on top of her.

"I'm Josephine Malloy."

He nodded in recognition. "You're Button-Eye Malloy. I've heard your name mentioned in several tent communities hereabout. You're the mender of shirts and the breaker of hearts, or so I'm told. I expect you're doing a thriving business to earn extra money. The brunette I saw you with in town must be Patches Wilson."

The blonde stared him down, making grand use of her elevated position on her demon horse. "At your service, Tremain," she said loftily. "Is there anything I can sew *shut* for you? In *that,* I can be bought for a fair price…but for nothing else."

He had to hand it to the minx, she gave as good as she got. He liked teasing her, just to watch those expressive eyes flash blue fire. He also liked the way her chin shot up in defiance. Not to mention the way she squared her shoulders, refusing to feel threatened, preparing herself for an oncoming challenge or debate. There was nothing docile or dull about Josephine Malloy.

"Maybe it's best that you don't accept any of the marriage proposals tossed at you," he advised. "I'm guessing you'd be as difficult to live with as your contrary stallion."

Josie studied the swarthy horse trader as he mounted the muscular buckskin, the coal-black mane and tail of which matched the color of Tremain's thick, shiny hair. She had to admit there was something intriguing about the man. He moved with the controlled grace and agility of a powerful predator. She reluctantly noted how his dark breeches, shirt and leather vest clung to his powerful body, accentuating his muscular physique. She didn't want to show the slightest interest in this man. Or any man, for that matter. She had more important things on her mind.

When Josie managed to drag her gaze off Tremain, she noticed his stallion behaved much better than Rooster did. "On second thought, I'll trade you straight out. My stallion for yours," she bartered impulsively.

He threw back his dark head and barked a laugh as he settled himself comfortably on his horse. His sea-green eyes, rimmed with thick black lashes, danced with amusement. Josie blinked in surprise when she saw the dimples creasing his bronzed cheeks. Tremain was actually quite handsome, in a rugged, earthy sort of way.

Not that she cared, of course. He could be God's gift to women and she wouldn't want him. She didn't need a man to complicate her life right now—maybe ever. The idea of a husband ordering her about, as if it was his natural-born right, didn't sit well with her. She wanted to avoid restrictive ties, so she could take complete control of her destiny and focus all her efforts on staking a claim for a homestead.

"Outlaw is worth a half-dozen horses like your cantankerous mount," Tremain insisted as he reined toward the string of waiting mustangs on the hill. He cast her a pointed look. "And you are not supposed to be out here, not even to exercise that ill-mannered animal."

"But *you* can be?" she challenged, as Rooster followed after Outlaw—probably looking to pick another fight, knowing him.

"I have a special trader's license, Josephine," Sol said, glancing at her over his broad shoulder. "*You* don't. Since you are trespassing, I might decide to tattle to Commander Holbrook. He can lock you up with the other sneaky Sooners and you can watch the run from behind bars."

"But you won't if I *what,* Tremain?" she asked suspiciously. "If I offer to provide some sort of services to you?"

His rakish grin did strange things to her pulse, for reasons she couldn't account for. More than a hundred men had tried to court her since she had set up camp beside the boundary line for the run. Yet this ruggedly attractive rascal appealed to her. Why? She couldn't say. She wasn't sure she even *liked* the man. Still, there was something about him that intrigued her—and that made her wary and defensive.

It likely stemmed from the fact that he had sprawled on top of her earlier, she mused. She had become fiercely aware that he was one hundred percent male. During their downhill tumble, Josie had found herself riding his muscular thigh, and her breasts had been mashed against his broad chest. It had been unnerving…and titillating. *Oh, for heaven's sake, don't think about that!*

She quickly turned her attention to the authoritative air that surrounded him like an invisible cloak. His demeanor reminded her of Captain Holbrook's commanding manner, which seemed odd for a wandering horse trader.

Her thoughts trailed off and she shivered, becoming aware of the evening chill settling around her. She wished she'd worn her jacket. It would have provided warmth, not to mention extra padding during her fall and wild tumble. Even now, her hip throbbed and her wrist ached from being hyperextended.

"You should buy one of the other horses I have for sale," he repeated belatedly. "Not Outlaw. He belongs to me."

She was disappointed he hadn't tossed out an inappropriate, off-color remark in response to her previous comment. Then she would feel justified in lashing out at him again. It would assure her that she had every reason to dislike him and would be well advised to maintain a cautious distance.

"No, thanks. I'm sticking with Rooster. He'll get me where I want to go the day of the race." She hoped.

"Or see you *buried*," Sol mumbled as he leaned out to grab the lead rope on the other horses.

"Muriel said something to that effect, but I intend to prove you both wrong," Josie insisted. She glanced curiously at him. "Are you going to make the land run?"

"Haven't decided yet. I'm not one to stay in the same place for long. Born under a wandering star, you might say."

Which meant he and Josie held opposing objectives in life. She dreamed of putting down roots and having a home of her own. She'd endured seven years of feeling unwanted, though she had stayed in a grand house where most women would delight in living. She had been overly anxious to escape that tormenting place. Nowadays, a sod house or crude dugout seemed like a welcoming palace to her.

"You can drop by my homestead after the run and see how well I'm managing without a man's help or intrusion," she invited. "Unlike you, Tremain, I want a place to call my own."

He studied her for a long, contemplative moment. His penetrating green eyes bored into her, as if searching out hidden secrets.

"So…Miz Josephine, where do you hail from?" he asked as they rode toward the tent community that had become her temporary home.

"Iowa. My mother died when I was ten. Three years later, Papa married a wealthy, influential widow who could improve his social standing." Josie wrinkled her nose in disgust. "Although Papa inherited property from my mother's family, he had no interest whatsoever in ranching. Eventually he sold it for extra money, after his new wife pressured him into it. Needless to say, my brother and I were hugely disappointed."

"You had constant conflicts with your stepmother," Sol said perceptively.

"Yes. She would have preferred if Papa didn't bring Noah and me into her grand house," Josie confided, and wondered why she was discussing her personal life with a stranger. Ordinarily, she kept her feelings to herself. She figured everyone had their own problems, and didn't want to hear about hers.

"It was *her* house, after all," she continued, surprising herself again. "She had a daughter and son by her first marriage, and she did her best to make my brother and me feel unwelcome and unaccepted in her circle of high-society acquaintances."

"*Her* home, *her* money, *her* friends," he said with a knowing smile. "She didn't want to run the risk of you outshining her children. She sounds anything but delightful."

"Needless to say, I leaped at the chance to join Noah and his then-fiancée, Celia, when they came south to make the Run of '89. They married after they claimed their adjoining homesteads."

"But you didn't claim property nearby?" he asked curiously.

"Couldn't. The Homestead Act states a single woman of legal age can stake land in a run, but I wasn't yet twenty-one at the time. Since Celia was, they could combine their property after they filed their individual claims. I helped them set up their farm, which is east of El Reno, and I lived with them until recently."

"And now it's your turn to follow your dreams."

"Exactly. I couldn't make the Run of '91, which opened land to the east of their homestead, either."

"Oh? Why's that?" he asked interestedly.

"Because I couldn't work the fields and erect buildings for barns, hog sheds and chicken coops by myself," she explained. "At the time, I didn't have the funds to hire workers, either. But I *can* raise cattle, train horses and build fences on the soon-to-be-opened range land." She stared at him, daring him to deny it.

He grinned and glanced meaningfully at Rooster. The horse had been tossing his head and sidestepping every chance he got.

"Yes, I can see how well trained this devil is. But you can claim twice as much land if you accept a marriage proposal and wed *after* the run, like your scheming sister-in-law did," he pointed out.

"She isn't a schemer, and that was different," Josie said defensively. "Celia loves Noah and he loves her. And don't think my prospective suitors haven't mentioned *repeatedly* the advantage of claiming more land for a ranch. But I'm not like my father. He married both times for position and prestige, the second even more than the first. I lost all respect for him when he practically deserted my brother and me to seek acceptance in society's highest circles."

Josie inhaled a calming breath, determined not to let hurtful feelings from her past upset her. She had a new life now and her always-critical stepmother was miles away.

"I had you and Miz Wilson pegged as clever opportunists." He inclined his raven head. "I was wrong to believe the worst without hearing the facts. I apologize."

"What about you, Tremain? What is your story…?"

Her voice trailed off when she saw Muriel trotting her dapple-gray mare over the hill—with none other than Captain Holbrook riding beside her. What the devil was her friend doing with *him?* And why were they out here?

Josie stared apprehensively at Tremain, wondering if he planned to accuse her of trespassing, as he'd threatened earlier. But he simply glanced at her, shrugged a broad shoulder and gazed curiously at the approaching twosome.

Dear Lord! Josie thought suddenly. Had Muriel taken her rash suggestion of proposing to the man she disliked as a tactic to fend off unwanted suitors? Muriel and she hadn't had time to hammer out the details of such a drastic plan yet. Perhaps Muriel had acted impulsively and persuaded Holbrook to become her temporary fiancé.

Josie tossed Solomon Tremain a speculative glance. Maybe she should follow her own advice. The aimless horse trader would make a perfect pretend fiancé. He wouldn't hang around after the run, and other potential suitors would be too busy establishing their own ranches to notice. She would be left alone to set up her homestead.

"Why are you looking at me like that?" he asked warily.

Josie flashed a wide grin and didn't reply, just turned her attention to the approaching riders—and wondered how Tremain would react if *she* proposed to *him*....

Chapter Three

Sol frowned after Josie shifted her speculative gaze from him to the approaching riders. He dearly wanted to know why the intelligent blonde had been staring at him with her lustrous blue eyes narrowed in thought. It made him nervous, reminding him of prisoners that were mentally plotting their escape.

Sol had an unblemished reputation of *not* losing prisoners. He brought them in alive or dead. Their choice. However, dealing with the feisty female was another matter entirely. She was up to something; he'd stake his reputation on it. He wanted to interrogate her privately, but Grant and her friend drew their horses to a halt in front of them.

"Thank God!" Muriel gushed as she looked Josie over carefully. "You are all right, aren't you? I was afraid that demon stallion might have left you in a broken heap on the ground." Her accusing gaze settled on Rooster.

The animal tossed his head proudly and ignored her.

Josie flashed a blinding smile that would have knocked Sol's knees out from under him if he'd been standing. Her face came alive and her radiant expression nearly stole his breath. He glanced at Grant to see if he had experienced the same stunned reaction, but the commander's focus was trained on the attractive brunette.

"I'm perfectly fine, as you can see," Josie assured her friend. "You're okay, too, I hope."

Muriel nodded reassuringly. "I finally regained control of my mare while she sloshed through the shallows in the river. But I was so worried about you that I headed straight for the garrison for assistance." She angled her head toward Holbrook. "Thankfully, I didn't have to ride very far before we crossed paths south of the fort."

No doubt Grant had been on his way to their rendezvous site at Shallow Springs, Sol mused.

"I asked the commander for permission to cross the border to ensure your safety," Muriel added. "He came along in case you were injured and I needed help transporting you to camp."

Sol scrutinized the two women closely. Especially Josie. It seemed that Muriel had answered an unspoken question, because her friend relaxed in the saddle. Whatever passed between the two women was meant to exclude Sol and Grant.

Here was yet another example of a puzzling reaction Sol didn't understand. But then, he had spent considerably more time with men than women, so he couldn't read their behavior quite as easily.

"I had no intention of crossing the boundary line," Josie assured Grant. "But the gunshots in camp frightened Rooster, and away he went without a care about what's off-limits and what's not."

"A rabbit bounding out of the grass and hopping across the prairie would set off Rooster," Sol commented as he stared at the horse, which refused to stand still. If it was possible for a stallion to strut, Rooster could pull it off, he decided. "Give me two days with that cantankerous animal so I can teach him discipline."

Josie rolled her eyes, then glanced at her friend. "Muriel, this is Solomon Tremain."

She smiled cordially. "You're the horse trader. I remember seeing you in town. And this is Captain—"

"We've met," Grant interrupted. "I checked Tremain's special license this morning. He's legal, but he's making a *killing* off his livestock."

"The horses aren't stolen, are they?" Josie asked, so innocently that Sol knew instantly that she was up to no good. "Heavens, I'd hate to think the man who saved me from fatal disaster was a thief."

Sol managed to maintain his trademark deadpan expression, but he inwardly fumed when Josie batted her eyes at him. What the hell was she doing? Fifteen minutes ago, she'd bitten his head off and insisted she didn't need rescuing. Now she was hailing him as a hero for saving her. He was beginning to think there were two women housed in that luscious body of hers—a witch and an angel—and you could never know which one would show up at any given moment. She sure as hell had him buffaloed.

"I'm not a thief," Sol insisted, while Muriel stared at him and Grant bit back a wry smile. "I'm half Cheyenne, and my people are offering their well-trained herds of horses for sale to the invading whites. We might as well make money off this outrageous theft of our land. Not to mention another peace treaty broken by the white government."

Sol shut his mouth so fast he nearly bit off the end of his tongue. Why had he blurted that out? He waited for Josie's and Muriel's reactions to his mixed heritage, and told himself he didn't care what they thought.

To his surprise, neither woman recoiled in repulsion, just stared at him for a few moments before nodding in acceptance of his announcement.

"That explains it," Josie said eventually.

"Explains what?" Sol demanded, a little too defensively.

She grinned at him, which made him nervous, because he couldn't figure her out…and it aggravated him that he *wanted* to be able to.

"That's why you dislike me," she continued, still smiling. "You resent my intrusion on Cheyenne-Arapaho land, and you're also taking your dislike out on my horse."

Sol snorted. "I find fault with that stallion because he is a disaster waiting to happen. Do yourself a favor and buy one of my horses. You'll be safe instead of risking your neck on that unpredictable misfit."

"You two will have to continue your debate else-where," Grant interjected. "You are on the wrong side of the boundary line and I have a meeting to attend." He glanced at Muriel. "Can you and your friend return to camp without an escort?"

"We'll be fine," she assured him crisply. "I already told you that in most instances we are perfectly capable of taking care of ourselves."

"But you should ignore the gunshots you'll hear coming from camp when we return," Josie suggested flippantly. "I plan to shoot the men who fired their pistols, spooked our horses and sent them racing out of control. I expect Muriel will stab those inconsiderate hooligans with her knife a few times for good measure, too."

Grant glanced at Sol after the women trotted off, with Rooster still tossing his head. "She's kidding, right?"

How was he supposed to know? Sol couldn't figure Josie out. "Your guess is as good as mine." He frowned when he noticed Grant was watching Muriel intently. "I thought you didn't like the brunette."

The commander swung his head toward Sol. "I don't. Personally, I think she delights in all that male attention, despite her claim that she isn't interested in accepting a marriage proposal before the race for land."

"Why do you care one way or the other?"

"Didn't say I did," Grant muttered defensively.

Sol let the matter drop, since the man appeared to be highly sensitive about the brunette, regardless of his insistence to the contrary.

"Did you find out anything about the gunslingers we spotted in town?" he asked as he led the way to their secluded rendezvous site near Shallow Springs.

Grant nodded soberly. "The gunmen met up with a Texas rancher named Carlton Bradley at the Oasis, a local brothel. Later, I saw Bradley chatting with several hopeful settlers at one of the tent communities while I was making my rounds."

"Which camp?" Sol questioned as he walked Outlaw into a copse of willows near the rippling springs.

"I think he's camped just north of the one where Josie and Muriel are staying."

Sol nodded pensively. "I need to find out what Bradley and his small army are up to. Robbery, maybe. He might be trying to familiarize himself with the settlers' routines. There are a lot of people about, carrying their life savings to make improvements on the land—*if* they manage to stake a claim without getting killed during the race."

"I talked to Sam Colby, the city marshal, this afternoon," Grant commented. "He mentioned that robberies were occurring with alarming regularity. Bradley and his thugs might be stealing all the money they can get their hands on before hightailing it back to Texas."

"The same sort of things happened in the two previous land runs," Sol reported, then frowned curiously. "What does this Bradley character look like?"

"He's about your height, with reddish-brown hair, a false smile, gray eyes and a square face." Grant rattled the description off. "I think he is as fond of females as he is of money. I see him flirting constantly with married and single women alike."

"Maybe we should sic Josie on him," Sol said drily. "I just met that firebrand, but I think she could put Bradley in his place in nothing flat."

"We'll send Muriel with her. She has tried to put me in *my* place on several occasions," the commander mumbled. "And I don't fling insulting innuendos the way Bradley reportedly does."

"If you come across anyone else that arouses your suspicion, let me know." Sol glanced back at his colleague as he reined Outlaw away from the springs. "By the way, my cousin spotted two squatters tucked in a ravine about eight miles northwest of the fort. Both men were heavily armed with pistols and rifles."

"I'll take out a patrol to confront them tonight," Grant promised. "After we overtake them, they can camp out in the stockade with the rest of their conniving kind."

"Good place for the bastards. You may have to expand the size of the stockade before this damn race for land takes place," Sol muttered before he rode off.

The moment Josie and Muriel reached the tent community, four would-be fiancés approached, eagerly offering to unsaddle their horses. One of the men thrust a tattered jacket at Muriel to repair. The eager suitor followed her like a puppy when she hiked off to fetch her sewing kit.

"If you don't mind, I need my privacy," Josie told the three who lagged behind.

The men bobbed their heads and backed away, much to her relief. She was not in the mood to be polite or listen to more flattery. She just wanted peace and quiet while she brushed down Rooster and staked out Bess, Muriel's mare, to graze.

Privacy was difficult to obtain these days, though. The area was jumping with people who anticipated the day of the run. More competition, Josie thought, disgruntled, as she groomed the stallion. She smiled, noting this was the only time he stood still. He liked the personal attention.

When weariness settled over her, depressing thoughts closed in. Josie wondered what she would do if she couldn't find a piece of property with a good water source and natural protection from inclement weather. What if she failed to stake a claim at all?

She'd heard in town that at least twenty-five thousand people were expected to make the wild run for free land. She knew some of them were settlers that had been unsuccessful in staking claims during the first two such events.

What if she and Muriel ended up with nothing?

Rooster pricked his ears and shifted sideways suddenly. Josie snapped to attention when she heard rustling in the underbrush. Now what? she thought in annoyance.

To her dismay, a scruffy cowboy, who looked part Spanish, staggered from the bushes. His shaggy black hair scraped the collar of his dingy shirt. His wide-set black eyes were at half-mast. He had a six-shooter strapped to each hip and he carried a near-empty whiskey bottle in one hand. Josie swore the hombre must have ingested most of the liquor, then used several drops as cologne, because offensive smells oozed from every pore.

"Well, well, well," the stocky cowboy drawled. "If it ain't Button-Eye Malloy all alone for once. I've had you in my sights for a week, honey."

"The answer is no," she said, out of patience with all men everywhere. "I'm not interested in marrying you. Go away."

"Marry?" He snickered, exposing a mouthful of jagged teeth. "Hell, honey, I don't wanna wed you. Just bed you." He discarded the bottle and advanced toward her.

Josie had found herself in similar situations on several occasions. Drunks with lust on their minds were more dangerous than overeager suitors. "Stay away from me or you'll be sorry," she warned, scooping up a fallen branch to use as an improvised club.

The unkempt hooligan just kept coming. Josie stepped around Rooster, using the horse as a shield. To her frustration, the ruffian swatted the stallion's rump. The flighty horse bolted sideways, knocking Josie flat on her back. She let out a yelp and tried to regain her feet before the ruffian sprawled atop her, but he overpowered her and trapped her beneath him.

She was reminded instantly of having Tremain fall on her, but this was not the same. She had felt a fierce physical attraction to the ruggedly handsome horse trader. She felt nothing but disgust and repulsion for this lusty drunkard.

He clamped a beefy hand around her leg, jerking it sideways to make room for himself between her thighs. Josie tried to whack him over the head with the tree branch, but he blocked the blow with his elbow.

"Get off me!" she yelled at the top of her lungs.

"Not till you give me a kiss," he growled. His shaggy head moved steadily toward hers.

Furious, Josie bucked beneath him and turned her face away. He grabbed a hank of her hair and yanked hard. She screeched in pain and outrage, and clobbered him on the shoulder with her makeshift club. Unfortunately, the blow only served to make him vindictive.

"You wanna play rough, do you, bitch?" he sneered. "Your choice—"

To Josie's surprise, her attacker suddenly levitated off the ground, flew through the air, then landed again with a grunt and a thud. She glanced up to see Solomon Tremain looming over her, looking like Satan arriving from the gates of hell. His eyes were narrowed slits of green flame and his facial expression was as hard as a tombstone. His menacing growl would have scared the living daylights out of anyone sober enough to realize Tremain was not a man to challenge if you valued your life.

"Get yer own woman," the drunkard spat as he climbed onto all fours. "I found her first!"

"Might be the *last* thing you ever do," Tremain

snarled ferociously. Then he swooped down on her attacker.

Panting for breath, Josie braced herself on her elbows and watched the horse trader clutch the front of the hooligan's shirt. He hauled him roughly to his feet and knocked the stuffing out of the brute, who hit the ground again—hard. The brain-scrambling blow caused his dark eyes to roll around like a pair of dice.

She watched in satisfaction as the ruffian shook his head to gather his wits, then gasped in alarm when he made a grab for one of the pistols on his hips.

"Watch out!" she called to her rescuer.

She wasted her breath. Tremain had lightning-quick reflexes and had already sprung into action. He shoved his boot heel against the man's wrist, dislodging the weapon and making him howl in pain. Tremain confiscated both pistols, then stepped on the hooligan's neck to discourage him from trying to gain his feet.

For a horse trader, Tremain was downright impressive when it came to hand-to-hand combat. Josie wondered if it was his Cheyenne training that prepared him to react so quickly and effectively. Probably, she decided. She could use a few lessons in self-defense from him. Clearly, she wasn't as good at fending off attackers as she'd thought.

"Do you have something you'd like to say to the lady?" Tremain asked in a low, vicious tone as he towered over the downed man like a seething thundercloud of doom.

"No, and you can go to hell," the man choked out.

"Already been there. Now it's your turn to see what it's like."

Josie pushed herself into a sitting position to massage her aching back, which had slammed into the ground one too many times in the past two hours.

"You okay, Miz Malloy?" Tremain asked, without taking his fierce glare—or his booted foot—off her tormentor.

"I've been better," she admitted. "But thanks for asking." She rolled to her hands and knees, favoring the wrist she'd hurt earlier that evening, and then rose slowly to her feet.

Her rescuer grabbed the drunkard and hoisted him off the ground. The man swayed as Tremain shook him, as if to clear his whiskey-saturated senses. Josie knew it wouldn't help. She had pounded her attacker with her makeshift club, but he had consumed a pint of whiskey, and the blows hadn't fazed him.

"Come with me," the horse trader demanded sharply. "You need to sober up, and a bath wouldn't hurt, either."

With satisfaction, Josie watched Tremain shove her assailant into the creek. The hombre landed with a splash and came up cursing the air black-and-blue.

When Josie heard more thrashing in the underbrush, she whirled around. Her yelps had drawn attention, apparently. A dozen men, weapons at the ready, appeared.

"You okay, Miz Malloy?" Orson Barnes, the leader of the group, asked worriedly.

"I am now," she assured the rescue brigade.

The settlers glared at the drunkard, who had slogged

ashore and stood there dripping wet, glowering at Tremain.

"There was no call to rough me up," he muttered, then gingerly examined his bloody lips. "I was just having a little fun."

"Well, *I* wasn't!" Josie huffed indignantly. "If my fiancé hadn't shown up when he did, I would have been mauled."

For the life of her, she didn't know why she blurted that out. Maybe because she had been mulling over the prospect during her ride back to camp. She had planned to see what Muriel thought of the idea, but they hadn't gotten around to the topic before they arrived and found themselves swarmed by four eager-to-please suitors.

For certain, Josie had shocked this latest group of men speechless. Whiskered jaws dropped. Eyes popped. Weapons sagged in the men's hands. In synchronized motion, the would-be settlers' stunned gazes swung to Tremain, who stared at her with that poker-faced expression he wore so well.

"Your *fiancé?*" the crowd crowed in unison.

"That's right," she confirmed, as she turned her back on them and walked up to Tremain. "My fiancé."

She cast him a please-don't-deny-it stare, then slipped her hand into his before she pivoted to face the baffled men. She noted that Muriel had arrived on the scene, along with another dozen men. The recent arrivals looked as shocked by the announcement as the first group.

Muriel didn't appear the least bit surprised, however.

She stifled a grin of wry amusement and hung back from the congregation of men.

"That true, horse trader?" someone called from the middle of the crowd. "You proposed and she accepted your offer over everybody else's?"

Josie held her breath, wondering if Tremain planned to humiliate her in front of their captive audience, or play along with her impulsive announcement.

"Didn't she just say so?" he asked, his deep, resonant voice carrying over the crowd.

She nearly swooned in relief, but tried her damnedest not to let her reaction show. Her relief turned to amusement when the men quickly switched their attention to Muriel, who flung up both hands and said, "Don't look at me as a potential wife. I accepted Commander Holbrook's proposal an hour ago, while we were riding." She flashed a beaming smile. "Josie and I are planning a double wedding after the land run."

Beside Josie, Tremain leaned down as if to whisper sweet nothings in her ear. "Are you proposing to me? Isn't that unconventional in white society?"

"Where is it written that a woman can't propose?" she challenged quietly.

"Nowhere I know. It's what I'd expect from a misfit like you…so I accept."

He draped his arm over her shoulder, drawing her closer. Ordinarily, she was inclined to step away when a man crowded her. She'd learned early on not to accept displays of affection, because suitors always wanted more than she intended to give. Oddly enough, however, she didn't object to Tremain's feigned interest. She felt safe and protected after her run-in with the foul-smelling drunkard, who would have molested her if Tremain hadn't shown up when he did.

"Does Holbrook know he recently became engaged?" Tremain murmured against the side of her neck, causing goose bumps to pebble her skin.

"I don't know," she replied, her voice a little on the unsteady side. "Muriel and I didn't have a chance to discuss anything privately. Four men approached the minute we dismounted in camp."

"You know this is going to cost you, don't you?" Tremain whispered devilishly. "Muriel, too, I suspect."

"*How much,* Tremain?" Josie asked, when she saw the wicked gleam in his sea-green eyes and the ornery grin twitching his lips. "I'm saving my funds for improvements on my homestead, *if* I manage to stake one."

"We'll work something out, trust me."

She flashed a smile for the benefit of the attentive males watching their every move. Then she said in a low voice, "Just so you know, I don't trust any man's intentions…."

Her voice trailed off when Tremain's raven head came slowly and deliberately toward hers, as if giving notice that he was going to kiss her in front of God and everyone watching. Not only that, but he was staking *his* claim on *her*. Josie waited, unsure if she wanted to know how he tasted, to know if he kissed the same way he fought—roughly and forcefully.

"You're a smart woman not to trust a man's motives,"

he murmured, his lips a hairbreadth from hers. "I myself don't trust *anyone's* motives, yours included. Just so *you* know…"

Then he kissed her, satisfying her curiosity—and stirring something wild and hungry deep inside her. She hadn't expected tenderness from a man who had reminded her of the flapping buzzard of doom a quarter of an hour earlier. Yet tenderness was what she received from Solomon Tremain. Though he was amazingly gentle, molten fire simmered beneath the surface. It seeped into her blood, bringing it to a quick boil, triggering white-hot sensations she hadn't wanted—or expected—to feel.

She didn't realize she had curled her arm around his neck to inch closer until she was there, enjoying the feel of his powerful body meshed familiarly against hers. She found herself wanting something she couldn't explain, and until this very moment hadn't realized existed.

Josie was sorry to admit she was dazed, dumbfounded and aroused by the gentler side of Solomon Tremain. Desire thrummed through her, raising her temperature another ten degrees. When he lifted his head and let loose a dimpled smile, it knocked her for another loop…until he looked over her head at the crowd of men and grinned in cocky male triumph.

"And *you* are going to pay for *that,* Tremain," she warned as she tossed him a smile for appearance's sake.

"Then we will have to owe each other, won't we, blue eyes?" he murmured huskily.

He dropped a featherlight kiss on her lips, then stepped away to quick-march her assailant to camp. The rescue squad fell in behind him, leaving the two friends alone together.

"Well," Muriel said. "I hope this scheme of yours doesn't blow up in our faces." She stared curiously at Josie. "What did Tremain say when you proposed to him?"

"I didn't actually propose." Josie shifted awkwardly from one foot to the other and avoided her direct stare. "It just sort of popped out of my mouth that he was my fiancé, after my ordeal with the drunkard."

Muriel gasped in amazement. "You gave him no warning? Just blurted it out in front of everyone?"

Josie nodded her tousled head. "You and I discussed the possibility this morning. Tonight seemed the perfect time to set the plan in motion," she reasoned. "The news will buzz around camp this evening and tomorrow we can enjoy some peace and quiet. For once."

"Maybe I shouldn't have yielded to the same reckless impulse," Muriel said worriedly. "Now I have to ride out to the garrison *at night* to confer with Holbrook… and face possible rejection. The captain might not play along the way Mr. Tremain did."

"You could send Tremain to propose for you," Josie suggested.

Her friend's shoulders slumped in relief and she bobbed her head. "I hope he'll agree to speak in my stead, because I'd rather not face Holbrook. I hope *your* pretend fiancé can square it with *mine*." There was a long pause as she stared anxiously at Josie in the gathering twilight. "Do you think we might have acted too irrationally with this scheme of desperation?"

"Most likely," Josie admitted. "But what's done is done. Hopefully, we have resolved the problem of so many unwanted proposals."

Her friend inhaled a bracing breath, squared her shoulders, then spun on her heel. "I'll go ask Tremain to be the bearer of surprising news."

"It'll probably cost you," Josie called after her. "It's what you should expect when you bargain with a wily horse trader."

Sol escorted Josie's assailant into camp, intending to tie him up, retrieve Outlaw and gather the horses he had stopped by to sell at the settlement. Damn good thing he had arrived when he did, he mused as he glared at his unkempt prisoner. Sol recognized the man as one of the six gunmen he'd seen loitering around the Saddle Burr Saloon earlier in the day.

"What's your name?" he demanded sharply.

"None of your business," the shaggy-haired hooligan said with a scowl.

"I'm making it my business," Sol snapped. "You tried to molest my fiancée, and we both take offense to that."

Fiancée? Damn, that sounded odd. Never in his wildest dreams had he expected to have one of those—ever. He knew absolutely nothing about dealing with females, especially one as high-spirited and quick-witted as Josephine Malloy.

"If that hellion is yer fiancée you shoulda kept closer tabs on her," the attacker snorted.

Sol scoffed. How many desperadoes who blamed him for their shortcomings had he encountered over the years? More than he cared to count. The bastards never wanted to own up to their sins and transgressions.

"You go near Josephine again and I'll shoot you a couple of times," he growled threateningly. "If you try to retaliate against her for fighting back, I'll slit your throat. If you touch her, you're a dead man. Do you understand me?" He stared at the hombre with fierce intensity. "And make no mistake, you won't be the first man I've killed, and you won't be the last. Now…what's your name?"

The defiant ruffian thrust out his stubbled chin and clamped his swollen lips shut.

Sol untied one of the horses he had for sale, then stabbed his forefinger at the prisoner, silently ordering him to climb aboard bareback. Scowling, the man mounted up, then swore foully when Sol coiled a rope around his neck, tied it to his wrists, then hooked it around the mount's neck and belly.

"We have our own ways of dealing with men who mistreat women," said a voice behind them.

Sol half turned to see the frizzy-haired, self-appointed leader of the rescue brigade, which had formed a semicircle behind him. "This man is headed for the stockade at the garrison," Sol declared authoritatively. "This area is under martial law, and vigilante justice is prohibited here and everywhere else." Damn, he sounded like a lawman, he realized. Sol told himself to watch what he said and how he said it in the near future.

The stocky man, whose face was covered with so much brown hair that he reminded Sol of a buffalo, lumbered forward to extend his hand. "Orson Barnes is my name. I guess you have a right to do as you see fit with this molester of women. And congratulations on your betrothal to Miz Malloy," he added begrudgingly. "You are the envy of all the single men in camp. I'm surprised she changed her mind, though. When I proposed to her this morning she said she wasn't ready to settle down anytime soon."

Sol smiled faintly as he looked past Orson and noted that he was receiving plenty of annoyed glances from Josephine's jilted suitors. The competition for a woman's affection in these mostly male tent communities was fierce, he reminded himself. "I must've caught her at a weak moment."

"Didn't know she had any weak moments."

Sol doubted she did, either.

"That's a lot of woman you got there, Mr.…?" Orson waited for Sol to fill in the blank.

"Tremain. I'm a horse trader." He inclined his head toward his prisoner. "Do you happen to know this hombre by name?"

"Harlan Kane," Orson replied. "He shares a tent with three other scruffy men on the north side of camp."

"Do you know their names?" Sol questioned.

"Bernie Hobart, Wendell Latimer and Ramon Alvarez." He rattled them off.

"You'd do well to mind your own business, too," Harlan muttered threateningly at Orson, who shrugged, undaunted. "My friends might pay you a visit when you least expect it."

Sol narrowed his gaze at his prisoner. No doubt threats of violence were this gang's specialty.

"You want me to keep an eye on Miz Malloy until you get back from the fort, Tremain?" Orson volunteered as the crowd of men behind him dispersed.

"Good idea. Thanks," he said as he mounted Outlaw. "I won't be back tonight, so tell my fiancée to sleep with her pistol under her pillow and one eye open."

When the man lumbered off to become Josie's temporary protector, Sol headed west. He halted Outlaw when he saw Muriel scurrying toward him, waving her arms to flag him down.

"May I have a private word with you, Mr. Tremain?" she asked anxiously, panting to catch her breath.

"Sol," he corrected. "Give me a minute to secure my prisoner."

Smiling to himself, Sol dismounted. He had a pretty good idea what Muriel wanted. He had to hand it to these two spirited women; there was nothing passive about either of them. They didn't sit and wait for the world to come to them, but grabbed the proverbial bull by the horns.

Sol predicted that any man who got tangled up with them would never experience a dull moment.

But hell, he wouldn't know what a dull moment felt like, even if it walked up and slapped him in the face, Sol mused. He existed in a rough-and-tumble world where flying bullets, slashing knives and hellish weather conditions prevailed. Becoming *engaged*—even to a lively spitfire like Josephine—couldn't be *that* bad…could it?

Chapter Four

Sol ambled over to tie his prisoner to a tree, horse and all. When Kane cursed him soundly, he ignored him and strode back to Muriel. She motioned for Sol to follow her to a clump of cottonwood trees that stood several yards away from a row of tents.

"I wonder if I could ask a small favor," she began, wringing her hands as she spoke.

Sol anticipated what she wanted, but he was ornery by nature and habit, and made her ask. "It depends on what the favor is. What is it you want from me?"

She expelled a gusty breath, then said, "Will you ask Captain Holbrook if we can be engaged? At least for—" She clamped her mouth shut and looked the other way.

"For how long?" Sol demanded. He figured his betrothal would terminate at the exact time Grant's did—when these clever females had no more use for their fiancés. They would discard Sol and Grant without the slightest regard for their pride or feelings.

Muriel winced, then stared at the air over his right shoulder. "What I meant to say was—"

"I know exactly what you meant," Sol interrupted sharply, resorting to the tactics he utilized when dealing with criminals. "Don't tell me. Let me guess. Grant and I will serve your purpose until right after the run, so you can go your merry way. Is that it?"

She shifted uneasily and refused to meet his intense gaze.

He leaned on her harder. "No? Until *when,* then?"

She clamped her mouth shut, reminding him a lot of Josie.

"If you want me to deliver your request to Holbrook and get him to agree to it, then you'll have to tell me the specific terms of these arrangements. Otherwise, I won't help."

She sighed heavily, then blurted, "Until the day of the run." Muriel looked relieved to have the truth out in the open. "Josie figures the men that keep hounding us with proposals will be too busy establishing and protecting their new homesteads to bother us for a few weeks."

"Oh, she does, does she?" Sol wasn't sure why the news of Josie's premeditated plot annoyed him so much, but it did. He'd be engaged for a week. And wouldn't you know this conniving scheme was *Josephine's* bright idea? No surprise there.

"Yes. After that, we won't be as easily accessible as we are in the tent community and in town," she explained.

"I can foresee all sorts of problems with this harebrained plan, which leaves you two separated and *unprotected* on your newfound claims," Sol cautioned. "You will become easy prey for claim jumpers trying to steal your land, because you won't have reinforcements to back you up."

Muriel tilted her head in a manner that instantly reminded him of the witch-angel that went by the name of Josephine. "We will stake adjoining claims so we can watch each other's backs."

"Right," Sol said, and snorted caustically. "Just like you were there to help Josephine fend off Kane tonight."

Muriel bit her lip and wrung her hands some more. "Next time I won't leave her alone."

"You just did," Sol reminded her with a stern glance. "I recommend you both become handy with pistols. Stabbing claim jumpers with sewing needles might not be discouragement enough."

When he turned around to walk off, Muriel called after him. "You *will* ask the captain for me, won't you?"

Sol halted, then frowned contemplatively. A wicked grin creased his lips when a thought occurred to him. He pivoted to face the attractive brunette. "I will square it with Holbrook *if,* and only *if,* you'll accept my stipulation," he stated.

Muriel eyed him warily. "What is your stipulation?"

"You can't tell Josephine that *I* know when you two plan to terminate these engagements."

"But she's my friend and I—"

Sol made a slashing gesture with his hand to silence her. "That is the condition. Take it or leave it."

Muriel blew out an exasperated breath, then tapped her foot in irritation.

"Well?" he prompted impatiently. "I propose for you, and you don't tell Josie what I know. Otherwise, the deal is off. *Decide*."

The brunette steamed and stewed for a full minute, then nodded her head in a way that conveyed her annoyance with him. "You drive a hard bargain, Mr. Tremain."

"I'm a horse trader. It's what I do," he teased, straight-faced.

"Very well, then, since you leave me with little choice," she said begrudgingly. "But I want it understood that it goes against my grain to keep secrets from my best friend."

"Duly noted," Sol replied with a slight inclination of his head.

After Muriel stamped off, he wheeled away. In this, at least, he planned to remain one step ahead of that clever minx who had drawn him into her scheme.

He and Grant would become the envy—and perhaps objects of vicious retaliation—of rejected suitors. Suddenly, Sol wondered if this might become the engagement from hell, after all, considering the feisty temperament of his supposed fiancée and the irritation of her legion of jilted beaus.

Luckily, he and Grant could roast over the same bonfire. He'd always heard that misery loved company.

Guess he was about to find out.

When Sol strode into the commander's office at the garrison, Grant was bent over the daily report, studiously jotting down information. He glanced up, clearly surprised to see Sol.

"What are you doing here? I thought you were going to snoop around the camp where Bradley pitched his tent."

"I decided to swing by Josie and Muriel's camp to sell a few horses before I headed north," Sol explained. "Good thing I did. A drunken cowboy that I recognized as one of the gunmen at the Saddle Burr Saloon this morning was attacking Josie."

Had it just been this morning? Damn, another long day.

"What?" Grant croaked in dismay. "Is she all right? Was Muriel attacked, too?"

Hmmm… Funny that you should ask, thought Sol. "No, she didn't make the same mistake, of tramping off alone to tend to her horse. Fortunately, I arrived to intervene before the bastard could do his worst and Josephine lost more than her temper." Sol cast aside the unpleasant memory of seeing the scoundrel force himself on her. "I brought Harlan Kane here so you can toss him in the stockade. I figured if I took him to town, his boss might try to *bail* him out of jail—or *break* him out."

"Well, that's one gunslinger down and five to go," Grant said as he pushed away from his desk and rose to his feet. "Kane can sober up in the stockade. Have you questioned him about his connection to Carlton Bradley?"

Sol shook his head. "He is belligerent about answering any questions. One of the would-be settlers gave me his name, and those of the other three men that share his tent in the same camp where Josie and Muriel live. But I've had too much on my mind tonight to concentrate on Kane."

Grant waggled his eyebrows suggestively and grinned. "It doesn't have anything to do with your encounter with Button-Eye Malloy, does it?"

"Laugh while you can, Holbrook. But you won't be so amused when I tell you what *your* future holds," Sol countered. "You only *think* you have problems, what with routing devious squatters, investigating robberies and breaking up fights between all these land-grubbing settlers that have gathered for the race, in hopes of finding their personal version of paradise."

Grant halted at the door, then pivoted to stare warily at him. "What's happened that's going to give me more headaches than I have already?"

Sol took wicked satisfaction in saying, "Miz Wilson asked me to deliver a message to you. And congratulations are in order. You have become engaged this evening."

"What?" Grant howled in disbelief.

Sol snickered while the commander staggered back against the door to steady himself. It didn't help much, he noted. "At least I'm delivering *your* engagement announcement in private. I received *mine* in front of a crowd of disgruntled men."

"Yours?" Grant bleated. "What the hell?"

Sol ambled over to park himself in the spare chair

in the office. Then he stacked his booted feet on the edge of Grant's desk. "It seems Miz Malloy and Miz Wilson decided to acquire pretend fiancés to counter the endless proposals they receive from the men trailing after them.

"It was *Josephine's* brilliant idea, I was told by your betrothed," he reported. "They plan to use us as props until the day of the run. After that, they will cut us loose, while they race off to stake their claims, or get trampled by wagon wheels or horses. Whichever happens first."

Grant stared at him, stunned to the bone. Sol snapped his fingers to jostle the man from his trance. "Are you hearing all of this, Holbrook? These two women don't seem to be holding out for the best match they can make, as you and I first thought. They are as independent-minded as two women can get."

The commander opened and closed his mouth like a fish, but no words came out.

"Consider yourself fortunate," Sol added, since Grant had been struck speechless. "I had to pretend I had prior knowledge of my betrothal. The crowd was hugely disappointed that one of the two most sought-after brides had been snatched off the marriage market. I should have denied Josephine's claim and made her look like a fool in front of that captive audience."

It's what she deserved, he assured himself. And after all, *he* was in the business of seeing folks get what they deserved. "But I was so damned shocked by the prospect of becoming engaged to anyone—especially *her*—that I just stood there and let her get away with it."

I should have embarrassed that sassy female, he mused spitefully. Why he cared about *her* feelings, when she had not the slightest regard for *his,* Sol didn't know. But he wasn't in the mood to delve into his reasons for giving her a free pass just now, for fear he might not like what he discovered about himself.

Deputy U.S. Marshal Solomon Tremain was not, and would never be, a sentimental softy, he assured himself confidently. That kind of attitude wouldn't fly—and could even get him killed—in his dangerous line of work.

When Grant finally regained his senses, he burst out laughing. "I wish I could have been there to see that."

"No, you don't. Soon as Josephine made her unexpected announcement, the men turned to Muriel as the last highly prized potential bride. She promptly declared that *you* had proposed to *her* an hour earlier, while you two were off riding together. You would have been caught flat-footed, the same way I was."

"She wants to marry me? She doesn't even like me," Grant mused aloud. "And personally, I didn't get the impression Miz Malloy was particularly fond of you."

"I was convenient," Sol replied, though the truth stung his pride. He frowned pensively, then added, "When you think about it, their scheme makes perfect sense."

"Then you should explain it to me, because I don't get it," Grant muttered as he reversed direction and plunked down in the chair he had vacated earlier. "Why would a woman purposely set out to marry someone she doesn't like?"

"Because it's easy to dismiss a fiancé you don't particularly want," Sol said perceptively. "We will serve their purpose until the morning of the run. There will be no sentimental attachment involved when they discard us at the last possible moment and race off to claim a homestead."

"So essentially, we are the two least desirable men on earth, so they want to marry us?" he paraphrased. "That isn't very flattering."

Sol grinned as he planted his hands on Grant's desk and then leaned toward him. "No, it isn't. Unless we turn out to be the very picture of charm and devotion...."

The commander frowned, bemused. "I'm not following the way you're drifting, Tremain."

"We outfox those vixens," he suggested. "We take part in their scheme and make sure every man in the area knows we are the perfect fiancés. We'll do our best to convince Josephine and Muriel that we are, too.

"I made Muriel promise not to tell Josie that I know about their plan to call off the engagement. We will pretend the engagements are for real." He grinned slyly. "We'll make them feel guilty and cold-blooded for using us as their shields against unwanted proposals. Then we break off the engagement the day *before* the run. Let those wily women field dozens of last-minute proposals while they prepare for the race. Serves those conniving females right, in my opinion."

"That is sneaky," Grant said, grinning wryly. "I love it! We'll take them into town for lunch and put on a show of devotion. Do everything right that their suitors did all wrong. I'll charm that woman's stockings off and make her regret dragging me into this scheme."

Sol would settle for giving that blue-eyed minx a parting kiss—like the one that still lingered on his lips and fogged his mind. That steamy taste of pleasure had fired his blood and sent his imagination running away with itself—and he still hadn't chased it down! Now he wished he didn't know how much he liked kissing Josephine. He wondered if he'd had the slightest effect on her. Probably not, calculating little witch that she was.

"Let's go see what Harlan Kane can tell us about his boss," Grant suggested, bounding to his feet.

"You'll have to question him," Sol insisted. "I need to protect my identity. As far as Kane knows, I'm just an outraged husband-to-be who wants vengeance and justice because he attacked my beloved fiancée. Let's keep it that way."

"Lunch at Land Run Café tomorrow then?" the commander said on his way out the door.

"We'll have to make it day after tomorrow," he replied. "I plan to discreetly gather information about Bradley from the settlers sharing his campsite. Also, I want the names of the other two hired gunmen who share the camp with him."

Grant nodded agreeably, then strode off to fetch the

prisoner. Sol remained behind, giving the commander time to march Kane to the stockade and fire questions at him. Then he veered toward Sutler's Store, beside the military compound, to replenish supplies.

A quiet chuckle rumbled in Sol's chest as he gathered several needed items. He had told that blue-eyed firebrand that her scheme would be a costly one. Nothing would make him happier than to break that little heartbreaker's heart.

That would teach her to trample on a man's pride and use him for her own purposes, he thought spitefully.

But first he'd have to shave, clip his shaggy hair and make himself more presentable. Josephine Malloy would be damn sorry she planned to toss him aside like a worn shirt, he promised himself. They'd see who broke off this ridiculous engagement first!

The next day Josie was busy mending a shirt for a customer who'd been roughed up the previous night. Thieves had practically ripped off his pocket to steal the money he had carried with him to town. She might have felt sorry for the young man, except he'd been wasting his money at one of the many saloons. He hadn't had his wits about him when he'd been attacked in the darkness. Worse, he couldn't provide the city marshal with accurate descriptions of his two assailants.

The thought reminded Josie of her unnerving encounter with Harlan Kane—may he rot in the stockade until hell froze over! She had been reminded of an important lesson: never let your guard down for even a moment with so many strangers milling around.

The crackle of twigs put Josie on high alert. As a precaution, she had laid her pistol in her lap—just in case trouble tried to sneak up on her while she was sitting beneath a shade tree a short distance from the tents.

A tall, square-faced, square-bodied rancher with gray eyes swaggered toward her. He had reddish-brown hair and wore stylish Western breeches, shirt and a leather vest decorated with silver conchos. He looked an inch or two shorter and a year or two older than Tremain…. And why that horse trader had become a yardstick for measuring other men, she didn't know. Maybe, because he was her fake fiancé, it was only natural to compare other men to him.

She found it disconcerting to realize Tremain left the others sadly lacking in physical appeal.

The newcomer practically undressed her with his eyes, then flashed what Josie presumed to be his most engaging smile. It fell short of the mark and didn't have the slightest effect on her—except to make her even more wary of his intentions.

"If you have a garment that needs repair, drop it off." After last night, Josie had lost most of her charm and all respect for men, especially one she didn't recognize as a member of this tent community. "You are fifth in line for mending, so don't be impatient."

The rancher flashed another beaming smile as he propped himself leisurely against the nearby tree that provided her shade. "My name is Carlton Bradley, Miz

Malloy. I came to talk to you about my friend Harlan Kane. He had a little too much to drink last night and behaved badly," he said with a distinct Texas drawl.

Josie stared at him critically. "You should find yourself a better class of friends, Mr. Bradley—"

"Carlton," he interrupted with a wink, then tossed her another glowing smile.

"Kane is nothing but a drunkard and a ruffian."

Her visitor shrugged his shoulders nonchalantly. "There is nothing much to do in these tent towns, and folks are jittery with anticipation of making the run." He flung her another cajoling smile—which was getting old quick, in her opinion. "You know men will be men, so let's let bygones be bygones, shall we?"

"No, we shall not," she countered sharply. "Now, unless you have need of my sewing skills, our business is concluded."

He leaned down, invading her space, so she pointed her needle toward his eye, silently warning him to back off.

He did, reluctantly. "Well, then, I'll make it worth your while to drop the charges against Harlan Kane, sweetheart."

Josie gnashed her teeth. Calling her sweetheart had the opposite effect of endearing her to him. She had known Bradley only five minutes and already didn't like him. She watched him make a big production of retrieving a leather poke from the inside pocket of his vest. Then he waved several banknotes in her face.

"How much will it cost to encourage you to drop the charges?"

She set aside the torn garment she was mending, then stood up. She clutched her pistol in her hand, letting her arm dangle beside her hip in warning. "You must be hard of hearing. This conversation was over long before you started flashing around money."

His granite-gray eyes narrowed and his expression transformed into a scowl. A moment later, however, the Texan gathered his composure and mustered a smile. "You're a strong-willed, spirited woman. I like that."

"Really? Most men don't," she replied, deciding she definitely didn't like the man and his air of self-importance. She wanted him gone. Now.

"I'll be honest with you, honey."

Sure you will, she thought, not believing Bradley for a second.

"I'm making arrangements to set up a ranch in the new territory. A woman with your beauty and spunk would make a fine wife for an ambitious man like me. We can double our land claims—"

"You're too late, Mr. Bradley," she took delight in telling him. "I have a fiancé and we are pooling our resources." She shooed Carlton on his way with her free hand. "Now, if you will excuse me, I have work to do."

When she turned away, he grabbed her arm to detain her. "Who is this fiancé of yours?" he asked suspiciously. "Last I heard you were still unattached."

She stared at the blunt-tipped fingers wrapped around

her forearm, then glared at him until he released her. "I'm marrying the horse trader."

Bradley barked a laugh. "He's a here-today-and-gone-tomorrow kind of man."

Which is precisely why I singled him out, she replied silently.

"Now me, I'm establishing a new ranch to rival the size of my father's spread in Texas. We'll see who holds more power and prestige when all is said and done."

His speech provoked her into a frown. She could hear the underlying resentment in his voice, but had no interest in his family problems. Josie had to deal with issues pertaining to her own father, so she wasn't about to become mixed up with his.

Furthermore, she didn't give a whit about this Texan's past—only his immediate departure and complete absence from her life in the future.

"How do you plan to acquire vast amounts of property when everyone is entitled to a claim of no more than a hundred and sixty acres?" she asked with wary disdain.

A crafty grin curved his thin lips as he brushed his forefinger over her cheek. But he backed off when she rammed the business end of her pistol into his belly.

"You were saying?" she prompted.

"If you stick with me, darlin', I can teach you plenty of things…about land acquisition, too."

The suggestive remark earned him a disgusted snort from Josie. "I plan to take my instructions in various subjects from my soon-to-be husband. It's time you—"

"Josie? Is everything all right?"

To her relief, she looked past Bradley's square physique—which was nowhere near as appealing as Tremain's muscular, power-packed build—to see Muriel toting a pistol of her own. Apparently, that was why she had made a trip to town this morning. After last night's fiasco, Muriel must have decided she needed to add another weapon to her arsenal.

"Everything is fine," Josie assured her friend. "Mr. Bradley—"

"Carlton," he corrected, as he leered at Muriel's shapely figure. Then he flashed her a come-hither smile that failed to move either woman in the least.

"Mr. Bradley was just leaving," Josie continued, ignoring the unwanted visitor.

Having dismissed the cocky Texan, she strode over to see what else Muriel had purchased in town. Scowling, Bradley brushed past her, knocking her partially off balance on his way.

Muriel frowned as she watched the Texan disappear between the rows of tents. "What did he want?"

"To convince me to drop the charges against my attacker. Apparently, they are friends."

"Which is all the more reason to have nothing to do with him," she advised.

"Amen to that," Josie declared. "Since I refused his request, he tried to bribe me into letting Harlan Kane go free."

Muriel harrumphed in annoyance. "My opinion of Carlton Bradley keeps getting worse."

"I'm not finished yet." Josie sank down on the wooden stool to finish mending the ripped pocket on the shirt. "When that tactic failed, he tried to persuade me to marry him, so I could reap the benefits of the sprawling ranch he plans to establish after the run."

Muriel smirked. "How many women is he planning on marrying to accumulate so much land? An entire harem?"

"I don't know what scheme he has in mind, but whatever it is, I doubt there is anything legal about it," she muttered as she stitched away.

"Didn't you tell him you already have a fiancé?"

"Yes, but that didn't discourage him from proposing."

"Maybe our plan won't be as effective as we'd hoped," Muriel fretted as she folded and unfolded the paper in her hand.

Josie frowned inquiringly. "What is that?"

Her friend handed her the note and said, "One of the soldiers from the fort dropped this by a while ago. What do you make of it?"

Josie read the message: *Captain Holbrook and Solomon Tremain request the pleasure of your company for lunch in town tomorrow. Your military escorts will arrive at eleven to accompany you to Land Run Café.*

Then she glanced up at Muriel. "I have no idea what this is about. Maybe we are going to be put on display to assure our rejected suitors that we are officially off the marriage market."

Muriel bit her lip worriedly, shifted from one foot to the other and then glanced sideways. "Josie…?"

"Don't start feeling guilty about this," Josie insisted, while she trampled her own nagging conscience with both feet. "I don't like having to resort to desperate measures any more than you do, but I'm fed up with men hounding us constantly. This is the first morning I haven't had to listen to a couple of proposals before breakfast."

"But Bradley was here to propose midmorning," Muriel pointed out.

"He isn't staying in this tent community and he hadn't heard the news," Josie explained. "But the fact is that none of the men who proposed to us have looked past outward appearances to discover who we are on the inside. How many times have men treated us as if we were interchangeable, when you reject a proposal and they turn around and make one to me?"

Muriel sighed audibly. "All too often."

"One of us is as good as the other when it comes to a man claiming a wife," Josie said cynically. "Heavens! I expect these male settlers will be more selective about the land they stake in the run."

"You're right, of course." Her friend gathered her resolve. "If I can't matter to a man, if I can't be someone special to him, then I want nothing to do with marriage."

"Same goes for me. I doubt I'll ever get past being so skeptical about the hidden agendas of men to consider wedlock," Josie remarked. "We'll find a way—somehow—to repay Holbrook and Tremain for running interference for us this week. We'll start by paying for our own meals at lunch tomorrow. We won't allow the temporary engagements to prove overly expensive for our fake fiancés. Fair enough?"

"Fair enough," Muriel confirmed with a decisive nod. Then she paced back and forth for half a minute. "But I'll still spend the whole day stewing. I don't know how the captain took the news of his sudden engagement to me."

Josie smiled wryly as she handed Muriel a tattered shirt that needed her attention. "I guess we'll find out tomorrow, won't we?"

Chapter Five

"My goodness, doesn't he look handsome?" Muriel gasped.

Josie was as astounded as her friend was. "Incredible," she mumbled when she first caught sight of Tremain and Holbrook, as the two soldiers from the fort escorted the ladies into town for lunch.

Their pretend fiancés stood on the boardwalk outside the Land Run Café. Josie admitted to herself that Solomon Tremain was the most ruggedly attractive man she had ever clapped eyes on. He was cleanly shaved today and had clipped his thick mane of raven hair. Not only that, but he was dressed in a fashionable three-piece black suit and shiny boots.

Dear heaven! thought Josie. Had Tremain gone to all this trouble and expense because he thought they were actually engaged to be married—*for life?* A wagonload of guilt weighed heavily upon her.

"That dress uniform makes him look like royalty, doesn't it?" Muriel said confidentially.

Josie blinked and came to her senses when she realized her friend wasn't talking about Tremain—who had immediately drawn Josie's eye and held her attention. Muriel was bedazzled by Captain Holbrook, who was decked out in white gloves, carrying his saber and wearing all the flashy trimmings of a military career officer. And yes, the captain was attractive. Yet in Josie's opinion he wasn't as eye-catching as Tremain.

Since the very first time she'd seen the horse trader, he had seemed larger than life. When he had made quick work of Harlan Kane two nights earlier, she'd realized he was definitely a force to be reckoned with. Josie wanted to always be on his side when fights broke out.

Then there was that wild tumble downhill after he'd brought Rooster to a halt. Josie well remembered the feel of the muscular planes and contours of Tremain's masculine body pressed familiarly to hers. Not to mention that sizzling kiss he had bestowed on her after her sudden announcement of their engagement.

The very thought of his erotic kiss sent waves of forbidden pleasure washing through her.

That swarthy horse trader had taught her the meaning of passion with one walloping kiss, awakening a vibrant desire that she hadn't wanted or expected to feel.

Now here she was, engaged to the man, deceiving him and using him for her selfish purposes. She wasn't on speaking terms with her conscience presently, because it tried to torment her nonstop. She owed Tremain an explanation of her plans, she knew. She needed to inform him of the terms of this engagement she'd sprung on him without warning. She hadn't given him the chance to accept or reject the idea, but had put him on the spot in front of a captive male audience.

Tremain, bless him, had agreed to the betrothal. Judging by today's fanfare, his clean-cut appearance and new clothing, he expected they would actually be *married*. Of course he did, she mused.

Josie swallowed hard, then glanced around, noting the rapt attention she, Muriel and their military escort had drawn. People lined the street to overflowing. It was as if the two soldiers were escorting Muriel and Josie down the aisle to meet grooms waiting at the altar.

It was as close to a wedding ceremony as it could get without actually *being* one. The thought nearly choked her.

The way Tremain was staring at her suggested she meant something special to him. He wasn't visually undressing her the way Carlton Bradley, that cad, had done the previous day. No, Tremain gazed at her with a welcoming smile that cut those becoming dimples in his cheeks. The masculine appreciation in his eyes felt complimentary and respectful, and made her feel special.

"I'm a nervous wreck," Muriel mumbled as she squirmed in the saddle. "Holbrook looks as if he's glad to see me, but he might be biding his time before he lets loose at me with that army-issued pistol for dragging him into this surprise engagement."

The comment prompted Josie to study the captain carefully. Holbrook didn't appear to be nursing a grudge. Instead, he stood there silently assessing Mu-

riel, who did indeed look attractive in the dainty pink
gown she had made herself.

Even Josie had set aside her mannish clothing to don
one of the nicest dresses she owned for this occasion.
Since she had received a formal invitation for lunch,
she'd made the effort to look her best. Besides, this was
about appearance's sake, to assure the hordes of men on
hand that she and Muriel did have prospective grooms.

"If this doesn't bring us the privacy from eager suitors we've craved the past three weeks, I don't know
what will," she mumbled.

Muriel dragged her enraptured gaze away from Holbrook, stunned to realize they were the center of attention. "Gads, we are definitely on display here, aren't
we?"

"Couldn't have planned it better myself," Josie said,
and then flashed Tremain a smile to rival the brilliance
of the sun.

Sol bit back a grin when Josie turned her blinding
smile on him. She was playing her role of smitten bride-
to-be to the hilt. He watched the procession cut an impressive swath down the middle of the congested street.
Hundreds of men had stopped to stare when Josie and
Muriel arrived with their military escorts. Even Rooster
was on his best behavior while wedged between the
other well-behaved horses.

The idea of pomp and circumstance had come to Sol
while he'd been tossing, turning and begging for sleep
two nights earlier—thanks to that sizzling kiss he had

stolen from Josie after she sprang the betrothal on him. He'd been hard and aching, and she was the cause of his discomfort. This was his revenge, part one. The woman didn't know it yet, but she would pay dearly for using him and Holbrook like pawns, then insensitively trying to toss them aside.

But…damn! Josie looked so stunningly lovely with her silver-blond hair piled neatly atop her head. She was wearing that frilly blue gown that accentuated the captivating color of her forget-me-not eyes, and fitted her shapely figure like a glove.

Hungry need clobbered Sol below the belt buckle, making him shift uncomfortably from one polished boot to the other. He had to bring the flower bouquet he held behind his back around front to conceal the erotic effect that gorgeous vixen had on him.

This public display closely resembled a wedding procession—as he intended. Unfortunately, it felt too real. Sol found himself speculating what it would be like to have Josie as his wife. To have her in his bed each night and to see her lovely face each morning for the rest of his life.

Snap out of it, Tremain! he silently shouted at himself. This was no more than his scheme to repay her for using him and Holbrook as pawns. There was no wedding day or steamy honeymoon in Sol's future. Hell, he didn't even own a bed for Josie to sleep by his side. He had a headquarters at three different hotels in eastern Indian Territory, where he tramped around with a saddlebag full of "John Doe" warrants issued by Judge Parker in Fort Smith.

Ordinarily, he was rounding up whiskey peddlers, murderers, rapists and thieves that illegally hid out in the Indian nations. The closest thing to "home" was an overnight stay at his cousin Red Hawk's cabin.

Sol gave himself a mental slap to shatter his wandering thoughts when the procession drew to a halt in front of him. In synchronized rhythm, he and Holbrook stepped off the boardwalk to fetch their fiancées.

Rooster jerked his head—the cantankerous cuss— and Sol grabbed the bridle, forcing the animal to stand still for once. Handing off the bouquet for the young soldier to hold, he reached up to lift Josie from the saddle.

He took his own sweet time easing her lush body against his before he finally set her on her feet. He tried to force himself to let her go, but his unruly body was screaming at him to kiss the breath out of her while he had the chance.

And he did—out of pure orneriness, or so he told himself.

From the corner of his eye, he saw Holbrook watching his every move. However, Sol became so distracted that he might as well have been alone with Josie on the street, for all the attention he was paying to what transpired around him. He kissed her as if there was no tomorrow, no land run, no assignment to concern him.

Then he raised his head and said, "I've missed you, Josephine." He kissed her again, as if he was starving for another taste of her—which he was, damn it! But he'd shoot off his gun hand before he revealed that information to the scheming little spitfire so she could use it against him.

His dazed brain finally registered the laughter and applause echoing around him, but he was too busy feasting on Josie's sensuous lips to remember this was supposed to be a charade. Apparently, *she* hadn't forgotten, because she looped her arms around his neck and kissed him back, in what he assumed was an attempt to convince her jilted beaus that Sol was her one and only.

Whatever her ultimate purpose, her embrace bombarded him with so much arousing pleasure that the top of his head was about to blow off, not to mention other body parts that were taking this steamy encounter in the street much too seriously.

When Sol finally came to his senses and raised his head, he realized only half the oversize crowd was rooting him on. The other half was glaring at him for stealing one of the two most attractive, eligible females in the area.

He might find himself shot in the back one dark night if he didn't watch out.

"Can we go inside and eat?" Josie's breathless voice indicated she wasn't completely unaffected by their kiss. Good. He'd hate to be the only one burning up inside. "I'm starving," she said, hanging on to his arm for support.

"So am I." *For more than lunch,* Sol mused. He could make a feast of Josie and you wouldn't hear him complain.

He glanced sideways, to see Grant and Muriel staring at each other, oblivious to the world around them. Oh, hell, Holbrook must have kissed his pretend fiancée and caused the earth to move beneath his feet. Obviously, it was shifting beneath Muriel's, too, because she couldn't see past the commander.

Sol reclaimed the bouquet to present to Josie. "For you," he said, handing her the flowers. Then he took the lead to the café, since Holbrook was still moonstruck.

"How thoughtful, but you shouldn't have spent money on a bouquet for me," she murmured, dodging his gaze and staring at the array of colorful flowers.

Did she look a mite guilty? Good. He hoped whatever served as her conscience was working her over. "I don't get engaged every day," he replied, pouring it on thick in an effort to shame her. "I want to do it up right."

"And the suit?" she asked. "You bought it specifically for this occasion?"

"It's brand spanking new, blue eyes," he told her, then let loose a dimpled smile. "I splurged, since I need one to wear to our wedding. I decided to purchase it in advance." He leaned close to add confidentially, "I thought you wanted to make our engagement widely known, so I decided to make a big splash to help you discourage unwanted suitors. The other men probably wonder what you see in me, but I'm trying to look civilized and presentable so I won't embarrass you."

Sol inwardly snickered when she refused to meet his gaze again. He intended to tie her conscience in knots over this grand scheme of hers.

Once they were seated inside, Josie leaned toward him to murmur, "Muriel and I decided to pay our share. No sense of you and Holbrook spending your hard-earned money, since we roped you into this."

Sol caught another whiff of the lavender scent surrounding her. He tamped down his unruly desires, which kept getting in the way of his attempt to shame the living hell out of her.

"Not a chance of that, my beloved betrothed," he said with a teasing wink. "Grant and I decided that since we are engaged to be married, we will do it properly. We will become your husbands, protectors and providers—"

"I shouldn't have forced—" she began, trying to interrupt, but Sol would have none of that.

"My people take marriage very seriously," he told her. "In our culture, this morning's procession is much the same as a lawful wedding ceremony. In the eyes of the Cheyenne, we are as good as married. Not to worry, Josephine, I've been taught to honor my obligations and responsibilities."

He bit back a chuckle when his supposed fiancée slumped back in her chair and stared at the flowers she had practically crushed in her grasp. He almost felt sorry for her, she looked so uncomfortable. Yet he refused to forget that she had asked for this, and he was a man who dispensed justice. After all, there were times when he had to become judge, jury and executioner while representing the long arm of the law.

This cunning charade wasn't criminal, but this beguiling, conniving beauty had committed a *crime* against his pride, and she was going to pay.

Sol cut a quick glance at Grant and Muriel, and decided the captain had become a fallen soldier. If that wasn't a lovesick expression plastered on Grant's face, he didn't know what was. Which meant it was Sol's sworn duty to torment the feisty female who had dragged them into this charade as her deserved punishment.

"A toast," he declared, loudly enough to snap Grant out of his mesmerized trance and bring Muriel to her senses. "Here's to our long and happy marriages."

Four glasses of lemonade clinked in midair. Sol watched Josie discreetly, noting her wobbly smile. He enjoyed seeing her stew in her own juice. It was the most fun he'd had in years.

"I'm not feeling well," she murmured, trying to scoot her chair away from the table. "I should return to camp."

Sol, still smiling, clamped his hand over hers. "Stay," he insisted. "You'll feel better after you eat, I'm sure."

A few more generous helpings of guilt should do the trick, he thought wickedly. Then he proceeded to order the most expensive meals in the house.

Two hours later, after parading up and down the street—in case any new arrivals had missed the mock wedding procession before lunch—Sol watched the military escort accompany Josie and Muriel back to camp.

Then he glanced at Grant and said, "You certainly

played the role of smitten fiancé to the hilt. You missed your calling in theater."

The commander dragged his gaze off the departing foursome. "I did, didn't I? You weren't too bad yourself. Especially when you spouted off about the Cheyenne marriage ritual."

Sol was surprised he had heard the comment, since the man had been so entranced by Muriel's every expression and remark.

"If I can make those two feel guilty as hell for using us, then I've accomplished my mission," Sol said as he strode beside Grant to fetch their horses.

"What other schemes have you dreamed up to stab our fiancées with guilt?" Grant questioned, a little too eagerly. "Should we go courting this evening, do you think?"

"Do what you want," Sol insisted. "I plan to let Josie fry in her own grease for a day or two. Besides, my job demands that I monitor Bradley, his small army of gunmen and other possible criminals to see what they're up to."

Sol's words reminded Grant that he had duties to attend to, as well—such as this damn land run! "By the way," he said as he swung into the saddle, "Muriel mentioned that Josie mended a shirt for a would-be settler who was recently robbed by two men in town, near one of the saloons."

And who, as if he didn't know, made the saloons and brothels their second home? Again, Bradley and his thugs.

"Could the victim identify his assailants?" Sol asked.

Grant shook his head. "No, he had been drinking heavily. According to Josie, he got what he deserved for wasting money that could have been used to make improvements on his claim."

What he deserved? Sol mused. Good thing the woman believed justice should prevail, because he damn sure intended to see that she tasted her just deserts.

"Before the women rode off, Josie hastily mentioned that another man proposed to her yesterday. Then he tried to bribe her into dropping charges against Harlan Kane. I didn't have a chance to question her further because they were in an all-fired rush to leave. Guilty consciences is my guess."

Sol frowned disconcertedly. "I wonder if it was Bradley who paid her a call."

"It could have been him or one of his ruffians." Grant reined his horse around. "I better get back to the garrison. I have Sooners to rout from their hiding places on the wrong side of the boundary line…." His voice trailed off when a soldier on horseback trotted toward him, dodging pedestrians in his haste.

"Is there a problem, Private Stotts?" Grant asked without preamble.

The young soldier nodded his blond head. "Yes, sir. The prisoner you stuffed in the stockade two nights ago is gone."

Sol bit back a curse. "Not Kane, I hope."

Stotts again bobbed his head. "Afraid so."

Damn it to hell! "That bastard might be out for revenge on Josie," Sol muttered. "How did it happen?"

Stotts shifted uneasily in the saddle. "The guard on duty said someone clobbered him over the head. He's in the infirmary nursing a hellish headache."

Bradley was behind it, whether he committed the offense or not, Sol was sure.

"I'll put a guard on Josie," Grant stated.

"I'll do it myself," Sol insisted—and then wondered why he had. It wasn't as if he didn't have enough duties to attend without camping out near Josie's tent at night to ensure her attacker didn't try to snatch her away under cover of darkness.

"Your call," Grant said, sending the soldier on ahead of him so he could speak privately with Sol. "Let me know when you think it's time to give the wheel of torture another spin to torment our fiancées."

With a wave, Sol reined Outlaw around, planning to head south, but pulled the horse to a halt when he recognized Carlton Bradley from the description Grant had given him a few days earlier. Sol couldn't believe his luck. This encounter would save him time—and he didn't have a lot to spare.

"I saw the formal procession this morning," the Texan drawled as he reached up to shake his hand. "I'm Carlton Bradley and you are a lucky man. More fortunate, in fact, than you even know yet."

"The name is Sol Tremain." He raised his eyebrows. "What makes me so lucky?"

"If you'll climb down and join me for a drink I'll explain it to you," Bradley invited.

Sol dismounted, then tied Outlaw outside the gun shop. When the broad, square-shouldered Texan gestured toward the Silver Dollar Saloon, he fell into step beside him.

"First off, I'd like to purchase two or three of your horses before the run. You can name your price, Tremain."

Sol flashed a wry grin. "I always do, so don't doubt it."

He wondered if Bradley intended to pay him with stolen money. Probably. After all, he might be spearheading a gang of thieves that preyed on would-be settlers.

"How much more fortunate am I going to get today?" Sol asked, with just the right amount of interest.

The man grinned as he reached inside his vest pocket. "In addition to the horses, I'll pay you to bow out of your engagement to Miz Malloy."

Sol hadn't expected that. However, if this was the man who had approached Josie with a marriage proposal, then tried to bribe her to release Kane, it made perfect sense. Since she had refused to drop the charges, Bradley—or one of his ruffians—must have sprung Kane from the stockade and cracked the unsuspecting guard's skull.

"What's your interest in my fiancée?" Sol questioned as he halted outside the saloon.

"I've decided I want her," Bradley declared frankly.

"I'm in the habit of getting what I want." He waved several banknotes in the air, then tucked them back into his pocket. "In most cases, I believe women serve a man's purposes and his pleasures, so one is as good as another. But this little spitfire openly challenged me, and we aren't finished yet."

Sol found himself wedged between the proverbial rock and a hard place. When dealing with criminals, he made a conscious effort never to let them know who or what was important to him, so they couldn't use his vulnerabilities against him. He had no choice now but to shrug nonchalantly and leave Bradley with the impression that Josie could be easily replaced, *if* he intended to wed her at all.

Besides, she *was* replaceable to him…wasn't she? She was *using* him, so surely had no special feelings for him, he reminded himself.

"What are you implying?" Sol said, staring pointedly at the concho-decorated vest where Bradley had stashed his roll of banknotes.

The man's expression turned hard. "I'm not *implying*," he corrected. "I'm *telling* you that I want the woman and a few horses. Simple as that."

Sol noted the veiled threat. He also recalled the dowry tradition in white and Indian cultures, and decided to use it to his advantage. "Buy a half-dozen of my horses and I'll break off my engagement…for a thousand dollars."

The Texan's brows shot upward and his gray eyes bulged.

"You think I couldn't sell off my fiancée to one of these love-starved homesteaders for more money?" Sol questioned confidently. "Men have been clambering all over each other, flinging proposals at her for weeks. She is extremely valuable property and you know it."

Muttering foully, Bradley handed him a down payment. "You drive a hard bargain, horse trader."

"I hear that a lot," Sol replied flippantly. "I'll give you a few days to come up with the rest of the money." He wondered if there would be a rash of robberies that he could link to Bradley's thieving brigands as a result. "I'm not calling off my engagement until the money is in hand, understood?"

Bradley gave a sharp nod. Clearly, he wasn't accustomed to someone standing up to him. Too bad. Sol wasn't accustomed to backing down to worthless criminals like Bradley.

However, Sol couldn't afford to anger or alienate the Texan, who was a possible suspect for robbery and a federal jailbreak. Sol needed to gather evidence to use against him. He was walking a fine line, and was not in the habit of allowing sentiment to sway his actions.

"And I'm not giving you a money-back guarantee if Josephine doesn't accept your proposal," Sol stipulated. "The woman has a mind of her own and she knows how to use it."

"That's a fact." Bradley scowled. "But she can be tamed with a firm hand, just like your horses, and I'm the man who can do it."

Sol inwardly winced, wondering if he was the kind

of bastard that took a whip to contrary women and live-stock. The thought of this arrogant scoundrel abusing Josie tied his stomach in knots. But with luck, he could gather enough evidence of bribes, robberies or land fraud to put Bradley away until the Texan was old and gray—or dead. Preferably dead, if he tried to mistreat Josie.

Yet Sol didn't want to bring him to justice at Josie's expense. She might deserve to be paid back for her cunning scheme and its effect on his male pride, but he wouldn't allow her to suffer abuse. His conscience wouldn't permit him to enjoy even one night of sleep for the rest of his life if that happened.

"I'll bring the horses later this week," Sol announced, as he tucked away the money in his drawstring pouch, then crammed it into the inside pocket of his stylish vest. "Where are you staying?" As if he didn't know.

"Just bring them into town in three days and I'll have the money by then," Bradley ordered brusquely. "You can find me at the Oasis." One of the local brothels.

Sol turned away to fetch Outlaw, cursing the whore-monger Texan at every step.

"What about that drink?" Bradley called after him.

"Maybe tomorrow. I have horses to gather now." He tossed the words over his shoulder, along with a silent *You can go to hell!*

The money Bradley had given as a down payment burned like a brand against Sol's chest. The lawman in him reminded him he had a job to do. Dealing with Bradley was an integral part of that important duty.

Still, the end would never justify the means if Josie became the sacrifice he made to see that cocky scoundrel behind bars.

Chapter Six

Josie was growing increasingly concerned about Muriel. Two days after their luncheon in El Reno, her friend was still wandering around in a daze. She rarely communicated and seemed unduly troubled. Josie was pretty sure she had fallen in love, after the kiss Holbrook had planted on her for all the world to see.

Something else was bothering her, too, Josie suspected, but all attempts to wheedle information out of her failed. Josie wondered if Muriel's conscience, like her own, was hammering at her for using the two men to avoid more proposals.

Having trouble sleeping herself, Josie listened to Muriel flop, flounce and finally collapse into a deep sleep. Still restless, Josie fled from the tent in her nightgown to enjoy the silence of the night.

She gasped in alarm when an unseen hand clamped over her mouth. Her attacker slammed her against his muscled chest. She squirmed and struggled to no avail as he dragged her farther from the security of the surrounding tents.

"Damn it, woman, what the hell are you doing, tramping around alone at this time of night? Looking to get molested?"

Josie slumped in relief when she recognized Tremain's voice hissing in her ear. When he loosened his hand, she glared at him. "What are you doing here? Molesting unsuspecting women who wander around at night?"

"I'm standing guard," he muttered, as he grasped her hand to draw her farther away from the tents.

"Why...? Ouch!" She grimaced when something sharp stabbed her bare foot.

He scooped her up and carried her off. Ordinarily, Josie would have objected. Yet the unexpected feelings she experienced while wrapped in Tremain's sinewy arms were oddly reassuring and comforting.

It still amazed her that she had broken so many of her hard-and-fast rules concerning men while dealing with this brawny horse trader. She wasn't sure what it meant, but refused to delve deeper to figure it out—in case she didn't like the answers awaiting her.

"Why are you standing guard at night?" she asked, when he finally set her on her feet on the edge of a clearing. The cool grass soothed the sting in her heel.

"Because you need a keeper. I'm your fiancé, so I'm it. You should have more sense than to wander around late at night," Tremain lectured as he led her on a zigzag path through the trees. "Unless, of course, you are a witch or evil spirit, as the Cheyenne refer to your kind, and you're on your way to some sort of witch's convention. Are you?"

Josie flashed him a withering glance. So much for that tender moment. "I'm not a witch, nor am I an idiot—"

"Couldn't prove it by me," he interrupted sardonically. "Just so you know, Harlan Kane escaped from the stockade. I wouldn't be surprised if he isn't lurking around, looking to have his revenge on you for pressing charges against him."

"Escaped? How?" she demanded.

"Someone jumped the guard and let him out," Tremain reported. "Holbrook said the two attackers wore black hoods to keep their identity secret. That's why I'm playing bodyguard. Can't have my beloved fiancée strangled or mauled or pitched in the river, can I? It wouldn't do my reputation as a protector a damn bit of good if something happened to you. In fact, *I* might be blamed for your demise."

The last comment ruffled her feathers and caused her chin to jut. "I can take care of myself, Tremain."

"So you say." He let loose a snort. "Are you packing?"

"Packing? Oh, you mean am I carrying a pistol. Not at the moment, no."

"Damnation, Josephine. Just because you gained yourself a fiancé doesn't mean men like Kane aren't waiting to take advantage of you."

Tremain stepped closer, until his powerful body was

only a scant few inches away. "Or is that what you want, firebrand? For a man to take advantage?"

She should have slapped him for the taunting remark. Yet what she suddenly wanted was to feel his sensuous lips moving over hers the way they had when he had kissed her so thoroughly during the public procession. It was unfortunate that her fascination for him chose this moment to overpower her.

Josie never invited physical contact with a man. So why did she drape her arms over Tremain's broad shoulders, then push herself up on tiptoe to steal another taste of him? She decided to sidestep the reasons for her impulsive actions, so she wouldn't have to face any messy emotions lurking in the depths of her mind. She just wanted to live in the moment, which sparkled with shadows and moonbeams.

"You win the argument," she murmured. Then she kissed him, employing the arousing techniques he'd used on her.

"I should make a note of this, since it's the first time you've let me win an argument," he teased, when she allowed him to come up for air.

Then he kissed her as if he were dying and she was his last breath. Josie was so caught up in the dizzying pleasure of his embrace that she didn't voice a single objection. Wouldn't have, even if she could have spoken. Instead, she leaned into him as if he were an indestructible anchor in a buffeting sea. She let loose her inhibitions and kissed him with all the forbidden passion bubbling inside her.

Someone moaned; she supposed it was she. Solomon's hands drifted up from her waist to trail boldly across the thin fabric covering her breasts, making her ache for more of his intimate touch. He brushed his thumbs over her nipples, provoking her to rub against him like a contented kitten.

"Damn, woman," he wheezed, dragging his mouth down her throat to the swells of her breasts. "You're killing me."

"You have it backward," she admitted. Her breath caught when he unbuttoned her nightgown to flick his tongue against her aching flesh.

A low rumble rose in his chest and echoed through her. "You like that, do you?"

"I'm not sure," she said raggedly. "Do it again."

He did, and she forgot to breathe when he drew her nipple into his mouth and suckled her. A burning ache coiled deep inside her being, then spread outward, intensifying as it went. She gasped when his splayed hand tunneled beneath the hem of her gown to skim over her inner thigh.

Josie swore she was staring cross-eyed at him when he lowered his head to take her lips in a devouring kiss at the exact same moment he glided his forefinger inside her throbbing core. She nearly came apart in his arms as he stroked her gently, repeatedly.

Desperate to ease the need raging through her, she twisted against his cupped hand and penetrating fingertip. She had no idea lust could assume complete control over her body, never knew she would want a man with such maddening intensity.

And suddenly, all the blazing-hot sensations ricocheting through her body converged, to strike like a lightning bolt. The most amazing feeling of pleasure rippled through her, undulating in all directions, leaving no part of her body untouched.

"Solomon?" she whispered in disbelief. "What…?"

He kissed away her question and savored the feel of her lush body shimmering around his fingertip. Need prowled through his body, craving release, but Sol willfully restrained himself. He would have preferred to bury himself inside her, to feel the liquid heat consuming him just as it consumed her. No doubt pleasuring her without satisfying himself would take its toll before the night was out, and unappeased desire would reduce him to ashes. But this was not the time or place. He was supposed to be her bodyguard, after all.

Already, Sol had gone places—intimate places—with this tempting beauty that he hadn't intended to go. But that didn't stop him from wanting more. He had no willpower whatsoever where Josie was concerned. That wasn't a good thing. He had learned the hard way—and he was as hard as a man could get right now—that he couldn't trust himself to be alone with her.

This alluring blonde had destroyed his restraint, his logic and his common sense—the very things he'd prided himself in perfecting the past thirty-two years. She had shot them all to hell in the course of one night.

Temptation had pushed him to the wall and left him aching.

Even while Sol stood there reading himself every line and paragraph of the riot act for taking intimate privileges, he couldn't make himself back away. Eventually, he removed his hand from beneath her gown—only to skim his fingertips over the full breasts that he had exposed a few minutes earlier.

Then he made the dangerous mistake of staring into her lustrous eyes that reflected the moonlight. He marveled at the silvery beams that formed a halo around the curly blond hair that cascaded over her shoulders. Sol couldn't remember ever craving someone to the point of obsession. He wanted to lay Josie down and make love to her until he'd expended every ounce of the raging desire pulsing through him.

"I should go," she whispered, then nearly killed him again when she reached up to limn the curve of his jaw, his cheekbones and lips.

She was torturing him with her light touch while he was trying his damnedest to be a gentleman—though never in his life had he ever aspired to *that!*

"You should have stayed put in the first place," he said, his voice not as stern as he'd hoped. But then, he was dealing with *Josie,* and his usual rules never seemed to apply to her.

He swung her around behind him so that her legs straddled his hips and he could carry her piggyback. He'd prefer to have her *riding* him in the most intimate manner possible, but Sol had learned years ago that he didn't always get what he wanted.

"Don't make the reckless mistake of wandering around at night again," he lectured sternly. "Especially not until Harlan Kane is back behind bars."

"Whatever you say, dear," she whispered in his ear, startling him with a playful side of her personality she hadn't revealed until now. Ah, just what he didn't need—another reason to like her.

Sol remembered his conversation with Bradley, and his attempt to leave the impression that he had no particular attachment to Josie. But he'd be lying if he denied to himself that she was getting to him.

Hell and damnation, he didn't need that kind of distraction—it was a weakness that could be turned against him. That's why he had been effective in law enforcement, by remaining hardhearted, cynical and detached. He wasn't some bleeding heart that fell victim to sad stories designed to manipulate and dissuade him from doing his duty.

Scowling because of his growing attachment to a woman who was using him, Sol set Josie on her feet beside his bedroll, then shooed her on her way. To his pleasure—or frustration; he couldn't decide which—she kissed him smack-dab on the lips, then strode quickly to her tent.

Sol dragged in a steadying breath, hoping to bring his rampant desires under some measure of control. It didn't help. Considering all the unappeased lust roiling through him, he doubted he'd be able to sleep at all during the night.

Turned out he was right.

Two days before the run, Josie rode Rooster into town to gather last-minute supplies that would sustain her when she camped out on her new homestead. At least she hoped she could stake a claim. She would be thoroughly crushed if she had to trudge back to her brother's farm and bide her time until the government opened another section of land sometime in the next few years.

That worrisome thought mingled with the arousing memory of her late-night encounter with Sol in the moonlight. Josie blushed beet-red, recalling how she had surrendered to the incredible sensations he had awakened inside her. Since that night, she hadn't ventured out after dark to see if Sol was still watching over her. But each morning she saw evidence of his presence—the crushed grass left by his bedroll and his muscular body. He had become her protector, allowing her to sleep secure in the knowledge that he was there if she needed him.

And she had *needed* him every blessed night. Yet she had managed to restrain herself from going to him after the erotic interlude beside the meadow, when she had practically begged for more of his sizzling kisses and intimate caresses.

To make matters worse, guilt bombarded her constantly. She was using Sol to run interference between her and the hordes of single men pursuing her. And she had used him for her own lusty pleasure, without offering him satisfaction in return. Not that she knew how, having spent more time rejecting and discouraging men than trying to satisfy them.

In two days, she would call off the short-term engagement, she reminded herself. She would saddle Rooster and ride hell-for-leather to find her promised land. That was her lifelong objective, and she had to stick to her guns if she wanted a home of her own....

Her determined thoughts scattered like a covey of quail when she reached the edge of town and glanced down the street, to see Sol standing outside one of the local brothels. Feelings of fury and betrayal assailed her when she noticed he was chatting with none other than Carlton Bradley.

Her heart twisted in her chest, and her growing affection for Sol went up in a puff of smoke. Josie silently cursed him to the deepest reaches of Hades while she watched Bradley reach into his vest pocket to count out banknotes, then drop them into the horse trader's open palm.

Cynical to the extreme, she presumed that Bradley had made Tremain the same kind of offer he'd made her—bribery for something, though she didn't know what. But there was no doubt those two shysters were in bed together. She supposed Bradley might be buying a horse from Tremain but there were no extra horses in sight.

For all she knew Sol might have decided to make

extra money by participating in the run, then selling out to the Texan—who intended to acquire more than his one hundred sixty acres by resorting to illegal means.

Josie had fumed the previous day when she had overheard some of the men in camp whispering about the money they would collect by handing over their future claims to a Texas rancher. She'd had no doubt that they were referring to that conniving scoundrel, Bradley.

Now she suspected Sol was part of the fraudulent scheme, damn his rotten soul! And here she was, tormented over the tender feelings she hadn't wanted to feel for him, not to mention the nagging guilt over using him.

For certain, she was going to take extreme pleasure in discarding him the morning of the run! It was what he deserved for becoming Bradley's cohort.

Silently cursing Tremain up one side and down the other, Josie watched him mount Outlaw and ride off. And good riddance, she thought spitefully. If she didn't have to tell him the engagement was off, she would prefer never to see him again.

And to think she had even speculated on what it would be like to *marry* this man who'd intrigued and excited her. Thank goodness she had discovered the horse trader was no better than Bradley, before she made a foolish mistake!

At least Muriel didn't have to deal with a double-dealing rascal. Captain Holbrook came around at least once during the day to check on her. Sol hadn't bothered, Josie reminded herself sourly. He was simply the ghost that hovered outside her tent after dark. Why he felt obliged, when he didn't seem to have many scruples, she couldn't imagine.

Smothering her anger and frustration, Josie left Rooster at the edge of town so the high-spirited horse wouldn't become nervous in the crowded streets. She hiked to the general store to gather supplies. She was on her way out with an armload of goods when Carlton Bradley fell into step beside her.

"Let me help," he insisted, taking several items from her arms while she strode down the boardwalk.

Josie reclaimed her supplies. "No, thank you. I can manage by myself." Her rude tone should have been hint enough that she had no use whatsoever for him.

However, he didn't back off. "I'm trying to be friendly," he said, quickening his step to keep up with her brisk pace.

"So am I," she told him. "This is the best I can do."

"You and I could be good together," he drawled as he touched her arm in what she assumed was meant to be a tempting caress.

Josie wasn't the least bit tempted. "You are wasting your time," she insisted, shrugging him off. "I told you, I'm engaged."

He snickered as he halted beside Rooster. The bright-colored sorrel stallion threw his head up and side-stepped, making his flaxen mane ripple. The animal was an excellent judge of character, she decided.

"I wouldn't count on marrying that shiftless horse trader," Bradley remarked in a confidential tone. "I keep telling you that you'll be better off with me, sweetheart. I have grand plans and you can be part of them."

"Count me out," she said sharply as she dumped her supplies into the gunnysack secured to the pommel. Then she swung onto the saddle and stared at Bradley from her advantageous position. "I know you're scheming to deprive honest settlers of their homesteads, but I refuse to be a part of fraud."

She wasn't like Tremain, who would sell *his* soul to benefit his selfish interests, damn him! And damn her for this unwarranted sentimental attachment she had developed for him. She was living for the moment when she could cut him loose. She'd prefer to look him up right this minute and call off the pretend engagement.

But that wouldn't benefit her interests, would it?

Bradley's granite-gray eyes narrowed threateningly. He grabbed Rooster's reins before she could trot away. "You just made the biggest mistake of your life, spitfire. Just like another traitorous female I know," he growled hatefully.

Josie had no idea what woman he referred to. His mother? A traitorous lover? It didn't really matter to her. She wasn't going to ask, because she couldn't care less.

"I won't forget that you've turned me down twice," he sneered. "You'll be sorrier than you can possibly imagine—"

Rooster, bless him, reared suddenly, nearly jerking Bradley's arm from its socket and forcing him to let go or be dragged down the street. Josie wheeled the horse about and headed to the tent community, which soon would be folded up and packed away, just like her tender affection for Solomon Tremain.

She squeezed her eyes shut and cursed mightily when her heart twisted in her chest. Feelings of disappointment, betrayal and outrage swamped her during the ride home. She kept telling herself she had no right to be angry with Tremain, since she had chosen this disastrous course when she'd made her surprise engagement announcement. Yet Tremain had seemed sincere about becoming her fiancé and following through with their marriage.

Guilt had consumed her for days on end. In addition, feelings of dishonesty had hounded her, knowing he had purchased new clothes and boots for their upcoming wedding, and had spent his money on her meal.

Tainted money, she amended, thoroughly disgusted with him.

So much for those silly, whimsical speculations about what it would be like to actually marry Tremain and spend her life enjoying the erotic pleasure he aroused in her so easily.

All he aroused now was anger and resentment.

"Fare thee well, Tremain!" she muttered, picturing with regret the sea-green eyes in a ruggedly handsome face. Then she nudged Rooster with her heels, sending him racing across the meadow at breakneck speed.

By the time Josie reached the tent camp beside the river, she had cooled down somewhat. She was still aggravated at herself, and at Tremain for disappointing her. It almost came as a relief to see Muriel dithering around in the clearing beyond the tents. At least Josie could focus on whatever problem hounded her friend instead of wallowing in her own misery.

"What's wrong?" she asked as she dismounted.

Muriel stopped pacing and glanced sideways, her golden-brown eyes haunted. "Just about everything," she muttered.

"Starting with—?"

"I think I'm in love with Grant," she burst out, then went back to her pacing. "How is it possible that I can love the one man who annoys me every time he opens his mouth?"

Muriel threw up her hands in exasperation. "Now I don't want to call off the pretend engagement the day of the run, as we originally planned." She glanced miserably at Josie and expelled an enormous sigh. "I can honestly say that although more than a hundred men have proposed to me, Grant is the one I want. But I know he knows—"

Her squeaky voice died abruptly. She stared guiltily at Josie, then turned away.

Josie went on instant alert. Good God, what else could possibly go wrong that hadn't already? she wondered. Tremain had fallen in with that shyster Texan, and the Texan had threatened retribution when Josie rejected him a second time. Now Muriel was beating herself black-and-blue over the situation with Holbrook, and whatever else she refused to confide.

Scowling, Muriel lurched around to pace in the opposite direction. An uneasy sensation skittered through Josie. She wondered why her friend looked so blasted guilty and upset, and why she had stopped talking in midsentence.

"What does Grant know?" Josie asked warily.

Muriel said nothing, just wore a rut in the grass while she paced some more.

"Muriel…" Josie said warningly as she approached. "What does Grant know?"

Muriel wheeled around, inhaled a gigantic breath, then expelled it in a whoosh. "He knows we plan to call off the engagement the day of the run."

"Did you tell him? *Why?*" Josie demanded. "I thought we agreed not to—"

Muriel waved her arms expansively, then shook her head, causing the hapless pile of dark hair atop her head to tumble down the back of her neck. "You are not going to like this. Or me, for that matter."

An edgy sensation coiled in the pit of Josie's belly. "I don't like it already," she muttered, sensing impending doom. "Tell me what is going on."

Muriel inhaled another bolstering breath, then said, "The only way Tremain would agree to convince Grant to go along with the pretend engagements was for me to tell him our plans. He made me swear not to tell you they knew."

"What?" Josie howled in outrage. "He *knew* we planned to call off the engagements, and he made me feel guilty for using and deceiving him? Why, that ornery devil!"

Josie swore under her breath. Tremain had bought new garments to prick her conscience about the extra expenses he'd incurred. Not to mention that he had practically seduced her one dark and steamy night. He had left her aching for more, and had probably delighted in making her vulnerable to his kisses and caresses. Curse him! She'd like to strangle him—for starters. Then she would blast him to smithereens for taking money from Bradley.

Who knew what that little transaction she'd witnessed in town was all about? More than she could possibly imagine, she presumed. Damn it all, that sneaky horse trader had played her for an unsuspecting fool. Now what was she supposed to do with the bittersweet feelings that were warring inside her?

"Josie? I'm so sorry," Muriel murmured brokenly. "Tremain swore me to secrecy. My conscience has been eating me alive because he forced me to betray you. I'm not worthy of your friendship, because I committed the unforgivable sin of keeping silent in the name of my own pride and embarrassment. Then I went and fell in love with Grant. I wanted our pretend engagement to be real, so I didn't tell you, since I knew you would call everything off and go for Tremain's throat."

Tears streamed down Muriel's cheeks and she drew a shuddering breath. "Last night Grant asked me to marry him for real, and I said yes…."

Muriel half collapsed after the truth gushed out of her like a geyser. "I'm so very, very sorry," she blubbered.

"Are you sure Grant is sincere about wanting to

marry you?" Josie asked cautiously. "This isn't part of Tremain's clever scheme to humiliate us for using them for our own purpose, is it?"

Muriel shook her head adamantly. More tendrils tumbled from the bun atop her head to dangle around her flushed face. "Grant says not. He says he wants to resign his commission with the army and stake a claim beside mine, so we can make a new life together in the new territory. He says he's tired of living up to his military family's expectations for him."

"And you believe that?" Josie scoffed. "That sounds like a well-rehearsed speech designed to lure you into whatever scheme Tremain and Holbrook have created to thoroughly humiliate us as payback."

Muriel wiped away the tears dribbling down her cheeks, then sniffed. "Do you really think so?"

"I wouldn't put it past them, considering they *knew* from the beginning that we planned to end the betrothal before the run," Josie replied, frowning pensively. "You'll have to test Grant somehow or another to find out for certain if he is sincere."

"How?" Muriel asked, while she blotted her eyes on her shirtsleeve.

Josie's mind raced, trying to devise a solution that would force the captain to put his feelings on the line or admit he was playing Muriel for a fool to repay her for her part in Josie's scheme—which she sorely regretted putting into action. Damn it, she would rather dodge another hundred proposals than see Muriel suffer unrequited love.

And she was holding Tremain personally accountable for her friend's torment.

"Ask Grant to move up your wedding day to tomorrow," Josie suggested suddenly.

"Tomorrow?" Muriel bleated. "The day before the run?"

Josie bobbed her head. "If he tries to put you off, then you can bet he has no intention of marrying you at all. Make him choose between you and the chance to double the amount of land you can claim if you postpone the wedding until after the run. That should test his devotion to you."

"What if he decides to have the last laugh by leaving me standing at the altar after I roped him into this pretend engagement?" Muriel grumbled, deflated.

Josie grimaced. "There is that possibility." And if that ornery scoundrel Tremain had anything to do with it, that was a very real possibility.

"That sneaky bastard," Muriel declared angrily. "Grant doesn't care about me at all. He has been playing a spiteful charade to teach me a lesson, I suspect."

Josie knew the feeling. Tremain didn't give a damn about her. He just wanted revenge.

"Like a naive, romantic idiot, I fell for his pretended sincerity," Muriel muttered. "He was born and bred into a military family and probably fed me that nonsense about being tired of living up to family expectations."

"I could be wrong—" Josie began, trying to soothe her tormented friend.

"In all likelihood you're not," Muriel maintained,

going back to her rapid pacing. "We will see who leaves whom at the altar tomorrow, after I insist we marry."

"Maybe we should—"

Muriel flung up a hand to silence her. "No, I'm definitely going to insist on holding the ceremony in town tomorrow," she decided. "If Grant tries to put me off until another day, I'll know he is part of the scheme of retaliation. And if he agrees too rapidly, I'll know he plans to leave me at the altar in hopes of disgracing me. It's what I deserve for withholding information from you. You, the only person in the world whom I actually trust. And I failed you!"

Josie watched her friend wilt to the ground and dissolve in tears. Obviously, Muriel's emotions had been run through the gristmill—thanks to that wily Tremain.

This is all his fault, she decided as she rushed over to console her best friend. And he was going to pay dearly.

"I will be there with you tomorrow to watch this scheme play out," she assured Muriel. "Now dry your eyes and pull yourself together before Holbrook makes his daily visit, like the model fiancé he's been portraying. You, my friend, are about to play the most important role of your life."

"He loves me, he loves me not," Muriel sobbed, then hiccuped. "I'm betting *not*. No more benefit of the doubt for any man who walks the face of this earth." She raised red-rimmed eyes to Josie. "What are you going to do about Tremain? Are you going to propose to him, too? Call his bluff and request a double ceremony tomorrow?"

"When? Before or after I kill him?" she said vindictively, then gave Muriel a consoling hug.

"Better kill him after," Muriel advised, breaking into a watery smile. "As his wife, you'll be entitled to everything he owns. His horse included. Outlaw will be easier to manage during the race than that contrary Rooster."

"You're right." Josie helped Muriel to her feet. "Better to see him wed, *then* see him dead."

"That's the spirit," Muriel declared, marshaling her composure. "Same goes for Grant—if I can entice him to the altar. Then I'll stab that deceitful soldier with his own sword."

Chapter Seven

"What am I going to do?" Holbrook asked as he walked circles around Shallow Springs during his nightly conference with Sol. "Muriel wants to get married tomorrow."

"Tomorrow?" Sol croaked in disbelief. "That's when we planned to call off the engagements." His gaze narrowed suspiciously as he watched his friend reverse direction, to pass counterclockwise in front of him. "What did you say to that?"

Holbrook drew up short to stare him squarely in the eye. "The only thing I could say. I said I only cared about marrying her and not about doubling the amount of land we could claim by waiting. I promised to meet her at the office of the justice of the peace midmorning to prove my feelings for her are sincere."

Sol studied him dubiously. "So now you are having a *pretend* wedding to go with your pretend engagement? And *she* asked *you?* Not the other way around?"

"I was stunned, of course. I've played along from

the very beginning, just as you said. I even told her that I would resign my commission and defy my military family's expectations so we could claim a homestead side by side—"

"What?" Sol crowed. "Are you loco?"

Holbrook puffed up indignantly. "You told me to sound convincing, so she wouldn't suspect I was leading her on to repay her for using me."

Sol scowled. Today had been a hellish day and the evening was deteriorating rapidly. It had taken considerable acting ability to assure Bradley at their conference outside the Oasis that he was glad to have an excuse to exchange money for Josie.

The haughty Texan had slapped banknotes into his hand, burning his palm and scorching his heart with feelings of betrayal. Even though Josie had used him for her selfish purposes and planned to discard him, he still felt guilty. No matter how many times he told himself that the beguiling blonde was getting what she deserved, the words didn't quite ring true.

He hadn't expected to enjoy Josie's company quite so much. He couldn't forget how much he'd liked having her soft and yielding in his arms the night they had almost become as intimate as a man and woman could get.

She still had the starring role in his fantasies every damn night. He awoke hard, aching and wanting her to the extreme. There was no relief in sight. Plus he hadn't tracked down Harlan Kane, so he couldn't take his frustration out on that brutish fugitive, either.

"I think I'm in love with her, Tremain," Holbrook confided as he stared at the toes of his polished boots.

"Well, hell."

Sol shook his head and sighed in dismay. He'd been afraid that might happen. From the very beginning, Holbrook had been fiercely sensitive to everything the shapely brunette said and did.

"I wonder if Muriel broke down and told Josie that I knew they planned to call off the engagement the day of the run," Sol mused aloud.

Holbrook snapped up his head and scowled. "You think she is playing me? She's planning to call the bluff and leave *me* standing at the altar?"

Sol frowned contemplatively. "I suspect Josie knows by now. Damn that woman!"

Sol felt vindicated and relieved when the heavy burden of guilt, regret and betrayal lifted from his shoulders. He'd outsmarted Josie for trampling his male pride. Now look where it had got him! Holbrook was miserable because he'd fallen hard for that golden-eyed brunette who had taken her needle and thread and stitched herself to his heart.

"If I refuse to show up for the ceremony, and Muriel is sincere about marrying me, then she will never speak to me again. I'll never convince her that I care about her, because she'll be too cynical to trust me," Holbrook said miserably. "If I go to the ceremony and she stands me up, then I'll look like a lovesick fool in front of the whole blasted town. I'll never live it down with the men under my command."

Sol swore colorfully. His scheme was causing Holbrook excessive grief. It wasn't doing Sol any good, either. Didn't he have enough going on with this undercover assignment, without tangling up his feelings? Damn it! He never became emotionally involved in his cases. Until now…

"Did Josie propose that you move up the date for your wedding?" Holbrook questioned curiously. "Is this a *double*-dealing deception?"

"No, she didn't." And damn it, why should he be feeling disappointed that she hadn't proposed to him? On second thought… "Which might serve to prove that Muriel is genuinely interested in you, and this isn't phase two of Josie's original plot."

Holbrook smiled hopefully, the pathetic chump. He'd worn his feelings on the sleeve of his military uniform. He'd placed his emotions out there in plain sight for the object of his affection to stampede over. Now he risked having his heart broken.

"I'm sorry that I've left you in this dilemma," Sol murmured sincerely. "You're right. You don't know what's coming. You could find love everlasting." If there was such a thing. Sol had seen little evidence of that, what with the domestic quarrels he'd witnessed in his profession. "Or you might become humiliated to the extreme. You can't be sure until it's too late."

Holbrook nodded broodingly. "Hell or heaven, and I won't know which until tomorrow."

"I really am sorry—"

Holbrook waved him off with a flick of his wrist.

"It isn't your fault that I tried to charm Muriel into believing I was heads and above the best choice for a husband. I charmed *myself* into thinking in terms of a true marriage with her. I was living a fantasy."

"I know what that's like," Sol mumbled. "It's murder."

"Pardon?"

"Nothing." Sol straightened, blew out a frustrated breath, then said, "I have no advice."

Holbrook looked at him and snorted sarcastically. "Really? You had all sorts of suggestions when you came to me with this devious scheme to retaliate against the women for using us." He pivoted on his heels like the soldier he was, and marched toward his horse.

"Forgot to tell you that I saw two more illegal nesters on the creek bank two miles north of the garrison," Sol called after him.

"Good. I'll go beat the bushes and flush them out with a stick," Holbrook yelled over his shoulder. "That should help relieve my frustration."

Swearing at the predicament he had unintentionally thrust Holbrook into, Sol mounted Outlaw. He needed to ride out to Red Hawk's cabin to gather the last string of horses, for sale the day prior to the run. Then he would stake them out and bed down near Josie's tent—just in case Kane showed up with vengeance and lust on his mind.

As he trotted off, Sol patted the inside pocket of his buckskin vest to make certain the money he planned to use as evidence against Carlton Bradley was where he'd left it. He was building an airtight case against that cocky swindler, who most likely had committed fraud and robbery to further his dream of a sprawling ranch in the soon-to-be-opened territory.

Bradley had paid Sol in full for the horses, and for the bribe to call off the engagement with Josie. That wasn't necessarily against the law. The arrogant Texan *hadn't* mentioned a bribe to claim land, then asked Sol to forfeit the property to him after the run. But now that Sol had gained his confidence, he hoped Bradley would approach him with such a proposition.

Unfortunately, the case wouldn't play out until after the run, when settlers actually forfeited their claims to Bradley for a price. Then Sol could arrest him and twist a few arms of would-be settlers, offering them clemency if they testified against him. Right now, all Sol had was suspicious speculation and hearsay from would-be settlers who had overheard Bradley making arrangements for land—if and when someone staked a claim near his one hundred sixty acres.

Sol wasn't sure how Bradley planned to circumvent the law about placing improvements—a house or a shed—on each parcel in order to lay legal claim to the title, as stated in the Homestead Act. No doubt the Texan had something devious in mind.

Sol kicked Outlaw in the flanks, urging the powerful animal to gobble up the ground at his swiftest speed. Sol wanted to outrun the convoluted feelings that cluttered his mind. He felt sorry for Holbrook and responsible for the man's misery. He even felt sorry for Muriel, if she actually had tender feelings for her fake fiancé. But he didn't trust that blue-eyed blonde who tangled his thoughts and feelings into hopeless knots.

True, he wanted her—badly. But that was just lust, he reminded himself sensibly. Plus, he didn't trust Josie not to complicate the dilemma between Muriel and Holbrook.

"I could come right out and ask her what part she's playing in tomorrow's supposed ceremony," he told Outlaw, when the horse slowed to a trot to catch his breath.

Unfortunately, the stallion offered no advice. Sol had nothing but years of cynicism to draw upon. He didn't take anyone at their word. Criminals lied through their teeth to save their worthless hides. As for Josie, she had devised a scheme that had snowballed into potential disaster and heartache for Holbrook.

"This wouldn't be so damn frustrating if I didn't actually *like* that firebrand—in an exasperated sort of way, of course," Sol told his horse. "I'm not even sure exactly when it happened. She just sort of sneaked up on me while I was trying to outsmart her before she outsmarted me."

Again, Outlaw failed to comment.

The only good thing about it was that tonight might be the last evening Sol felt obligated to stand guard over Josie. Tomorrow, everyone would be packing their belongings to break camp in anticipation of the run the following morning. Twenty-five thousand hopeful souls would line up for a wild, dangerous race for free land—or quick death, depending on how many overturned wagons and accidental tramplings occurred during the run.

Sol gnashed his teeth. He'd be damn glad when this land rush was over. Within a few days, he should have collected the evidence and witnesses needed to bring formal charges against Bradley—and whoever else was running a scam to separate decent settlers from their homesteads. Sol would place the criminals behind bars, and he'd be anxious to leave the woman who had tormented his thoughts and dreams.

Well, he hoped she found *her* dream of a homestead and ranch on his people's land. Sol was anxious to close the book on this chapter of his duties as a deputy U.S. marshal. He'd been unable to remain emotionally unattached in this case. Nevertheless, he would do his damnedest to get on with the next assignment, and hope it took him miles away from the woman with forget-me-not-colored eyes and curly, silver-blond hair. Yes, he decided, time and distance would cure what ailed him.

Josie eased off her bedroll and moved quietly toward the tent flap so she wouldn't disturb Muriel, who had worn herself out fretting about what tomorrow would hold. As for Josie, she was determined to repay Sol for putting her and her friend through an emotional meat grinder.

To her surprise, he hadn't bedded down at his usual site. That said a lot, she supposed. He must see no reason to keep up the pretense of acting as her noble protector. Apparently, he planned to let Harlan Kane have at her, if and when the drunken bully showed up with revenge on his mind. She'd be dead and Sol could pretend to be the bereaved fiancé.

Too restless to return to bed, Josie ambled down to the river. To her surprise, she saw Sol standing in midstream, waist-deep in the water. His torso was bare and probably the rest of him was, too. She ducked behind a bush to keep from being seen.

The tantalizing sight of him threatened to mesmerize her, but she willfully battled her reckless desire. This man had conspired with Carlton Bradley and accepted money for whatever swindle the Texan was running, she reminded herself sensibly. Also, this same rascal had twisted Muriel's arm a half-dozen different ways to pry information from her....

Josie's bitter thoughts trailed off when Sol lathered his muscular chest. Silver streams of water cascaded over his washboard belly, leaving shiny bubbles circling around his waist. Ripples of moonlight undulated away from him and Josie cursed the arousing effect the man had on her. If she were as cold-blooded as he was, she would use his body for an experiment in passion, then walk away without looking back. Just as he had done the night he had awakened her feminine desires and left her feeling vulnerable and out of control.

Sol hadn't come around to check on her, as Holbrook had done with Muriel. Instead, he had slept by her tent. Probably because the scoundrel had needed a place to bed down, and she had made it easy when she had announced their fake engagement.

Her mind froze and her eyes popped when Sol walked toward the shore, revealing his masculine physique inch by tantalizing inch. The water swirled around his lean hips and she waited expectantly to see him come ashore.

To her surprise, he glanced at her hiding place in the underbrush and said, "You want to see me in my entirety, blue eyes? Or do you want to turn around before it's too late?"

Josie blinked. "How did you know I was here?"

He grinned, displaying those damnable dimples that no self-respecting, double-crossing devil rightfully should have. She hated that she was so affected by his smile…and his well-sculpted body. His mind-boggling kisses and bone-melting caresses… She hated that she wanted to see him in the altogether. For feminine curiosity's sake only, of course. It was nothing personal.

"I'm part Indian," he told her as he came forward, causing the water to ripple and shift, teasing her with lusty anticipation. "I've grown eyes in the back of my head. It's part of my training as a Cheyenne warrior and for the Bowstring Society."

"Bowstring?" she questioned, completely distracted.

"Special fighting force. To be more specific, I was a Wolf Warrior in the military society that protected and defended our people against our enemies." He rinsed off the suds. "Why are you here, Josephine?" he asked abruptly.

"Why am I here?" she repeated stupidly.

Her mind went blank while her helpless gaze zeroed

in on Tremain's magnificent body. She noticed the battle scars left by bullets and knives, but that didn't diminish the forbidden desire rolling through her. Josie couldn't seem to control her reckless yearnings for a man she couldn't trust.

"Josephine?" he prodded.

She gave herself a mental shake, gathered her bravado and walked determinedly toward him. She had reached a decision. She intended to have a fling with her pretend fiancé, then cast him off because he had tried to outfox her, and had caused Muriel excessive anguish in the process.

Not to mention that he was Bradley's cohort, damn him. Yet for tonight—*and only tonight*—he would become her instructor in intimate passion. She would get him out of her system for the last time, so she could devote her thoughts and energy to staking her claim and building a ranch of her very own.

Casting caution to the four winds, Josie sauntered toward him. His thick raven brows climbed up his forehead when she positioned herself on the riverbank in front of the clothing he had draped over Outlaw's saddle. She crossed her arms and tapped her bare foot impatiently.

"Are you coming out, Tremain? I think a fiancé is like a horse. I'm entitled to see what I'm getting. You, being a horse trader, should understand that logic."

He studied her for a long moment, then nodded, as if he had arrived at a decision—like she had. "Remember, Josephine, you asked for this, so don't go crying to Orson Barnes, claiming I took unfair advantage of you."

Oh, he most certainly had done that, she reminded herself righteously. He had played her for a blundering fool, turned her emotions inside out and tempted her with his brain-boggling kisses and body-scorching caresses. Now she was going to behave like a man—one who used a woman's body for his selfish, temporary pleasure, then walked away without a backward glance.

Every thought, spiteful or otherwise, flew right out of her head when Tremain emerged from the river, naked as the day he was born. He was aroused, no question about that. Her gaze swept up and down his muscular form, which glistened with water and sparkled like diamonds in the moonlight.

Josie forgot to breathe—couldn't remember why it was necessary—when he moved deliberately toward her. He didn't halt, just strode right up, to gather her in his sinewy arms and kiss her with so much heat and hunger that she could do nothing but respond—instantly, instinctively.

"I want you like crazy, Josephine. But you can see that for yourself, can't you? This is your last chance to run for your life," he warned when he came up for air.

Sol waited, half hoping she'd race off in the direction she'd come from, and spare him whatever game she was playing with him now. But she didn't turn tail. She trailed her forefinger over his body, making a dedicated study of the planes, contours and scars on his chest and belly.

"What do you want from me, blue eyes?" he rasped, as ravenous need throbbed through him.

When she met his gaze, he fell into the fathomless depths of her eyes. "I want you, Solomon Tremain," she whispered against his lips.

There was a catch, he reminded himself cynically. There was always a catch. But he was long past too-far-gone to question her motives.

When her hand curled around his pulsating shaft, his heart slammed into his rib cage—and stuck there. She stroked him gently, and a rumbling purr rose from his chest, giving away far more than he intended about his reaction to her.

There was no question that she had an inescapable hold on his body—literally and figuratively. He craved her touch with an obsession he didn't understand, savored her caress like an addict. She touched him experimentally and left him battling the scalding sensations that resulted. She was curious and creative, and he loved every moment of her erotic explorations of his body.

When she knelt in front of him and took his throbbing length into her mouth, Sol's knees threatened to buckle beneath him. Somehow, he managed to maintain his balance while her tongue flicked at him playfully and her hands trailed up and down his inner thighs. The intense sensations caused blood to roar in his ears.

Sol swore he couldn't survive another moment if he let her continue having her way with him. Already his breath came in ragged spurts and desperate pleasure enflamed his body, threatening to burn him to a crisp.

With what willpower he had left—which, admittedly, wasn't much—he drew her to her feet, then towed her with him to his horse to fetch his bedroll from behind the saddle.

"One of us is overdressed," he rasped as he spread out the pallet with a snap.

Then he made swift work of pulling her nightgown over her head and casting it aside, to make a study of her lush, curvaceous body. That was when his thought processes broke down completely. Sol stared at feminine perfection in its purest form.

Entranced, he reached out to skim his thumb over her beaded nipples. When she gasped, he lowered his head to kiss one and then the other. All the while, his hand drifted up and down her soft swells and contours. To his delight, she arched against him, silently asking for more.

He was all too eager to accommodate her.

"You are the devil," she panted as his fingertips drifted lower to circle her navel. "And yet here I am, yielding to wicked temptation."

"I'm not the devil." His hand brazenly ventured lower. "But I'm well acquainted with some of his closest friends," he murmured, thinking of the long list of criminals he'd arrested over the years.

"You make me want—"

Josie's voice dried up when his hand glided between her thighs. Need, so deliciously tempting, bombarded her as he eased his fingertip inside to stroke her, arousing her to the brink of torment. Josie closed her eyes and her mind to all except the extraordinary sensations of desire Sol provoked with his skillful touch. Then he eased two fingers inside her as his questing tongue drove demandingly into her mouth.

Desperate for him, Josie linked her arms around his neck and gave herself up to the indescribable pleasure burgeoning through her. She could feel her traitorous body arching shamelessly toward him, seeking that delirious pinnacle of rapture she had discovered in his arms.

Yet that was no longer satisfaction enough. Whether he had betrayed her trust and deceived her was of no consequence in the heat of the moment. She wanted— no, she *needed*—to have his powerful body meshed intimately to hers. She longed to ride the wild storm of passion that she sensed awaited her.

Anxious to show him exactly what she wanted from him, she curled her hand around the hard, satiny shaft that nudged her hip. Her bold touch triggered his low growl. Before she could blink, she found herself lowered to the pallet and looking up to see Sol's face, surrounded by hair the color of midnight, hovering over her.

It seemed to her that he was waiting for permission or acceptance or *something*. She didn't know what, having never in her life been naked with a man. Something about his hesitation and unspoken question touched her carefully guarded heart. Whatever he was, he was considerate enough to let her decide how far she wanted this encounter to go. She adored him for that, even though instinct constantly warned her to be wary of his hidden motives.

Josie didn't trust herself to speak, for fear she would destroy the unique moment between them. So she framed his rugged face with her hands and brought his lips to hers, silently welcoming him. She moaned huskily when he traced her heated flesh with his thumb and fingertip. She trembled uncontrollably when he brought her body to a feverish pitch once again, provoking her to cast aside every cynical thought and throw caution to the wind, so she could appease the ravenous need she felt.

"Come here," she gasped in mindless desperation.

When Sol did as she commanded, she felt the hard length of him pressing intimately against her. She tensed momentarily, then melted when he glided his tongue into her mouth at the precise moment he penetrated deeper, filling her with his heat. Then he lifted her to him, guided her legs around his hips and drove deeper still.

He set such a hypnotic rhythm that Josie found herself caught up in the intimate dance of two bodies moving together as one, creating pleasure and sensations beyond description. He clasped her tightly to him, rocking her against him, leaving her aching to discover where it was that her body seemed to want to go, what it needed to reach the pinnacle of complete satisfaction....

And suddenly she was there, riding the crest of frothy waves that rolled toward shore, showering her with amazing sensations that converged as they had once before. It was like lightning striking, only so much more intense. She cried out Sol's name the instant the world spun off its axis and left her tumbling through space.

She heard Sol groan, felt him shudder against her. Pleasure, like the tide rolling out to sea, left her motionless and spent in his encircling arms. All the tension and frustration that had plagued her throughout the day drained away. Josie closed herself to everything but the remarkable feelings of rapture that enveloped her.

Her last thought was that she would likely face humiliation, betrayal and embarrassment at Sol's hand in the near future. But for this one moment out of time, she had discovered the amazing power and erotic pleasure of wild, reckless passion.

A wry smile quirked her lips as she dropped off to sleep. She had traded one untamable stallion for another. A fair bargain, she supposed, when dealing with a horse trader.

Sol cursed himself ten times over while he eased away from Josie, listening to her rhythmic breathing. He stared down at her luscious body, watching moonlight glow on her bewitching face and glisten in the flaxen hair that spilled across his pallet.

He should be shot. He had taken her innocence, when he knew in all likelihood this fiery, independent female had never been intimate with a man. It damn sure hadn't bothered his conscience ten minutes ago, had it?

Sol rose to walk back into the river—where he should have stayed in the first place. He'd figured she was up to something when she'd appeared unexpectedly tonight. He thought maybe Josie had decided to propose a hasty wedding ceremony to him, after all. But no, not this minx. She wanted his body, strictly to satisfy her feminine curiosity. On second thought, maybe *she* should be shot!

He reminded himself that he was thinking in terms of double standards, and that if a man could take his pleasure in a woman, then turnabout should be fair play. Yet that didn't make him feel better. Hell, he didn't know what would!

Battling conflict, confusion and frustration, Sol submerged himself in the river. He hadn't been able to figure Josie out since the moment he met her. He was no closer to insights or revelations now than he'd been then.

Some investigator he'd turned out to be, he thought with a self-deprecating snort. Of course, in his defense, the woman always made him crazy, and he couldn't think straight when she came within five feet of him.

All he knew for sure was that if she decided she wanted him again before they returned to her campsite, she could have him as many times as she pleased. She could conduct all the erotic experiments she wanted, and she wouldn't hear him voice a single complaint.

Sol swam to the surface and shook the water from his hair. For a man who once prided himself on second-guessing fugitives and staying one step ahead of criminals, he had played right into her hands—quite literally. And he'd enjoyed every sensuous, sizzling moment.

Nonetheless, he didn't trust her true intentions for seeking him out tonight. He had lost his focus the moment Josie had crooked her finger at him. He had been at her disposal from that moment on. The worst part was he had discovered the difference between reckless sexual encounters and mind-blowing, body-scorching passion. Now he wished he didn't know there was a difference, because he was ruined for life.

He was going to lose the woman who had bewitched him, he predicted. To be sure, there would be hell to pay for what he'd done. There always was, Sol reminded himself. Ordinarily, *he* was the one who brought hell down on sinners, but everything had changed in his dealings with this blue-eyed blonde who was bursting at the seams with indomitable spirit.

His gaze drifted to the riverbank, where the gloriously naked female was sleeping on his bedroll. The enticing sight of her inflamed his passions once more, and impulsively, Sol walked ashore to scoop her up in his arms.

Her thick lashes fluttered and she looped her arms around his neck. "Where are we going?" she asked drowsily.

"Back to where we've been," he whispered as he walked into the river with her cradled in his arms.

"Oh? And where's that, Solomon?"

"To paradise." He left her adrift on the water, then made a feast of her body, one kiss and caress at a time.

Encouraging her to open herself to him, he tasted her very essence, using every erotic technique he knew—and a few he created specifically for her. To his delight, she shed every inhibition while they turned the river to steam with the flames of their passion for each other.

As Sol drove into her, his self-control so far gone he knew he'd never get it back, he told himself that for this one magical night he could soar in motionless flight. There were no regrets, no self-restraint, only rapture in its purest, wildest form.

Whatever the future held, he would accept it, because no matter what, he had found his personal version of paradise tonight.

Chapter Eight

Josie retrieved her nightgown, quickly pulled it over her head and smoothed it into place. Thirty minutes earlier, she had been frolicking like a carefree nymph in the water, boldly teasing and touching Sol while he taught her all the wickedly delicious ways he could pleasure her body.

Then reality showed up in the aftermath of their lovemaking. Sexual encounter, she hastily corrected. The time had come for her to explain to herself how she had drifted so far off course when she'd sought out Sol at the river.

Josie had prided herself on being practical and sensible, but nothing about her whirlwind affair with Sol was logical. Mercy! Who was this woman who had overtaken her this evening? How could she have been so angry and mistrusting of Sol all day, yet succumbed to selfish pleasures tonight?

"There's only one explanation," she muttered to herself. "I've gone crazy—"

She started when Sol's sinewy arms slid around her waist and he pulled her back against his bare chest, to spread butterfly kisses along the side of her neck.

"Did you call me?" he questioned as his hands strayed over her breasts in such a possessive manner that she should have pushed them aside. So why didn't she? Why did she savor his touch? Because she *was* crazy, she reminded herself.

"I want to ask you something," she murmured.

She felt him go utterly still, though he didn't retreat, just held her in his arms. A half second later, he nuzzled his chin against her shoulder and said, "Ask away, Josephine."

She marshaled her courage, turned in the circle of his arms and pasted on a sincere expression, or at least hoped to give the impression she was sincere. "I know this is sudden, but I was wondering if you would marry me tomorrow."

He did retreat then. "Why? Because of what happened between us just now?" His voice was so carefully neutral that she had no idea what he was thinking or feeling. But then, she never really knew with Solomon. He was a master at concealing his thoughts and emotions, damn him.

"No, because I am fond of you. And I *did* propose to you, after all. Well, sort of," she amended. "We were set to marry eventually. What happened between us wouldn't have happened if I hadn't wanted it to."

Oddly enough, that was true—in part. She kept struggling with this love-hate conflict that tangled her thoughts and emotions. She would never forgive Sol for throwing in with Bradley, but no other man made her feel the wild, reckless ecstasy she had discovered in his embrace. She'd felt safe and secure, protected and satisfied, despite her independent nature, which usually assured her she needed no man to make her life complete.

"You might have noticed that I have a habit of making up my own mind about what I do and what I want," she added, almost as an afterthought.

He chuckled as he fastened his shirt. "I might not be too observant, but I did notice that." He tossed her a quick glance before he scooped up his socks and boots and put them on. "I've become fond of you, too, Josephine. But you know what I am. I will be here today and gone next week. My horse-trading business takes me hither and yon for several days at a time. We can use the extra money to build improvements on our homestead. Are you sure that's what you want to tie yourself to—a come-and-go husband?"

"Yes." After all, she'd decided the first day she met him that he'd be the perfect candidate for a fiancé to discourage other suitors.… Wait a minute, what was happening here? He was confusing her with his questions and comments. Confound it, this was supposed to be a test and a tactic to counter his mischievous scheme that had poor Muriel twisting in the wind and keeping secrets she hadn't wanted to keep.

"Now let me see if I have this straight," he said very deliberately as he came to stand in front of her. "We are having an impromptu wedding tomorrow, then making the run? You are well aware that as my wife you can't claim separate property."

"If that was an issue with me, I would have married the first man who asked. But you're the one I want." Besides, she knew he wouldn't go through with the wedding. She was calling his bluff. He wouldn't even show up for the ceremony. She'd bet her life savings on it.

"After the wedding I'll ride off to train and sell horses, while you set up housekeeping? Is that about right?"

Sol watched her closely, wishing it were daylight so he could read her expression more clearly. Not that it would help. He'd had trouble figuring out this perplexing female since day one. Damned if he wasn't pleased she had asked to marry him tomorrow, though. Nevertheless, he suspected he was about to receive the same treatment as Holbrook—being left at the altar. He supposed the only way to test her sincerity was to agree, and see what happened the next morning.

Still, he was willing to bet that *she* knew that *he* knew about her original plan to cancel the engagement at the last minute, so she could ditch him and make the run.

Then there was the complication of Bradley paying him to break the engagement with Josie, Sol reminded himself. Yet whatever conflict arose, he knew he was going to accept—whether he should or not.

"All right. Shall we seal the promise with a kiss?" he asked as he angled his head toward hers. "I'll be there in my best clothes if you will, blue eyes."

"And I'll be there if you will," she replied, just before his lips settled possessively over hers.

Sol shoved aside his cynicism and doubt and kissed Josie for all he was worth. Let her think she had him wrapped around her finger. Let her think she had outsmarted him and would humiliate him. That was tomorrow. No matter what happened, he had lived his wildest fantasy tonight.

For sure and certain, Sol would never be able to bathe again without recalling their mystical lovemaking—sexual encounter, he quickly corrected—in a pool of water that had very nearly turned to steam in the heat of their fiery desire for each other. He had been her first, and he didn't plan to let his soon-to-be or soon-*not*-to-be bride forget it.

"Do you mind a double wedding?" she asked as she leaned back in his arms. "Muriel and Grant are getting married tomorrow, too."

"Are they? I haven't talked to Holbrook lately. No, I don't mind sharing the limelight. What time are we getting hitched?"

"Ten o'clock, at the office of the justice of the peace."

Sol inclined his head. "I'll be there."

He retreated, to scoop up the bedroll and fasten it behind the saddle. Leading Outlaw behind him, he took Josie's arm and walked her back to camp. When she disappeared into her tent, he unrolled his pallet.

As he stretched out, he tried to recall another time in his life when he'd been this anxious to discover what tomorrow held. Josie would either disappoint him beyond words or surprise him to the extreme. One way or another he would find out exactly where he stood with her.

Married? Him? The whimsical prospect captured Sol's imagination and fueled his fantasies. Yet he was a realist. He lived a different existence than most folks and had learned to expect the worst from the criminals he dealt with on a daily basis. That's what he usually got, too.

Time would tell which category the blue-eyed whirling dervish of a female fell into.

He'd know tomorrow.

"I'm not going to survive this, I swear," Muriel muttered as she wriggled into her best gown. "I *think* I'm attending my wedding. But maybe not. The not knowing is driving me mad!"

Josie experienced the same nervous apprehension. She fastened the delicate buttons on the scoop neck of the gold dress she had worn to her brother's wedding, and asked herself if she would be pleased or disappointed if Sol didn't show up.

Her friend halted in the process of fluffing wrinkles from her emerald-green gown and stared wide-eyed at her. "My gracious, you look amazing."

"Thanks. So do you." Josie grinned wryly. "Nothing like being all dressed up and no one to wed."

Damn, she should have kept her mouth shut. Muriel's face fell and she shifted from one foot to the other. "Well, if all else fails, at least we can still look forward to making the run," she said mournfully.

"That has always been our primary objective, after all," Josie reminded her as she fastened the last button. "If this wedding doesn't work out we will still have our homesteads."

"Maybe, maybe not," Muriel murmured. "Thousands of people have gathered to make this run. You said yourself that hundreds of them failed to stake property in the first two races."

Josie grinned, trying to lift her friend's spirits. "Well, yes, but I've heard rumors that more tribal reservation land will be available in the future. We'll keep trying if we fail tomorrow. Agreed?"

Muriel nodded her dark head, then inhaled a huge breath, nearly popping the buttons off her dainty gown. "I suppose we should ride into town to see if anyone is waiting for us at the altar."

Resigned to being disappointed in Sol, yet hopeful that Muriel could marry the man she'd come to love, Josie exited the tent. People scurried about, packing their wagons with supplies they wouldn't need until after the great race. Josie planned to do the same, after waiting a few minutes in town to see if Sol showed up for their wedding.

She was betting against him, of course. She expected he was betting against her, too. And why on earth had she even asked him? It had been her impulsiveness that got her into this situation, she realized. Although she had been aggravated with him, she'd still yielded to temptation and then requested his presence as her groom at the ceremony.

Who would have thought that she, a woman who valued common sense and practicality, would become a captive of wicked desire and reckless whimsy?

Josie gave herself a mental kick in the derriere, then went to fetch Rooster. The sorrel stallion was in fine form on the way to town. He tossed his head and pranced sideways, making his striking flaxen mane and tail ripple and swish. She reminded herself that she had neglected to take the spirited animal for his nightly run. Now she was paying for it.

When she and Muriel reached the edge of town, Josie was dismayed to see a huge crowd filling the streets. It seemed the population had swelled by ten thousand! Afraid to ride Rooster any farther, for fear he would mow down anyone in his path if he became startled, she dismounted.

Bemused, Muriel glanced down at her. "Have you changed your mind?"

"No, I just don't trust Rooster. I plan to tether him here and walk to the middle of town…."

Her voice trailed off when a freckle-faced, red-haired boy, who looked to be about ten years old, slipped through the crowd. Waving a folded paper in his hand, he halted in front of Josie.

"Mr. Tremain asked me to deliver this to you," he reported with a beaming smile. Slightly out of breath, he presented the missive to her. Then he proudly displayed the quarter clutched in his fist. "He even paid me to make sure you got his message."

"What's wrong?" Muriel asked from atop her dapple-gray mare.

Josie read the note quickly, then frowned. "Sol wants me to meet him behind the church." She huffed out an exasperated breath. "Now what game is that rascal playing?"

She shooed Muriel on her way. "You better check to see if Grant is waiting for you. It will take time to wade through this mob. If you dally he might think you deliberately abandoned him."

"If he's there at all," Muriel grumbled fretfully.

"I'll be along as soon as I can," Josie promised, tethering Rooster to the hitching post outside the bakery.

She noticed a dozen people exiting with loaves of bread to sustain them during the day of the run. She should grab a few loaves herself. They were lightweight and wouldn't weigh Rooster down when he bolted across the prairie at his swiftest speed.

Josie set off toward the church, wondering how Sol planned to embarrass her this time. She threaded her way through the throngs, bumping into one person and then another before finally reaching her destination.

"What game are you playing, confound you?" she muttered. She waited a moment, then strode around back, past the crates and trash cans from the blacksmith shop that butted up against the church.

When she poked her head around the corner on the opposite side, she heard quiet footsteps approaching behind her.

"It's about time you got here. Why did you—"

Before she could turn to face Sol, a hard blow landed on the back of her head. Pain exploded in her skull and stars sparkled in front of her eyes. Her last thought was that Sol had never had the slightest intention of marrying her—not that she planned to go through with the wedding, either. But still, this was a rotten way to repay her for using him. He could have just *not* showed up!

Josie blacked out, cursing his name as she crumpled into an unconscious heap in the dirt.

Sol leaned against the wall outside the Saddle Burr Saloon, his gaze fixed on the pinewood building that housed the justice of the peace. While Holbrook had chosen to wait on the boardwalk, his fool heart on the line, Sol had taken the cautious approach. Quite honestly, he didn't expect Muriel *or* Josie to show up for the supposed ceremony. Still, he had fastened himself into the fancy trappings he had purchased a few days earlier.

He sagged in relief when he saw Muriel, all dressed up to be wed, moving slowly through the crowded street on her gray mare. Sol glanced from her to Holbrook, noting the way the captain's face lit up like fireworks on the Fourth of July. Sol also noticed that Josie was conspicuously absent.

That said it all, didn't it? That devious little witch had played her charade to the extreme. She had even sacrificed her innocence in the name of spite, just so she could set him up for the greatest fall of all—to be left at the altar.

Well, the joke was on her, because he did not intend

to set foot in that office. Sol told himself he wasn't surprised Josie hadn't made an appearance. But deep down inside, he was disappointed. He had wanted to trust her. Obviously, he'd turned into a hopeless, pathetic romantic.

Him? The world's worst cynic? How had that happened?

Looking gallant in his dress uniform, Holbrook stepped off the boardwalk to lift Muriel from her horse. He glanced around, obviously realizing, as Sol had, that Josie wasn't coming.

Scowling, Sol wheeled away when Muriel and the commander, arm in arm, walked inside to say their I do's. Sol fingered the gold band he'd impulsively purchased for the occasion—in case Josie showed up to actually marry him. For a jaded lawman who never planned to wed, he had changed his tune for Josie. And look where the hell it had gotten him. Rejection stung like a wasp and he cursed her deception, even when he had expected it.

Well, he was done with that conniving firebrand as of this moment, he told himself. He was here to do a job and he wouldn't give her another thought—

A gunshot exploded in the near distance, jostling him from his bitter musings. Suddenly, silence descended over the crowd, followed by hundreds of conversations erupting at once.

Out of habit, Sol grabbed a pistol from one of the holsters draped on his hips, then took off running in the direction of the sound. He used the alley to save time and avoid the crush of people clogging the street.

Behind the church, he skidded to a halt and stared in disbelief at the scene in front of him.

The first thing he noticed was Josie sitting in the dirt, wearing a fancy golden gown that suggested she *had* planned to go through with the wedding. Then he saw the pistol in her hand and smelled the scent of gunpowder in the air.

A sinking feeling settled in the pit of his stomach when he saw Harlan Kane, drunkard and molester of women, lying toes-up in the dirt.

"I hate to admit it, Kane, but you deserved a good shooting," Sol muttered as he studied the dead man, who stared sightlessly skyward. "You're looking the wrong direction, though. You'll never nest in the heavenly roost."

He turned his attention to Josie, who wore a dazed expression. Apparently, this was her first shooting. Killing someone tended to take the starch out of most folks when reality set in.

"Nice of you to dress up for our wedding," Sol said caustically as he strode toward her. "Too bad you had to detour to shoot Kane first."

Josie's gaze dropped to the pistol in her hand, then she stared at the dead man. "I didn't shoot him."

"No? Sure looks like it to me." Damn, how many times had he heard claims of innocence from those who were guilty as original sin?

"Oh, my God! Button-Eye Malloy committed murder! Behind the church, of all places!" someone called out from the crowd that had gathered behind Sol in the alley.

"That's the man who attacked her by our tent community," someone else added. "Guess she got even with him, didn't she?"

Scowling, Sol noticed Kane's empty holster. Josie must have swiped his pistol, then shot him before he could do his worst to her. Sol reminded himself that she was a spit-in-your-eye kind of woman who didn't back down from trouble. He shouldn't be surprised that she'd repaid Kane for abusing her. But hell! Couldn't she have punched him a couple of times instead of shooting him?

Josie stared blankly at Sol while he hoisted her to her feet. "You're all dressed up," she mumbled in bewilderment.

"I was planning to get hitched," he grumbled, "not attend a shooting."

"I didn't shoot—"

"Do not say another word," he ordered sharply, then grabbed her elbow to steer her through their captive audience. Sol veered into the alley behind the newspaper office, where, to his frustration, he saw the city marshal striding toward them with his pistol drawn.

The lawman looked to be five or six years older than Sol, fifty pounds heavier and several inches shorter. His hazel eyes narrowed beneath caterpillar-like brows that swooped down on his wrinkled forehead.

"Ma'am, I'm Marshal Sam Colby and you're under arrest," he said grimly. He glanced briefly at Sol. "Did you see what happened?"

"No. I showed up after I heard the gunshot."

Sol wanted to wield his legal authority to override the marshal, but he had been given specific instructions to tell no one but Captain Holbrook who he was and why he had been sent to oversee the opening of the Cheyenne-Arapaho reservation land.

The stern-faced lawman grabbed Josie's arm. The fact that she went along peacefully assured Sol that she was guilty. Damn it all! Why did she have to kill Kane in a town jumping with people, only minutes before their wedding? Allowing the marshal to take the lead, Sol trailed behind, cursing Josie with every step for taking the law into her own hands.

Hell and damnation! He'd been keeping an eye out for Kane for several days. He'd even bedded down near Josie's tent to catch the bastard if he came looking for revenge. Unfortunately, Josie had found him first. She had shot the son of a bitch with his own gun. Sure, that was true justice, but the law frowned on that sort of thing nonetheless.

As the marshal veered into another alley, taking a shortcut to reach the brick building that housed the jail, Sol saw Muriel and Holbrook emerge from the justice of the peace's office a few doors down. Their smiles turned upside down when they noticed the marshal marching Josie across the street.

Holbrook met Sol's gaze, then darted an apprehensive glance at Marshal Colby.

"I'll take care of it," Sol insisted. "You and Muriel are on honeymoon."

So much for *Sol's* honeymoon. He should have known Josie hadn't planned to follow through. Now that he thought about it, he figured she must have dressed up and come along to *witness* Muriel's wedding—and then became sidetracked when she'd spotted Kane.

Sol would have preferred that she skip out on him without killing somebody. But as excuses went for not showing up at her wedding, this was original. He'd give her that.

He tried to ignore the snide comments from jilted suitors in the crowd, who claimed Button-Eye Malloy was receiving her just deserts. She would be spending the day of the run behind bars if Sol couldn't talk the marshal out of holding her prisoner for a minor misdemeanor…such as *murder.* Hell!

"This way, ma'am," Colby said as he opened the door and shoved Josie inside.

It was at that moment that she appeared to emerge from her trancelike state, wheeling around to dart off. She managed to wrench free of Colby's grasp, but Sol hooked his arm around her waist before she could make a jailbreak.

"Don't resist arrest," he growled in her ear. "Trust me on this. You'll only make things worse."

She glowered at him as if he were the one who had committed murder. "Trust you? This is your fault, damn you!"

"Mine?" Sol chirped as Marshal Colby jerked her away from him to stuff her in a cell.

"That's a woman for you," the lawman said, and

gave a rude snort. "Always blaming a man. She could be my wife."

Sol stared at the woman in the gold gown, framed by iron bars. "She was almost *mine,*" he said.

He didn't know if he was relieved or disappointed. Now that she had blasted Kane to hell and gone, he couldn't say for sure.

Chapter Nine

Josie's head pounded so much that it hurt to think. The one thing she did know was that Sol, in his spiteful effort to repay her for using him the way she did, had set her up for murder.

How could he have done this to her?

Thanks to him, the sneaky scoundrel, Josie was staring at the world through iron bars. Now she wouldn't be able to make the long-awaited run to claim a homestead. Sol knew how much having a home of her own meant to her. He knew how anxious she was to chase her dream. And he had used that confidential information against her, to have his revenge.

And there he stood, outside the bars, acting the innocent for the marshal's benefit.

"I ought to kill you," she muttered as he walked toward her.

"One murder a day isn't enough?" Sarcasm dripped from his deep voice. "And how the hell can you twist this disaster and make it *my* fault?"

"Because *you* sent me the note to set me up!" she snapped, despite the extra pain her loud voice added to her pounding headache.

His dark brows shot upward, then he frowned, supposedly bemused—consummate actor that he was. "What note?"

"The one you had that freckle-faced, red-haired kid deliver when Muriel and I reached the edge of town for the weddings." As if he didn't know.

"What did it say?"

She rolled her eyes in annoyance. "You know perfectly well what it said."

"Refresh my memory."

She glared daggers at him—him in his three-piece suit, all dressed up for *her* hanging! "It said you wanted me to meet you behind the church. And then you set me up!"

"I did no such thing," he stated, and scowled. "Someone else sent that note, and I guarantee that if you could find the kid and get a description of the man who passed it along, it wouldn't be me."

Sol sounded so sincere that she almost believed him. She walked over and dropped on the lumpy cot, her dazed mind struggling to make sense of the situation. "Then who disposed of Kane?"

Sol clamped his hands around the bars. His sea-green eyes zeroed in on her. "One of his double-dealing cohorts, perhaps. Tell me exactly what happened from the time you received the note."

Josie dragged in a restorative breath, wishing her

head would stop pounding in rhythm with her heartbeat, and cease tangling her thought processes. She frowned in concentration. "I halted on the edge of town because the oversize crowd was making Rooster nervous. I was afraid to continue down the street, for fear he'd trample someone while I was on my way to the justice of the peace—"

"So you *did* plan to attend the ceremony?" Sol interjected, using a terse voice reminiscent of a lawman conducting a serious investigation.

She jerked up her head—carefully, on account of her blinding headache—to study him with a pensive frown.

He shrugged. "Sorry, but every detail is important."

"I planned to see, at a distance, if you would show up," she admitted.

She noticed the quirk of his sensuous lips, and wondered what that meant.

"*I* was standing in the side alley beside the Saddle Burr Saloon, waiting to see if *you* would show up."

"To leave me at the altar and watch my humiliation?" she asked, before she could bite back the words.

Curse this blow to her skull! It had jarred her usual caution and common sense, and sent them catapulting into oblivion.

He grinned wryly. "To avoid my own embarrassment, in case you didn't show up…. Go on. What happened next?"

"After I read the note from you—"

"From my imposter," he corrected hastily.

"—I told Muriel to proceed without me, because her

mare isn't as nervous in crowds as Rooster is." Josie squeezed her eyes shut and defied the throbbing pain in her skull, trying to recall every detail, as Sol asked. "Muriel was anxious to see if Grant was waiting for her, so she rode Bess on down the street. I took the board-walk to the church, then veered into the alley, where I glanced around the corner near the blacksmith shop."

Josie inhaled a deep breath, battling the nausea, then continued. "I thought you were tormenting me, the way you'd tormented Muriel by refusing to let her tell me that you knew we planned to call off the engagement tomorrow. I thought the mysterious note was part of your spiteful revenge." She glowered at Sol. "That was a terrible thing to do to Muriel, by the way. You tortured her no end and she barely slept all week."

He shrugged. "You had it coming, and so did Muriel, for leaving me to spring the news of the surprise engagement on Holbrook. Luckily, he is head over heels for your friend and they are married now."

"At least that worked out," Josie mused aloud.

"You were in the side alley…" Sol prompted, getting her back on track and sounding like a professional interrogator once again.

"There were crates and trash cans against the back wall of the blacksmith shop, and you were nowhere to be seen," she reported. "I was aggravated with you because I'd planned to be on hand to watch Muriel marry, even if you didn't show up. I walked into the back alley, then strode over to glance around the far side of the church, to see if you were waiting for me there. Then I heard your footsteps—"

"For the last time, Josephine, that wasn't me!" he barked irritably.

"I was about to turn around and scold you for the mischievous delay," she went on. "Before I could face you, you clubbed me on the back of the head, and I cursed you before I blacked out."

"It wasn't me!" he all but yelled at her, sending pain ricocheting through her sensitive skull. Then he spun around. "Marshal Colby! Please open this cell. Someone knocked my fiancée on the head. We need to check her injury to see if she needs medical attention."

The lawman's skeptical gaze bounced back and forth between Sol and Josie, but he reached for the keys hooked to his belt loop. When the door swung open, both men advanced toward her. Sol sank down beside her on the cot to run his hand over the back of her skull.

"She's right," he confirmed. "Someone struck her."

When he examined the wound closely, Josie recoiled. "Ouch! That hurts."

"Sorry." Sol withdrew his hand to note telltale blood on his fingertips. "So someone knocked you out. Then what happened?"

Josie looked up to see the marshal's hazel eyes boring into her. "Then someone stuffed something under my nose that jerked me back to consciousness. But I was so confused that I couldn't seem to function physically or think straight. I saw Kane lying at my feet, bleeding all over himself," she informed the marshal.

"Then I heard Sol's voice and saw the pistol in his hand. I thought he'd shot Kane after he knocked me out. I assumed that he'd try to lay the blame on me after he placed a gun in my hand."

"Thank you so much for your confidence in me," Sol said, scowling yet again.

"I had no other explanation for how the weapon might have come to be in my hand, unless you put it there," she retorted.

She supposed this was good practice for defending herself when she wound up in a courtroom, on trial for a murder she didn't commit.

"Did you hear the gunshot?" the marshal questioned intently.

Josie shook her head gingerly. "No."

"Then it's settled," Sol said in a decisive tone. "Josephine didn't do it. Someone set her up, no question about it."

"Oh? And who do you suppose did that?" Colby asked caustically.

"Carlton Bradley is my best guess," Josie insisted. "He proposed again to me yesterday and I turned him down. Then he told me I'd be sorry I rejected him." Her gaze settled on Sol's grim expression. She hoped he felt guilty for accepting that bribe she'd seen him take the previous day at the Oasis.

"How can you be so sure it was Bradley, whoever the devil he is?" Colby said dubiously.

"Kane is one of Bradley's hired hands," Sol explained.

How did Sol know that? Josie wondered. Because he'd spent considerable time with Bradley and his thugs, that's how.

"You're trying to convince me that this Bradley character killed his friend?" the marshal challenged in a skeptical tone.

"Perhaps he did. I don't have the slightest idea what happened or why." Josie stared pointedly at Sol. "Maybe there was a falling-out among scoundrels, and Kane lost the fight and I was set up."

Sol said nothing, just gazed at her with that damnable deadpan expression he wore so well.

Curse it, just when she began to soften up toward him—and reluctantly admit she cared for him—she found herself wondering how much he knew about the Kane-Bradley connection. She didn't recall mentioning it to him. Furthermore, Sol's morals and ethics were still in question. She would be an absolute fool to trust him.

"We don't know for sure that Bradley killed Kane. That's speculation," Sol remarked, still staring intently at Josie for reasons she couldn't comprehend. Then he surged off the cot and exited the cell. "I'll be back in a minute, Marshal. Don't let her out just yet."

"Wasn't planning to," Colby called after him. "She was the one caught with a smoking gun in her hand, you know."

When Sol left, the lawman plunked down beside her to check for himself if there was a knot on her head.

"Ouch!" she yelped when he touched a tender spot.

"Sorry," he mumbled. "Now that Tremain is out of

earshot, why don't you tell me the truth? He's the one who shot Kane, right?"

"I don't know," she insisted. "I didn't see who shot the man."

"You're trying to cover for your fiancé, because you don't think I'll hold *you* for murder, so *he* can get off scot-free." Colby's bushy brows flattened over his slitted eyes. "Well, think again, little lady. I just transported a female prisoner to the capital at Guthrie last month. She killed her husband when she found him in bed with another woman, who happened to be her own sister. So if you think a judge and jury will turn you loose because you're prettier than most, you're in for a rude awakening. This may be a new territory, but we take law and order seriously here."

"I am not covering for Tremain," Josie stated emphatically. "This knot on my head should be evidence enough."

"Unless he put it there to confuse the issue," the marshal said speculatively.

Josie did admit Sol probably would like to put a knot on her head. But he had shown up, dressed to kill....

She inwardly winced at her careless choice of words. *Correction,* he had arrived in fashionable clothing to attend the wedding. Josie wasn't sure exactly what that implied. Maybe he'd intended to be Holbrook's best man, not her groom.

Yet what if Sol actually did like her, the way she had begun to like him? Despite her issues of trust, of course. Did he simply want her physically, because other men chased after her and male pride demanded he claim her as his prize?

Or maybe spite still motivated him, she mused. Maybe he wanted to marry her because of her initial insistence that she didn't want to marry anyone. Blast it, she couldn't figure out his motives, and this hellish headache wasn't helping in the least.

"Look, Marshal, Kane attacked me last week, and Tremain stepped in to rescue me before I was molested," Josie explained. "Then Kane broke out of jail and we feared he would return to exact revenge."

"Ah-ha! Now we're getting somewhere," Colby said, coming to attention. "So Tremain had good reason to retaliate against Kane and defend your honor."

"For a marshal, you certainly jump to a lot of conclusions," she said under her breath.

When the door to the jail creaked open, she glanced through the iron bars to see Sol and an unfamiliar, well-dressed gentleman. Bless Sol's soul! Maybe he'd found a good lawyer to defend her against this ridiculous charge of murder. With luck, Josie wouldn't have to rot in the calaboose, and could make the run tomorrow.

"Now what?" Colby asked, his wary gaze leaping from Sol to the newcomer.

Sol hitched his thumb toward the barrel-bellied, gray-haired gent that stood behind him. "This is the justice of the peace. He is going to marry us."

Sol watched Josie's reaction carefully. Her striking blue eyes nearly popped from their sockets. Her mouth dropped open wide enough for a sparrow to roost in it.

Yet she didn't recoil or protest. He took that as a positive sign.

Damn it, he wasn't sure why he'd given way to this impulse—or insanity. People tied the matrimonial knot for dozens of reasons, some sensible, some pragmatic and some not. Nevertheless, *he* was going to marry this lovely, spirited but troublesome misfit because he *wanted* to.

It was as simple and complicated as that.

Speaking of complicated, this was definitely going to undermine his investigation of Bradley and his goons, he reminded himself. Yet he kept remembering what he had said to Josie last night. *I'll be there if you will.* Then she'd said it back to him.

She had shown up in that formfitting gold gown that displayed her lush curves to their best advantage. He'd dressed in fancy trappings for a wedding. So he decided that sealed the deal. Sol wasn't going to let a little thing like murder interrupt their wedding day.

The marshal's eyes bugged out as he studied Sol suspiciously. "I don't know about this marriage ceremony taking place in my jail. It's highly irregular."

So is my bride-to-be, Sol thought to himself. "I appreciate the fact that you are trying to do your job, Colby, but the bump on Josephine's head is indication that she was a pawn used to cover up a murder committed by someone else."

"Such as you," the lawman said accusingly. "She just informed me that she had a run-in with Kane last week and you arrived to rescue her in the nick of time."

Sol waved him off. "The note delivered to her and the weapon planted in her hand are dead giveaways that there were underhanded tactics involved, and you know it."

Colby harrumphed. "'Dead' is right, and I don't know anything for certain yet. Kane could dispute your story, and hers, but he isn't around to protest, now is he?"

"We didn't come to town to kill Kane," Sol insisted. "We came to get married before we stake our claim tomorrow." He glanced quickly at Josie. "We're crazy about each other, aren't we, sugarplum?"

"Right. Absolutely crazy, my love," she said, and flashed a wide smile. "Does this mean *you're* going to make the run tomorrow to claim our land, if I'm still stuck in here?"

"That's exactly what it means, my beloved." He turned his attention back to Colby. "Why would Josephine or I become sidetracked and murder someone on our way to our wedding? That would spoil the festive mood, wouldn't it?"

"The fact remains that Kane previously attacked your fiancée, and you both might have plotted revenge against him," Colby theorized. "You're using the wedding plans as part of your alibi. Clever but not foolproof."

Damn, the marshal was intelligent and thorough. Just what Sol needed—an experienced lawman determined to question each supposed fact, as *he* was in the habit of doing.

"Muriel saw the boy hand the note to me," Josie interjected. "She will vouch for me."

"She's your loyal, true-blue friend, I suppose?" the marshal said in a mocking tone. "How fortunate for you."

"Can we get on with this ceremony?" Sol demanded impatiently. "There is a killer running loose and the trail is growing colder by the minute. If I were you, Marshal—" he stared meaningfully at Colby "—I would snoop around to see if there are footprints to indicate someone might have been lurking behind the crates or trash cans in the alley. The clutter might have provided the perfect hiding place to lie in wait to dispose of Kane and put the blame on Josie. She received the note that lured her to the scene of the staged murder. It sounds premeditated to me."

"Seems to *me* you are the only two people with opportunity and motive." Colby cast Sol a pointed stare. "If you are married, I can't force you to testify against each other. Convenient. But then, I suspect you already know that, don't you, Tremain?"

Sol expelled an exasperated breath. Staring at Colby was like looking at himself in the mirror. Now he knew what it was like to be on the wrong side of an intensive investigation. He preferred to fire questions, not field them.

"I agree that we look suspicious, but I promise to do all I can to help with the investigation, as soon as we're married. Josie can stay in jail—"

"Now wait just a blasted minute!" she protested hotly.

When she bolted to her feet, the color drained from her face. She grabbed her head in both hands and sank back on the cot.

"Marry us before she passes out again," Sol demanded of the justice of the peace. "Then I'll canvass the area. Afterward, I'll try to locate Muriel to get her testimony."

Colby stabbed a beefy finger at Sol's chest, then narrowed his eyes threateningly. "You better not be thinking about planting evidence, or you will be spending your honeymoon in a cage with your new bride. Hear me?"

"Loud and clear," Sol replied with a mock salute.

He strode into the cell and clutched Josie's hand, urging her to her feet. When she wobbled, he curled his arm around her waist to steady her. "I knew you were trouble the day I met you," he whispered in her ear. "I never dreamed I'd be marrying a jailbird. You have to admit a ceremony behind bars is unique."

Josie smiled feebly. "This will be a memorable event to be sure. We can exchange handcuffs rather than wedding bands."

Which reminded him… Sol fished in his pocket to retrieve the gold ring he had purchased. She blinked in surprise when she saw it. Hell, he was surprised he'd bought it, too.

When he tried to slip it on her finger, it was too large, so he tried her middle finger. He eventually found a fit on her index finger.

"At least it's on your left hand," he murmured after

the rotund justice of the peace pronounced them man and wife. "Considering this unconventional match of ours, I think an oversize ring handed over in a jail cell might be the best we should expect."

Then he kissed her—that was his favorite part. All the frustration, conflicting emotions and confusion that were eating him alive melted away. He was *married*. Didn't that beat all? He'd never expected it to happen. Nonetheless, he was lawfully wed—to a murder suspect. He would become one himself, if Colby had anything to say about it. Which he did.

The irony was almost amusing to a lawman who was not at liberty to tell anyone, including his wife, who he really was and why he was here.

"I'm coming with you, Tremain," Marshal Colby insisted. "I want to make sure you don't try anything sneaky."

Dropping one last kiss on Josie's dewy lips, Sol stepped away, then closed the barred door between them. "You stay here, wife. It's the one place I can be sure you won't get into more trouble."

Following that remark—which incited her to puff up with indignation—Sol lurched around and headed out the door to see if he and Colby could find something—anything!—that would divert suspicion from his bride-behind-bars.

Three hours later, Josie woke up from what she was sure was a nightmare of misadventures. Then she glanced sideways to see the iron bars, and realized it hadn't been a bad dream. It was reality.

Sweet merciful heavens! she thought as she threw her legs over the edge of the cot to sit up. How had she become caught up in a whirlwind wedding ceremony? And when would this atrocious headache ease up?

Sol was off playing pretend deputy to the city marshal. Obviously, Sol enjoyed all manner of pretense, she decided as she stood up to pace the narrow confines to relieve her restlessness. She needed to pack her gear in preparation for the run so no one would steal her belongings. She wanted out of here—now!

Josie glanced down at the gold band on her index finger and smiled reluctantly. *Married.* That hadn't been on her list of things to do before staking her claim on a homestead. Yet here she was—wed, and jailed for a crime she would have liked to have committed, but hadn't. If Sol couldn't find evidence that provided her with the benefit of the doubt, she could be here indefinitely.

She had fretted for weeks, wondering if she could complete the race without being thrown from Rooster's back before she thrust her stake in the ground to claim her property. Now she wondered if she would be allowed to approach the starting line, or if Sol planned to make the run for her so he could sell their jointly owned property to Bradley—

Her fretful thoughts broke off abruptly when Marshal Colby and Sol entered the jail. She turned so quickly to confront them that the cell seemed to spin furiously, and she had to grab the bars for support. She was still dizzy and light-headed. For certain, if she wasn't back to her old self tomorrow she wouldn't be able to control her high-strung stallion.

To her vast relief, the marshal lumbered over to unlock the jail cell. "You're free to go, Mrs. Tremain," he told her, not sounding very enthusiastic. "We found the note wadded up in one of the trash cans by the blacksmith shop. But in my mind you're not in the clear, because I still maintain the note could have been planted."

Despite his suspicion, Josie nearly fainted in relief— and she was not a woman prone to the vapors. Her gaze leaped to Sol. His new clothes were covered with grime. From the look of him, he was the one who'd scoured the garbage looking for evidence.

Impulsively, she dashed through the cell door and threw her arms around his neck. "Thank God! And thank you!" She gave him a loud, smacking kiss on the lips, hugged the stuffing out of him and then leaned back to wipe away a smudge of soot from his chin.

"You're welcome, Josephine." He grinned wryly. "You look much better outside iron bars than you do inside."

Colby pivoted to toss the ring of keys onto the scarred desk that sat in the back corner of the room— facing the door, in case someone burst in with guns blazing to break a prisoner out of jail. "We also found two sets of men's boot prints in the powdery dirt. One set was Kane's. The others don't belong to your husband. So for now, you can go free."

Elated, Josie smiled widely, then bounded over to hug the marshal. "You have restored my faith that justice does prevail. Sometimes at least."

She thought she saw the slightest hint of a smile twitch his lips before she turned toward the door. Toward freedom and her grand plans for tomorrow.

"I hope you catch the culprit, Marshal Colby," she said as she whizzed off, then screeched to a sudden halt to face him. "Did you search Kane's pockets or check for a blow to the back of his head? He wasn't clobbered, then robbed, was he? I sewed a pocket back on a customer's shirt recently, after thieves had overtaken him. Perhaps Kane was the victim of a robbery gone bad and I was lured there to take the blame."

The marshal gave her a clipped nod. "I'll check him and his clothing at the undertaker's office."

Josie stepped outside and inhaled a deep breath of fresh air to combat the stench of sweat she had encountered in the jail cell. It did wonders for her headache.

"Can you make the trip to the tent city without me?" Sol asked hurriedly as he veered off to fetch Outlaw. "I have some business to attend to. I don't know when I'll return."

Josie had to admit she was disappointed that her honeymoon had been shunted aside in favor of "business." The lingering doubts about Sol's integrity gathered like storm clouds in her mind. Maybe she should follow him and see what he was up to. She'd feel a dozen times better if she thought she could trust her new husband.

"Sure, do what you need to do," she insisted with a

dismissive wave of her wrist. "I have to pack up the rest of my belongings for the run."

Keeping an eye on Sol, Josie zigzagged through the crowded street, to find Rooster wedged between two other horses. He did not look happy. Josie could only imagine how he would react when thousands of horses banged against him, jockeying for position on the starting line before cannons exploded and the report of rifles filled the air.

The thought made her grimace as she grabbed Rooster's reins and led him down a side street, in hopes of monitoring Sol's activity. A sinking sensation settled in the pit of her belly when she saw none other than Carlton Bradley sauntering toward Sol. Hell and damnation, what was going on with those two?

She reminded herself once again that since she and Sol were married they could claim only one quarter section of land—which amounted to one hundred sixty acres—as man and wife. His name would be on the deed alongside hers. Like some of the other shysters circling like vultures, he might plan to sell the property for profit, so Bradley could increase the size of his sprawling ranch.

Feelings of betrayal flooded her. She swore under her breath when she saw Sol and Bradley head off to an alley to hold their private conference. Towing Rooster behind her, she tried to get as close as she could without calling attention to herself.

Bradley's stance suggested hostility toward Sol, who stood toe to toe with him. They were likely haggling over money, she speculated. Maybe they would have a showdown and she would be done with them both, she mused resentfully.

Whatever tender feelings she had developed toward her new husband fizzled out while she watched the men conversing. She was back to mistrusting Sol's intentions.

Bradley she didn't trust at all!

The two men moved deeper into the alley to continue their conversation, making it impossible for her to overhear. Angry and disappointed, Josie swung onto Rooster's back to return to the camp. Whatever scheme the two men were hatching in the shadows, she vowed to remain on high alert.

No one was going to deprive her of her dream. *No one*. Not even her new husband, who appeared to be in a league with the devil—if Tremain wasn't the very devil himself!

Chapter Ten

Sol listened to Bradley chew him out for a few minutes before gesturing for the irate Texan to follow him deeper into the alley behind the Silver Dollar Saloon. If the man's anger resulted in gunplay, Sol didn't want an innocent bystander shot.

"You're done hurling curses," Sol told the fuming rancher.

"I'm just getting started, damn your double-crossing hide!" he snarled hatefully. "I paid you to break off your engagement, and you married the wildcat I wanted for myself!"

"I was forced into it," Sol growled defensively, then retrieved the money Bradley had paid him. "Returned in full," he added as he slapped the banknotes into his hand. "If not for that drunkard attacking her last week, and somehow getting himself shot this morning, this wouldn't have happened."

Sol feigned ignorance of Bradley's connection to

Kane and continued, "My wife wouldn't have ended up in jail, if not for her conflict with the man."

"It's what she deserved." Bradley sneered derisively as he pocketed the money.

Sol gave a sardonic smirk. "For what? Being mauled by that thug? And what the hell did you expect me to do when she landed in jail, beside herself with fear?"

"Having a murder suspect as a fiancée was the perfect excuse to break the engagement," Bradley snapped. "If you had any brains, horse trader, you would have figured that out for yourself."

Sol wondered if that had been part of the scheme that landed Kane at the undertaker's and in Boot Hill Cemetery—eternally. Sol would dearly love to drag a murder confession from Bradley, here and now. It would save time and effort.

The man might have *ordered* the execution, which would be difficult to prove without testimony from the actual murderer. Until Sol knew how and if Bradley was connected to Kane's death, his hands were tied.

Hell! Sol had known that marrying Josie would invite complications and conflict with Bradley. Sure enough, it had. All Sol wanted was to be with Josie all day long and all through the night, as a groom rightfully ought to be with his new bride.

So much for exotic whims.

"If you had been at the marshal's office when Josie begged me to help her, you would have knuckled under, too," Sol said, giving the truth a creative twist. "Even the marshal expected me to stand up for her, and asked me to accompany him to the scene to look for clues to substantiate her story that she had been knocked out and set up."

Sol gauged Bradley's reaction carefully. The Texan's gray eyes narrowed, and then he glanced away. An indication of guilt? Or at the very least, prior knowledge of the incident? Sol wished he knew.

"Josie maintains that she didn't kill the man, though she admitted she would've liked to after Kane assaulted her last week," Sol added.

"Did you figure out who did it?" Bradley questioned.

He shook his head. "We didn't find the note she said she received, luring her into the alley," he said, lying. "But we saw two sets of boot prints. One belonged to the dead man. The other must belong to the real killer." Sol scowled for the Texan's benefit. "In a town bulging with land-hungry strangers, it will be difficult to locate the murderer. By this time tomorrow, thousands of folks will line up for the run. They'll scatter all over the area and the marshal will have damn little to go on to solve the case."

Bradley's square forehead furrowed. "That still doesn't explain why you married the woman when I *paid* you *not* to."

"While it's true that I'm a hard-nosed trader and everything I own is for sale, excluding my best horse, I discovered I'm a sucker for a woman's tears. Josie broke down, cried and asked me to go through with the wedding because she decided she needed a man's protection after the fiasco in the alley," he said, giving the truth another deliberate twist. "Plus she wanted me to make the run for her if the marshal didn't release her."

If Bradley was responsible for killing Kane and setting up Josie, Sol wanted him to think his scheme had backfired. Served the bastard right. Even if he wasn't directly responsible, he was still trying to rob hapless victims and defraud homesteaders of property. Sol wanted evidence to put him away.

"I still hold you responsible for reneging on our agreement," the man said angrily. "So now you owe me a favor, Tremain. I expect you to do as I say or *you* might end up dead. And I will be there to console your widow."

The worst cutthroats humanity had to offer had threatened Sol over the past decade. This cocky Texan didn't intimidate him in the least. Sol's one true fear was for Josie's safety. Independent and spirited as she was, she could provoke this conniving, self-important rancher and he might retaliate.

Josie had become Sol's Achilles' heel, and he felt protective of her. Of course, he'd cut out his tongue before he let her or Bradley know that.

"What is it you want in exchange?" Sol questioned.

"I want you to make the run with your new bride and forfeit your land to me," Bradley demanded. "I'll pay you for it, of course. If Josie wants the property as badly as she says she does, then *she* can deal directly with me and meet my demands."

Sol rubbed his chin pensively. "You realize she's

going to be spitting mad if she loses the homestead she wants so desperately, right?"

A devilish grin spread across Bradley's thin lips, making them all but disappear. "I'm counting on that. She turned me down twice, but if I own the land she wants, she will change her tune. She'll come to me submissively after you abandon her."

Submissively? Josephine? Ha! That'd be the day, thought Sol. "Twice? I thought you said you only asked her once," Sol said, feigning ignorance every chance he got.

Bradley shrugged nonchalantly. "It was once or twice. The point is I don't like being turned down, turned away or turned *against*." He eyed Sol meaningfully. "If you know what's good for you, you won't forget that."

"When will I collect my fee for forfeiting the claim to you?" Sol asked. "I already told Josie I would hang around this area only until she settled on the homestead. She knows my job takes me hither and yon, and I can't offer protection indefinitely."

Sol noticed the gleam in Bradley's eye. *Take the bait, you bastard,* he thought to himself.

"You'll line up tomorrow, south of me and the men who agreed to my terms," he instructed. "I want all the parcels I claim for my ranch to be adjoining."

"Makes sense," Sol said with a lackadaisical shrug. "Have you selected a site for your headquarters?"

Under his breath, Bradley muttered, "I had two, er,

friends sneak inside the boundary line, ready to claim the prime property, but the army captain ran them out."

Sol smiled inwardly, hoping he was the one who'd tipped off Holbrook. Had Sol known in advance that Bradley had hired the heavily armed squatters, he would have had the captain interrogate them thoroughly.

"I have a special license to cross into the area," Sol informed the Texan. "Describe the place to me and I'll lead Josie in that direction."

Bradley smiled wickedly. "Maybe you aren't so bad, after all, Tremain."

Maybe not, but you are, thought Sol.

"The choice property is about eight miles northwest of the fort. It has a good water source and the rolling hills will provide exceptional forage for my cattle."

"I know the place," Sol replied. "I'll see that we stake our claim nearby."

"I'll be counting on that, horse trader," he said sternly. "You already crossed me by marrying that spitfire. Don't cross me again."

"I'll see you sometime tomorrow." Sol pivoted around, but kept an eye on Bradley, just in case the rancher decided to shoot him in the back. "I have a few more horses to sell to eager settlers before the night is out."

He walked away, wishing Bradley had left first, so Sol could check his boot prints. He might have time to circle back later, but right now he needed to put out feelers to locate some of the men Bradley had bribed—or strong-armed—to stake claims they would be forced to forfeit for violating the stipulations of the Homestead Act.

"So much for my wedding night," Sol muttered as he mounted Outlaw, then trotted off to fetch his string of horses.

When he circled back a few minutes later to check for prints, he scowled in frustration. A would-be homesteader and his family had set up camp in the alley. It wasn't an unusual occurrence, Sol reminded himself. The town was crawling with hopeful settlers. But damn it, possible evidence had been smeared in the dirt!

Josie was surprised to find Muriel, dressed in her usual attire of breeches and shirt, in the tent when she returned to camp. Yet there she was, dashing toward her with open arms.

"Oh, thank heavens you're all right!" Her friend hugged her excitedly. "I'm so glad the marshal released you. I was afraid you'd be in jail during the run." Muriel jabbered on without taking a breath. "Grant insisted we leave town and let the marshal and Tremain sort out what happened…."

Her voice fizzled out when she noticed the gold band encircling Josie's index finger. "What does this mean?" Her gaze narrowed suspiciously. "That sidewinder didn't coerce you to marry him, the same way he coerced me to keep silent in exchange for squaring my engagement with Grant, did he?"

Josie mulled that over for a moment. Truth be told, the blow to the skull had dazed her severely. The memory of the fiasco was blurred in several places. Just how had the wedding come about? She tried to recall, but the incident was fuzzy.

Before she could figure it out exactly, Muriel rushed on. "Or did that rascal demand certain favors if he helped set you free?"

"We have an arrangement of sorts," Josie hedged. "Sol makes the run with me tomorrow so I can stake my claim. Hopefully, he will stay around long enough to help me make a few improvements on the property. Then he'll go his own way. This afternoon he helped find evidence that indicated I didn't kill Kane, so I owe him my freedom."

Muriel threw up her hands in exasperation. "I knew it! I should have stayed in town after my wedding ceremony. I could have corroborated your story of receiving that note, so you wouldn't have to depend on him to spring you from jail."

Josie gestured dismissively. "Everything worked out well enough, so there's no need for you to fret." She glanced around the tent. "Where are your belongings? And did you misplace your husband already? Some honeymoon this is."

"We took up residence in officers' quarters at the fort. We got to spend some time together before his duties pertaining to the run demanded his attention."

Josie noted her friend's blush. Obviously, the bride and groom had enjoyed a few hours of privacy before Grant rode off looking for Sooners.

"Grant can't make the run with me, but he promised to watch out for me after signaling the start of the race."

"You are still planning to stake a claim beside me, right?" Josie questioned.

"Of course," Muriel insisted. "I also plan to store our extra supplies at the garrison until we set up housekeeping." She gathered some of the belongings she knew Josie wouldn't need until after the run. "I plan to spend the night—" her cheeks turned beet-red again "—with Grant, but I will meet you at the site where we usually exercise our horses, and we can move to the starting line together."

"Agreed." Josie scooped up the nonessentials to stack outside. "We might as well fold up the tent and pack it away, too. I can camp out under the stars beside Rooster, and save time in the morning."

"At least Tremain will be here to watch over you," Muriel said. "Just like he was on hand the night Kane..." She frowned distastefully. "I can't say I'm sorry that ruffian met a bad end."

"Amen to that," Josie murmured.

"When will Tremain return?"

She forced a casual smile. "I'm not sure. He has last-minute horse sales to make." *Among other things I doubt I'd approve of.*

She wasn't sure she could trust herself to be civil to him if he did show up. She knew he had met with Bradley, and that infuriated her. She wondered what wicked plot those two scoundrels had hatched. She hoped beyond hope that Sol wasn't planning to cheat her out of her future homestead for his own selfish profit. The torment of not knowing if she could trust her new husband was killing her, bit by excruciating bit.

Muriel pulled down the tent braces, then stepped outside to watch their temporary housing collapse on itself—which was too symbolic of the possibility of Josie's dream imploding.

She turned away to inhale a bolstering breath.

"After I store the tent and extra belongings at the garrison, Grant should be free, so we can spend the afternoon together.... You'll be all right by yourself, won't you?"

She flashed Muriel a beaming smile. "Of course. I'll fill my canteen, then lead Rooster around, while people are milling about. It will help him become accustomed to the crowds he'll face tomorrow."

"Good luck acclimating that flighty horse to abrupt sounds and motion." Muriel shook her head. "I might not be pleased with Tremain for manipulating both of us—"

You think you *are displeased?* thought Josie. She could strangle him for what she was afraid he'd try to pull while conspiring with Bradley. She shouldn't have married him on a whim, thinking he could make the run in her stead if she was still stuck behind bars.

This is likely the worst mistake of my life!

"—but I'm thankful Tremain will be riding beside you to help keep Rooster under control," her friend finished.

Muriel hoisted up the folded tent and spare supplies.

Together they tied them onto the packhorse Grant had loaned her.

Josie watched her friend ride across the boundary line without being waylaid by the patrol guarding the soon-to-be-opened territory. She smiled, thinking there were certain advantages to marrying the fort commander.

She, on the other hand, had married a horse trader who might sell her property out from under her if she didn't take care.

She frowned curiously when she recognized the two soldiers who had accompanied her and Muriel to lunch earlier in the week. They were escorting several men off the forbidden land.

"These individuals will not be allowed to seek a homestead until day *after* tomorrow," the young, blond-haired private announced to all within earshot. "Same goes for the other Sooners, who won't be released from the stockade until tomorrow. *After* the run begins."

"If you see anyone who has defied the laws regulating this run, and tries to cheat honest settlers out of their property, report the incident to the garrison," the red-haired corporal added in a booming voice. "All offenders will be stripped of their claims."

It was an idealistic proclamation, thought Josie. The early birds faced the disgruntled jeers and glares of law-abiding citizens waiting to make tomorrow's great race, but no one could follow all the Sooners to keep them honest. The area was jumping with land-hungry people—twenty-five thousand of them. It was impossible for the cavalry to keep track of them all.

Josie stared pointedly at several men in the tent community that she had overheard discussing their "arrangements" with that scoundrel Bradley in the past few days. She wasn't sure how his sidekick, Tremain, fit into the scheme, but she had seen him skulk off with the Texan today. She condemned Sol to the farthest reaches of hell for keeping company with him rather than his new bride.

The thought stung her pride like a swarm of hornets.

Muttering a salty curse, Josie scooped up her small amount of supplies and the colorful stake she had created to mark her claim. Arms overloaded, she strode down to the creek flowing into the river. Rooster whinnied when she approached.

"Be thankful you're in isolation. For now," she told the sorrel stallion. "Tomorrow you better not bolt and run the opposite direction when the race begins."

Josie recalled several high-strung Thoroughbreds that had been shipped in by rail for the Run of '89. The excitement had been too much for the animals. As soon as the cannon boomed, two Thoroughbreds had reared, wheeled around and shot off in the wrong direction. Considering Rooster's temperament, that was an alarming possibility.

Josie brushed down the stallion to calm him—and herself. She had a bad feeling about tomorrow. About Tremain's hidden agenda. She wanted to trust him.

Wanted to believe she wasn't such a bad judge of men—more specifically, the man she had impulsively married.

If Tremain betrayed her, if he shattered her hopes, dreams and expectations, she would do him bodily harm....

Josie expelled a troubled sigh. "Best not make vicious threats," she advised herself. She had spent more than enough time behind bars already. She didn't want to do it again, even to have her revenge on Tremain if he disappointed her.

"Come on, Rooster," she murmured as she headed toward the hustle and bustle of the tent community. "You need to learn to deal with loud voices and noises and you better learn fast!"

The next morning dawned cloudy. After spending the night tossing and turning on her flimsy pallet on the grass, Josie paced nervously on the creek bank. She wondered if Tremain planned to show up. Where the blazes was he? He hadn't sought her out the previous night. Their *wedding* night! Thanks to his inconvenient absence, she had slept with a pistol in her hand, her newly purchased dagger in her boot, and one eye open, just to be on the safe side.

She blew out an exasperated breath as she stared warily at the flighty sorrel stallion that sidestepped around the tree where she had tethered him. She knew the animal wasn't every would-be homesteader's dream mount, but the ornery horse was all she had. Now she didn't even have a husband to line up beside her for the race!

Swearing she would be tempted to chew Tremain up and spit him out if he finally bothered to show up, Josie led Rooster around the disassembled campsite. Hundreds of hopeful settlers milled about, sorting nonessential supplies from necessities. Women and children packed covered wagons and buckboards, while husbands and fathers prepared their horses for the great race.

Josie shook her head in dismay as she watched some of the men pile their belongings into their only mode of transportation—a rickety wagon hitched to plow horses. There were even some folks with bicycles. Some were seated in wobbly buggies and others were on foot. They would be lucky indeed if horses and wagons didn't trample them.

Glancing at her pocket watch, Josie gave up waiting for Muriel and Sol. Neither of them had shown up on time. She led Rooster toward the boundary line, where the military patrols had marked off the starting points. A cannon sat on a rise, waiting to break the apprehensive silence.

Josie smiled in satisfaction when she saw a second cavalry troop, led by Grant Holbrook, escorting two more Sooners from their hiding places on the wrong side of the boundary.

"These illegal squatters are banned from making the run *at all*." Grant's authoritative voice boomed over the gathering crowd. "The rest of you are urged to notify

me or my men if you come upon other Sooners who
defied the rules."

Josie glanced around the crowd and swore under her
breath. It was an hour until the race and still neither Muriel nor Tremain had shown up. The rumble of thunder
caught her attention and she stared skyward. While she
wouldn't mind rain to settle the powdery dust caused
by thousands of riders and hundreds of wagons, she
preferred not to dash off to claim her homestead in a
downpour.

Anxiety assailed her as she led Rooster westward to
find a starting place. The wild-eyed stallion sidestepped
when he came in close contact with other horses. Josie's
dreams were on the line today and she was counting on
Rooster. He was all she had, especially since it looked
as if Tremain had his own agenda and had decided not
to race alongside her.

A rain shower pelted the settlers as they jostled for
position. Josie didn't care that her hair became a wet
mop and her breeches and shirt clung to her like second skin. She *did* care that the crowded conditions had
Rooster whinnying, throwing his head and half rear-
ing each time another horse bumped into him. It was
all she could do to stand her ground and keep him from
breaking loose.

"I told you that stallion was a disaster waiting to
happen."

Josie tightened her hold on Rooster's bridle, then
glared over her shoulder to see Tremain straddling Out-

law. The buckskin didn't seem to mind that other horses jarred him; he simply held his ground.

"I'll trade my entire savings for your horse," she offered in last-minute desperation.

Sol grinned wryly. "You don't need my horse. You have *me*."

"Not sure that's such a grand bargain," she muttered bitterly.

She scrutinized his five o'clock shadow, now a day old. His raven hair was disheveled and his sea-green eyes bloodshot. It looked as if he'd spent all night in a saloon—or somewhere like the Oasis, celebrating their honeymoon without her. She'd like to shoot the rascal where he sat.

Josie reflexively touched the pistol she had stuffed into the band of her breeches. She was tempted to use it on Tremain, before facing down possible claim jumpers that might encroach on her property after she staked it. *If* she staked it.

"Don't even think about it, wife," he said warningly. "In this public setting, there are too many witnesses. Marshal Colby would tote you off to jail, for sure. Or these would-be settlers might hang you before they dash off to claim my tribe's land."

"Perhaps I would be justified, husband," she retorted as she held on to Rooster—and her temper—for dear life. "You look like you've been up all night."

"I was," he said curtly.

Josie wasn't satisfied with that. "Did you spend the

evening at the Oasis? Did I mention I saw you and Bradley together there last week?"

She swore she saw him grimace before he masked his expression with that infuriatingly blank stare he wore so well. "Would you care if I did, Josephine?"

Yes, damn it all. She would. She didn't want to care about this untrustworthy rapscallion, but she did. Fool that she was, she secretly wanted what Muriel had—a real marriage with two-way affection. Instead, Josie had bargained with the devil, and who knew what else he wanted besides her soul?

"There you are!"

She spun around at the sound of Muriel's voice, relieved that she didn't have to answer Tremain's question.

"I've been looking up and down the line for forty-five minutes. I was delayed by this surging crowd, and couldn't reach our meeting site on time," her friend declared as she tried to wedge in beside Josie. "You would not believe how many people are lined up—for miles!"

Muriel pointed south. "There's even a six-horse team hitched to a small *house* on wheels a half mile from here. Incredible! Considering the rough terrain, I can't imagine how it could hold together during a bouncing ride at swift speed."

"We are moving north on the line," Tremain announced abruptly. "Josie, pile on Rooster. Muriel, follow me."

"I'm satisfied with where I am," Josie muttered, annoyed by his dictatorial attitude. It never failed to incite her contrary nature.

"Trust me, I've been all over the area that's about to be opened for the run. I know where I'm going."

To line up beside Bradley? she thought suspiciously. Along with other fortune hunters that planned to exchange claims for money?

"I told you already that I don't trust the selfish motives of men, especially ones that spend their wedding nights elsewhere," she sniped, for his ears only.

"I wasn't sure I'd be welcome," he said, and grabbed Rooster's reins the instant the horse acted up again.

"Probably not, considering the company you've been keeping lately."

Josie clamped her mouth shut and told herself to bide her time. She didn't want to have a domestic quarrel out here in public. No matter how angry she was with Tremain, no matter how disappointed that he'd barely showed up in time, and how suspicious she was about where he'd been since the wedding ceremony, she had an important race to run. She was on the verge of realizing her dream, and she refused to let her misguided affection for this black-haired rascal spoil it.

Tremain confirmed her worst fears when she saw Bradley mounted on a strapping black gelding, surrounded by several men she had overheard discussing the sale of their upcoming claims to him. When Tremain nodded mutely to that sneaky bastard, Josie itched to go for both men's throats simultaneously.

She forced aside her bitter thoughts when she saw Grant riding his roan horse toward the mounted cannon that would officially signal the start of the race to her promised land—if Tremain didn't find a way to swindle her out of it.

All around them the tension was palpable. She glanced sideways to see a string of riders as far as the eye could see. Horses shifted, champed at their bits. Wagons, carts and buggies were jammed hub to hub. Every settler knew, as she did, that there were only half as many homesteads available as there were riders to claim them. She could come away with nothing.

A dog yapped somewhere behind her and another one barked in reply. The entire line of riders and horses surged forward, until Grant stood up in his stirrups, waved his arms in wide, sweeping gestures and shouted for everyone to hold the line or be disqualified. Josie glanced at Muriel, who was gazing proudly at her military husband.

Her friend was happy, decidedly so. Pleasure glowed in every inch of her face.

Josie wished she felt the same, but didn't. She didn't know what Tremain had been up to during his absence last night. Bradley kept casting her the same insulting stares she had endured during her recent confrontations with him, and Sol didn't seem to notice. Or care. He simply gazed west, awaiting Grant's signal to begin the race.

Swallowing hard, Josie retrieved her pocket watch to check the time. Two minutes until high noon. Blast it, uncertainty and anticipation were killing her. She might be bucked off Rooster and trampled five minutes from now, but at least the run would be under way. The waiting was pure agony.

She focused her attention on Grant. She watched one of the soldiers under his command step up between him and the cannon. Others up and down the line drew their carbines from their saddle holsters, awaiting their commander's signal.

Kaboom! The cannon exploded and the reports of rifles filled the air. The roar and rumble of thousands of horses and wagons echoed around Josie as Rooster reared up on his hind legs and screamed in terror. She threw herself forward to grab the stallion's quivering neck, determined to stay on board. She wouldn't be able to set even one foot inside the new territory, she realized frantically when Rooster reeled in the opposite direction. The jittery horse was going to leave her in the dirt, to be run down by the team of plow horses hitched to the wagon behind her!

Chapter Eleven

⤸⤸⤸⤸

"**D**own, you cussed animal!" Sol growled fiercely. He yanked on Rooster's reins, forcing him in the right direction, while Josie kept a death grip on the panicky horse.

A wall of humanity lunged forward, spreading across the virgin prairie like a wind-driven wildfire. Sol scowled when the horse directly behind him slammed into Outlaw's rump, trying to shove him out of the way. Sol reached out with his free hand to press Josie facedown on the flighty stallion she insisted on riding—to her own death, if she wasn't careful.

He swore a blue streak when his leg was squeezed between Rooster and Outlaw. Luckily, he managed to keep Josie in the saddle as their stallions plunged forward, jockeying for position among the other horses and wagons. Sol glanced worriedly at Muriel, relieved that she had reined her dapple-gray mare into Rooster to restrain him from bolting sideways.

The tidal wave of humanity swept the threesome

along at dangerous speeds. Horses and wagons thundered and rumbled across the prairie that was knee-deep in damp grass. Behind him, Sol heard the frightened shrieks and wild shouts of hapless riders who had taken a fall and had to scramble to avoid being trampled.

Wagons and carriages overturned, launching drivers through the air. Sol's training urged him to stop to help the less fortunate, but he had his hands full trying to hold position without being run down himself. Plus he had to battle to control the frightened stallion beside him.

He breathed a gigantic sigh of relief when Rooster and Outlaw set a swift pace, separating themselves from the multitude of hard-riding land grabbers behind them. He glanced back to find Muriel's mare close behind, letting the two faster horses cut a swath for her to follow.

"Turn right when we reach the crest of the hill," Sol shouted over the pounding of hooves.

Josie glowered at him as if he was a traitor of the worst sort. But no matter what she thought of him, he was determined that she should claim the homestead he had specifically selected for her.

"No," she yelled belligerently as she tried to yank Rooster's rein from his hand. "*My* land. *My* dream. You will not betray me, damn you!"

Scowling, he leaned sideways and forced Rooster to veer right at breakneck speed. Sol ignored the unflattering curses Josie spewed at him. He glanced right, noting Bradley was enjoying the fight on horseback between husband and firebrand.

"I'm on your side," he growled, while maintaining a death grip on Rooster's reins.

"Liar," she spat, then scowled when she failed to re-gain control of her horse.

To hell with it, thought Sol. His first order of business was to stake a claim so Bradley could pay the sum they had agreed upon. Josie could pitch as many fits as she pleased, but he had a job to do—for her and the other honest homesteaders at risk of being defrauded, roughed up and possibly killed for their newly acquired property.

"Damn you," she muttered as he cut sideways, drag-ging Rooster with him.

He raced downhill toward the tree-lined creek in front of them.

While other settlers rode straight ahead to find a place to cross the swift-moving stream, Sol headed north to a bend in the creek. Water splattered over him and the two women as their mounts splashed through the shin-deep water, then lunged up the far slope.

To Sol's relief, they emerged from the creek valley two hundred yards ahead of the hapless riders that were unfamiliar with territory that had once been Cheyenne stomping grounds. Sol was pleased to note that Josie ceased glaring arrows at him when she realized they had taken the lead in the race across the rolling hills and valleys.

The expression that settled on her flushed face tugged at his heartstrings. He saw this land as she was seeing it for the very first time. She looked exhilarated, delighted by the prairie sprawling endlessly in front of her. She even tossed him a smile, indicating that she wasn't as outraged at him as she had been before he'd forced her toward the shallow crossing.

"Oh, my goodness, Josie," Muriel shouted above the sound of thundering hooves behind them. "This is heaven!"

"At least as close as I'll ever need to come," Josie replied as she twisted in the saddle to retrieve her stake, prepared to make her claim.

"Not yet," Sol insisted. "I have the perfect places picked out for both of you."

There were shadows of suspicion in her blue eyes. He could see the conflict in her expression. She was afraid to trust him. Afraid he would betray her, because she knew of his encounters with Bradley. But damn it, he had her best interests at heart, even if she refused to believe it.

"How much farther?" she demanded warily. "If you're pulling a fast one on me, Solomon, so help me, I'll—"

"Two miles ahead," he interjected. "It will be worth the wait and you can thank me later." He flashed a dimpled grin, but he failed to charm his new wife.

"You better be right, is all I can say. Don't doubt that I will ever let you hear the end of it if you're wrong."

Sol was greatly relieved that he was able to unclamp his hand from Rooster's reins and take the lead up the steep incline of another grassy knoll. He pointed toward the meandering creek and thick grove of trees on the downhill slope.

Josie eyed him skeptically, then glanced over her shoulder to see Bradley and more than two dozen men closing in fast.

"Muriel," Sol yelled over the rumbling thunder of pounding hooves. "Place your stake on the corner marker." He indicated the stones that signified the survey site joining four quarter-sections of land.

Muriel slid off Bess to ram her stake—decorated with a patchwork flag—beside the designated stone. Sol held his breath and waited to see if Josie would defy him on general principle or follow his instructions. He smiled inwardly when she listened to him—for once— and dismounted with her stake in hand. She shoved the wooden stick, decorated with a banner of buttons and buttonholes, into the ground beside Muriel's.

Then his wife, spitfire that she was, drew her pistol and held the approaching men at gunpoint, in case they considered stealing her claim. Several of the saddle tramps who'd been riding with Bradley glared at her, but she jutted out her chin, defying them. They veered north to find other homesteads.

"*You* might consider this prime property," she said as Sol dismounted. "But I'm quite certain I'm not going to like my new neighbors. And I'm going to hold you personally responsible for making me settle beside them."

"I expected you to say something like that."

Sol reached behind the saddle to grab the small, rolled-up tent he used on forays, while chasing criminals in Indian Territory. With swift efficiency that came from years of practice, he set up housing.

"Our first home," he declared teasingly. "Shall I carry you over the threshold?"

She smirked in reply, then turned her back on him to help Muriel retrieve the canvas tarp. Together they spread it out like a picnic blanket on her corner of the claim.

An hour later, an uneasy sensation skittered down Sol's spine when three riders he knew worked for Bradley rode toward him, looking grim and determined. Sol positioned himself a good distance away from Josie and Muriel, in case gunfire broke out.

Apparently, Bradley had decided not to waste time claiming this property. He had sent his hired guns to confront Sol and take over the claim immediately. No doubt Bradley felt justified, since Sol had married Josie, despite their earlier agreement. That was the kind of reasoning Sol expected from that two-legged Texas rattlesnake.

"These two quarter-sections are already taken," Sol declared brusquely. "Go look somewhere else for a homestead."

The three gunslingers halted twenty paces from him. Out of the corner of his eye, Sol saw Josie reach for her pistol.

"The boss decided he wants this piece of property now," the spokesman, a thin-faced, gangly pistoleer who looked to be about Sol's age, announced. "Get off this claim...or else."

While digging for information from the patrons at

the Saddle Burr Saloon, where Sol had spent half the night buying rounds of drinks, he had loosened a dozen tongues. He knew the names of Bradley's hired guns and of several shysters who had thrown in with him. Kane, of course, hadn't survived to stake a claim for Bradley. The undertaker had planted Kane in the ground early this morning.

This spokesman, with his sandy-blond hair, close-set eyes and large ears, was Wendell Latimer. He had threatened several would-be settlers to forfeit their property to Bradley, immediately after they were instructed to pay their two-dollar claim fee at the land office.

Grant already had picked up another one of Bradley's thugs, Felix Baldwin, and his recruited sidekick after they had fleeced several would-be homesteaders of money. They had hidden out behind the boundary line, but the captain had brought them in.

Bernie Hobart, the round-faced kid of twenty-five or thereabout who rode beside Latimer, wore a billy-goat goatee and a mustache. The young tough had thin brown hair and a belly that avalanched over his belt buckle. Sol had dealt with bullies like him before, and doubted the cocky kid would live to see thirty.

From beneath the brim of his oversize sombrero, Ramon Alvarez was eyeing Muriel and Josie insultingly. No question as to what he planned after they sent Sol packing.

"Guess you didn't hear us, hombre," the stocky Mexican growled threateningly. "The boss wants—"

"I heard," Sol snapped. "Your boss and I have an arrangement. Apparently, you aren't well informed of it. Now clear out. You aren't welcome here."

The three men snickered, indicating they weren't leaving.

Beside him, Sol heard Josie gasp. He knew what she thought of him, but it couldn't be helped. Sol was walking a fine line here. His connections to Bradley and his hired muscle helped him build an airtight case. Yet he needed to protect Josie and Muriel from harm. He hoped like hell he'd be quick enough to defend the women and take down these gunslingers all at once.

When the three men dismounted to make a stand, Sol thought, *Here we go.*

Grinning wickedly, the ruffians separated so they wouldn't become three ducks in a row, making it easy for Sol to fire off rapid shots and blast them to kingdom come. Or to hell, to be more accurate.

"Sol," Josie grumbled. "What do you think you're—"

"Quiet," he growled. "You wanna keep this property or not?"

"Yes, but not at your expense, even if I don't trust you."

He was pleased that she didn't want to see him blown to smithereens, but refused to respond, keeping his gaze trained on the three hooligans.

"Well, lookie here," Hobart, the cocky young gun, taunted. "Yer bride is standin' up for ya. You gonna hide behind her skirt? Oh, wait, she ain't wearin' one. Guess we know who wears the breeches in this family, don't we?"

The mocking comments didn't faze Sol. He'd heard all manner of insults during his years of law enforcement. And he was too intent on keeping Josie and Muriel safe to fret over bruised male pride.

"You have a choice, *boys,*" he muttered, his hands hovering over the pearl-handled peacemakers in the double holsters strapped to his thighs. "You can ride off or be dragged off. Decide now."

The three men snickered.

"You think you can take us, horse trader? You'll find yourself planted six feet under this plot of land," Latimer jeered. "I'll fetch a shovel."

Josie tensed, her gaze leaping back and forth between Sol and the men. Her husband had to be crazy if he thought he could take on three ruthless gunfighters and live to tell about it. Experienced Cheyenne brave that he was, the odds were *not* in his favor. And damn him for becoming mixed up with Bradley. None of this would be happening if he hadn't.

Now he was being double-crossed, and he'd end up *dead* for his selfish interests, whatever they were. She still didn't know for sure.

Pistol clamped in her hand, Josie focused pensively on Sol, trying to figure out which gunman he planned to shoot first. It looked as if he was concentrating on the two older men, not the arrogant young buck that made the insulting remark about who wore the breeches.

Beside her, Muriel aimed her weapon in the same direction as Josie. She doubted her friend had shot at anyone before, but knew Muriel was ready and willing when it came to defending their homesteads.

To Josie's surprise, Sol let out a sharp whistle. Outlaw reared and raced toward him, drawing the gunmen's attention. She was stunned by the lightning-quick speed and accuracy Sol displayed, his two six-shooters clearing leather a full second before the other three men could respond. Sol hit the two older men in their gun arms before they could fire off a shot.

Although Josie wasn't an expert marksman, she cocked her pistol and blasted away at the young thug while he was aiming at Sol. She hit him in the kneecap. A half second later, Muriel fired her pistol, missing her target by a mile.

The young gunman clamped hold of his bleeding leg, cursed foully and swung his pistol toward Josie, promising death. Frantic, she tried to cock her weapon to fire another shot, but found herself staring down the business end of his pistol.

"Bitch," he snarled—and aimed at her heart.

Gunfire exploded in the air again. Josie staggered back, certain she had been hit, though she didn't feel burning pain. *Maybe that's the way it happens,* she thought. *You don't realize you're dead until you already are.*

Stunned, she glanced down at her torso, but didn't see any blood oozing out. The young gunman had two gaping wounds in *his* chest, however. His knees buckled beneath him, his pistol dropped in the grass and he collapsed facedown on top of it.

Still dazed, Josie swung her gaze to Sol. Smoke drifted from both barrels of his peacemakers and his expression was as cold and hard as a tombstone. She had never seen him look so vicious.

"You two wanna slap leather again?" he snarled at the wounded gunslingers. "I have two shots left...with your names on them."

Sol tried to remain focused on Latimer and Alvarez, but wanted to breathe a gigantic sigh of relief that Josie hadn't been injured—or killed. She had taken an awful chance by shooting Hobart and drawing his fire. Yet she had provided a distraction, allowing Sol time to deal with the two older hired guns before turning his attention to the young tough. Sol had gotten off two shots at Hobart before he could blast Josie for shooting him in the kneecap.

Damn her daring hide! She had scared Sol half to death. And she was going to hear about it, in great length, after he dealt with Latimer and Alvarez.

The two wounded men favored their injured arms as they backed toward their horses. Thankfully, they'd lost their nerve after witnessing firsthand how skilled Sol was with his guns. Sol had cut his teeth on thugs like them, and had graduated to some of the most menacing and bloodthirsty criminals ever to hide out in Indian Territory.

He bit back a grin when he noticed Josie and Muriel, aiming their pistols at the two retreating men. Neither of the women was a shrinking violet. Good. The faint of heart wouldn't survive in this untamed territory, he assured himself.

"Nice shot, by the way, Josephine," he said, without taking his eyes off the retreating gunmen.

"I was aiming for his heart," she informed him. "I'm aiming right between the Mexican's eyes now. Wonder what I'll hit this time."

Sol inwardly chuckled, but again refused to become distracted while the gunmen were still on the property.

Before the two could turn tail and ride away, Captain Holbrook and a troop of six soldiers raced downhill toward them. Sol would have preferred if they had put in an appearance five minutes earlier, but it was better than not showing up at all.

Holbrook's brows shot up and disappeared under the brim of his military hat when he took in the scene before him. His Adam's apple bobbed twice when he saw his bride holding a pistol on the two men left standing.

"Trouble?" he asked unnecessarily.

"Not now," Sol replied, while he watched the soldiers hold the claim jumpers at gunpoint. "What took you so long?"

"We came across two other ruffians trying to force a man off the homestead he'd claimed." The captain noticed the gunslinger lying facedown in the tall grass. "Who's that?"

"An overconfident young gun named Bernie Hobart. Josie blasted him." Sol stared at the prone figure unsympathetically. "I was afraid that cocky kid wouldn't live to see thirty. Sure enough, I was right."

"Josie shot him?" Holbrook chirped, clearly incredulous.

"I had to," she retorted. "Sol faced three-to-one odds. Your wife fired, too."

His eyebrows disappeared under the brim of his hat again as he gaped at her. "Muriel? Dear Lord!"

"But I missed the man completely," she complained, staring accusingly at the weapon in her hand. "I think I need target practice, dear."

"And you shall have it, sweetheart," Holbrook promised, looking like the lovesick sap he had become.

Sol turned his attention back to the gunmen. "You claim Bradley sent you, right?"

Both men clamped their jaws shut in defiance.

"Fine, then." Sol glanced from them to Holbrook. "These men arrived to tell me their boss, Bradley, decided he wanted this property now rather than later. You can lock them in the stockade. We'll deal with them tomorrow. We have bigger fish to fry before this is over."

Sol noticed the befuddled glances he was receiving from Josie and Muriel. Obviously, neither of them could figure out why he had the audacity to issue orders to a military commander. Frankly, Sol was tired of Josie believing the worst about him, when he was trying to protect her, help her to secure her homestead, and catch several deserving crooks all at the same time. But his detailed explanation would have to wait awhile longer. He and Josie had claims to defend, and Holbrook needed to escort his wife and prisoners to the garrison.

Sol watched the captain and his troop jackknife Hobart over his saddle and secure the two other prisoners to their horses. Then Sol turned to face Josie, who was studying him warily.

"I demand to know what is going on, Tremain," she muttered impatiently.

"I'll be back this evening to stand guard over my new property," Muriel interrupted as she mounted Bess. "I'll bring some of your extra supplies, Josie, if Grant will loan me the army pack mule."

"You are not coming out here," Holbrook said emphatically. "It's too dangerous, as you just found out."

Sol swallowed a snicker when Muriel thrust out her chin in defiance—just as her mentor was prone to do.

"Don't take that tone with me, Grant," she said tersely. "This is why I came to the Twin Territories in the first place. This is *my* claim and *I* shall defend it."

Holbrook scowled sourly. "Not without target practice, you won't."

"Then we are wasting time dallying, aren't we, dear?"

When the soldiers and Muriel rode away, Sol was forced to deal with the question Josie had posed before the interruption.

"Well?" she prodded, one perfectly arched brow elevated. "I'm waiting, Tremain."

He blew out his breath, then whistled to bring Outlaw to him.

"You're stalling, blast it," she snapped, her blue eyes narrowing in irritation. "Why are you giving orders to Holbrook of all people? And how did you get so fast with a gun? Dear Lord! Am I married to a hired gun-slinger?"

Sol was well aware that he had been instructed not to tell anyone who he was until he'd completed his assignment. But enough was enough. Knowing Josie, she would badger him to death if he didn't explain what was going on.

If a man couldn't trust his wife not to betray him, then who could he trust?

He inwardly flinched, remembering several cases he'd worked where wives had turned on their husbands to collect rewards, protect secret lovers or take control of their husband's money and property. Then he reminded himself that Josie's sole reason for being here was to claim her homestead. As long as he didn't stand in the way of that, he should be safe. Sort of.

"I'm a deputy U.S. marshal," he confided. "Holbrook is my only contact. Judge Isaac Parker in Fort Smith sent me here to work undercover and build cases against criminals trying to defraud honest settlers of their land and their money. The last two runs were lousy with dishonest scoundrels, so I was assigned specifically to the task because of my familiarity and connection with the Cheyenne and Arapaho reservation. There are other law officers planted at the north and south borders of the area."

Josie's eyes nearly popped out of her head. Slack-jawed, she gaped at him for half a minute. Her lush mouth opened and shut repeatedly, but she uttered not a single word.

Sol grinned, proud that he had managed to leave this spitfire speechless. For once. Maybe the only time ever, he predicted.

"I spent yesterday evening at the Saddle Burr Saloon, buying drinks for men I have linked to Bradley. Several of them confided that he was going to pay them to ride out and claim property, then forfeit it to him."

"You bought drinks for the three men you just confronted?" she rasped.

"No, they weren't there," he answered. "They are part of the small army he brought with him from Texas. They did their drinking at the tent camp a mile north of where you stayed."

"Those men were going to kill you at Bradley's command," she wheezed as she wilted, cross-legged, onto the tarp Muriel had left behind. "Dear God!"

"There are at least two dozen opportunists claiming property for Bradley as we speak," Sol reported as he sank down beside her. "According to what I learned last night, Bradley has instructed them to erect a piddly shack on the land, as the Homestead Act requires. Since the law doesn't stipulate size, they will build a four-foot-by-four-foot structure. When they officially turn over the property to Bradley in six months, they plan to find someone else willing to offer them the same deal in the next run."

Josie was still staring owlishly at him, so he continued speaking. "According to rumors in Washington, the Cherokees will be forced to take allotments like the other tribes. The government will open up land for free homesteads in the reservation just to the north."

Sol blew out a frustrated breath. "I sent a formal request through Judge Parker to Washington, recommending a lottery instead of a run to distribute Indian land. *If* it has to be opened at all—"

"Which you prefer not to have happen," she finished for him, when she recovered her powers of speech.

"Exactly. But I was notified by telegram yesterday that my suggestion will be taken under advisement *after* the Cherokee Outlet is opened by run next year. That's why I want all these shysters rounded up, jailed and serving sentences before that time comes."

Josie's gaze drifted over the lush prairie grass waving in the wind. Out there, riders and wagons were moving ever westward, searching for unclaimed land. "And you will be given another assignment after you gather the necessary evidence to put Bradley and his hired men behind bars?" she asked.

Sol studied her expression, trying to determine if she looked pleased or disappointed by the prospect. He wished he knew for sure.

"That's my job, Josephine. Ordinarily, I rattle the bushes in the Indian nations east of the lands opened in the Runs of '89 and '91."

"Doing what?"

"Tracking murderers, rapists and thieves that commit their crimes in Kansas, Arkansas, Missouri and Texas, then hide out in the Five Nations," he explained. "I also arrest whiskey peddlers who are taking advantage of members of the tribes. They have their own creative schemes to swipe land from the Choctaw, Chickasaw, Creek, Cherokee and Seminole."

"For instance?" she asked curiously.

"Like marrying an Indian maiden, then conveniently disposing of her because some tribes allow whites to marry Indian women and lay claim to their property. Then there are ruthless bastards that hold Indians at gunpoint or knifepoint, demanding they sign over the deeds to their land in exchange for their lives. Then they kill them in cold blood, anyway. I particularly enjoy bringing those cutthroats to justice."

"I saw firsthand that you are extremely skilled with your peacemakers," Josie murmured, meeting his gaze. "I was impressed and immensely grateful for your protection in that showdown."

He smiled, unable to keep himself from reaching out to skim his forefinger over her creamy cheek. "Thanks to you, I lived to fight another day. Granted, I've faced three outlaws at once before," he said, "but you never know when you'll come up against one that is faster than most."

"Glad to help a deputy U.S. marshal," she replied, smiling up at him. "And naturally, you will always be welcome on this claim. After all, you are entitled to half of it."

Sol shook his head. "This land belongs to you, Josephine. It's your dream come true. But if you think you are free and clear of trouble, think again. Until I bring formal charges against Bradley and other greedy scoundrels like him, you will face problems. Not to mention other claim jumpers who see a woman alone on the prairie as easy prey."

"Perhaps I'll have to fight for what I have, but thank you for making this happen," she said softly.

Then she leaned over to kiss him appreciatively. Sol wanted more than gratitude, but he took what he could get. After Hobart had tried to shoot her earlier, he was relieved she was still alive and kicking. Which reminded him…

"You took an awful chance in that showdown," he said gruffly. "You scared me witless. Don't do it again."

"Sorry, dear. I was only trying to protect you from harm. And maybe Muriel isn't the only one who needs an intense round of target practice." Josie tossed him a teasing smile, then traced his lips with the pad of her finger. "Can I count on your position of authority to get me off if I'm arrested again? The same way you did when Marshal Colby tossed me in jail for murder? That is, if and when the situation arises where I'm forced to shoot someone for encroaching on my property?"

"Sure," he said, falling victim to her infectious smile. "I'd prefer advance warning, though. Let me know when you plan to blast someone to smithereens, wife."

"I'll do my best to accommodate you, husband."

Sol would enjoy it thoroughly if she *would* accommodate him, but he didn't think she meant it that way.

Chapter Twelve

 Josie bubbled with pleasure as she rode Rooster around her one-hundred-sixty-acre homestead that afternoon, while Sol stood guard at the markers that verified her and Muriel's legal claims. The broad, sweeping hills, sloped valleys and tree-lined creek would provide plenty of pasture and water for her cattle and horse herds.

She was anxious for her brother and sister-in-law to visit her property and bring along the small herds of livestock she had purchased and bred over the past three years. She had scrimped and saved, thanks to Noah and Celia's generosity. Now Josie had her own land, free and clear. This would be her home.

Well, she amended, for now it was just a tent. But there was timber available on her property to construct a small cabin. Provided she had saved enough money from her sewing and mending to hire a reputable carpenter.

This was her new beginning, she mused, as she dismounted, then ambled down to the spring-fed creek to splash cool water on her face. The only problem was that Sol wouldn't be here to share her dream. He had generously scouted out and provided her a prime location in the new territory.

But he would be long gone all too soon.

The depressing thought sat like a disagreeable meal in the pit of her stomach.

"Greedy fool," she chastised herself, provoking Rooster to toss his head and glance at her. "Be satisfied with what you've got. You can't always have everything your heart desires."

Yet her friend Muriel had her claim *and* a husband who loved her as much as she loved him. Josie had a federal deputy marshal for a husband, one who would ride off to a new assignment after he wrapped up the loose ends on this case.

Would he miss her when he left? She doubted it. She had given him little reason to return her affection, because she had been suspicious of his motives, and had refused to let him know how she really felt about him. Even now, cynic that she was, she considered asking to see his badge, just to make sure he wasn't feeding her a line.

Josie rolled her eyes heavenward, wondering if a day would come when she allowed herself to trust a man with her life and her heart. She had spent too many years sidestepping men, mistrusting their intentions, to change her opinion overnight. Yet with that raven-haired horse trader—or rather, deputy U.S. marshal—she secretly longed to try to make a true marri—

Her whimsical thoughts broke off when she heard crackling twigs and saw Rooster tense up, ready to bolt and run at the first sign of trouble.

And trouble was what she got. An Indian, carrying a rifle pointed at her chest, emerged from the bushes. He had a pistol and a dagger strapped to his hips, and she predicted he knew how to use both weapons skillfully. He wore buckskin breeches, moccasins and a doe-hide shirt trimmed with fringe and colorful beads. He was tall and muscular, and his dark, narrowed eyes promised danger.

"You are about to trespass on a staked allotment belonging to White Eagle," he growled at her. "Go find somewhere else to live, paleface."

"She staked her claim beside the allotment, Red Hawk. This is my wife."

Sol's voice rolled over her, making her jump in surprise. She twisted around to see him trotting toward them on Outlaw. A dimpled smile creased his ruggedly handsome face and caused a hitch in her heart. Josie had made the crucial mistake of falling in love with Sol, and it was going to torment her no end when he rode away.

She refocused her attention on Red Hawk, whose Indian heritage was far more obvious than Sol's, with his complexion a shade darker and his eyes coal-black.

"Your *wife?*" Red Hawk howled in disbelief. "Why wasn't I informed?"

"It happened rather suddenly," Sol admitted.

The Indian studied Josie critically, then frowned at Sol. "When did you marry her?"

"Yesterday."

He harrumphed. "Do you even know this woman, or did you just marry her on a reckless whim? She's *white,* you know."

"I noticed," Sol replied drily. "Attractive, isn't she?"

"I suppose, if you like white women," Red Hawk mumbled sullenly.

Sol glanced in Josie's direction. "Josephine, this is my double cousin. He is the chief of the Cheyenne Lighthorse Police. They're responsible for protecting and defending our people and their allotted property. His father was my father's brother—both of them white. His mother was my mother's sister."

"Was?" Josie questioned gently.

"Was," Sol confirmed in a bitter tone. "Thanks to George Custer's bloody massacre on the Washita, our village was burned, our food supplies destroyed and more than seven hundred horses were shot on the spot. Worst of all, we lost our parents."

"Along with dozens of warriors and more than forty women, children and elders. Our fathers, white though they were, were killed alongside our mothers, as if they were traitors," Red Hawk muttered resentfully. "Custer tried to pass off the massacre as a *battle,* to explain the deaths, to further his military career and to guarantee his promotion. Of course, the blond-haired coward refused to provide reinforcements for the troops he sent out to determine if there was another vulnerable village he could attack that same day."

"By then, the sounds of gunfire alerted other nearby

camps," Sol added, his voice brimming with contempt. "Our people countered the attack and swarmed the small patrol of soldiers. Custer turned tail and raced off, leaving his men without reinforcements."

"Our people are convinced that the curse we placed on Custer was responsible for his demise against the Sioux and the northern Cheyenne at Little Big Horn," Red Hawk insisted.

Josie digested the information, which was very different from the story reported in white newspapers. She wondered how many times Indians had been misrepresented, to conceal atrocities that whites had committed against them—such as massacres officially ruled as "battles," and so-called treaties that swindled tribes of their land and forced them to accept smaller allotments in order to make white settlement available.

And *she* was benefiting from the injustice, she thought with a grimace.

"Married," Red Hawk mumbled, still stuck on that surprising revelation. "Why?"

"That isn't very flattering," Josie said in mock indignation. "He's crazy about me. After all, he broke me out of jail after the marshal incarcerated me for murder. If that doesn't signify he likes me, I don't know what does."

Although Sol chuckled at her mischievous comment, Red Hawk gaped at his cousin as if he had gone loco.

"She was innocent," Sol informed him. "Unfortunately, I haven't had time to ferret out the real killer."

"Come. Sit," Red Hawk invited abruptly. "I have a rabbit roasting on my campfire."

When Sol's cousin pivoted around to lead the way across the shallow crossing and through a dense clump of towering cedars, Josie fell into step behind him. She blinked in amazement when the densely wooded slope dropped off into a canyon lined with gypsum cliffs and sandstone walls. Springs flowed into a splashing stream which tumbled over a series of small waterfalls, then meandered through a plush meadow where two dozen horses grazed on buffalo grass and wild blue sage. Flat-topped mesas rose up from the canyon floor, breaking the rolling terrain.

"Oh, my gracious." Josie breathed in awe as she surveyed the sights and listened to the sounds that filled the panoramic box canyon, which formed a natural corral and adjoined her new property. "This is the most spectacular place I've ever seen!"

"You can't have it, paleface," Red Hawk told her sternly. "This is a Cheyenne allotment that belongs to White Eagle, as I told you. I'm protecting it from invasion until the land-hungry settlers stake their claims on reservation land that was *supposed* to be ours as long as the moon and stars lit up the night sky."

"My cousin is as displeased as I am with the takeover of Cheyenne land," Sol said. "It's hell being half-white and resenting the part of your heritage that turned on the Cheyenne to satisfy the greed for property."

Josie could understand the internal conflict Sol and Red Hawk faced. Their resentment of the invasion of their reservation by whites couldn't have been more obvious. She could imagine how outraged she would be if someone tried to take her precious homestead away from her. In addition, she felt guilty that Sol and Red Hawk had to sacrifice their favorite haunts, hunting grounds and sacred sites when the government insisted on opening part of their land for settlement.

She wondered if her white heritage was another reason Sol could never love her, as well as her being waspish and mistrusting of him since the first time they'd met.

If that greedy, ruthless bastard Carlton Bradley managed to take her property and force her off her land, she would be as bitter as the Cheyenne who had been forced to give up much of their reservation. Injustice ran rampant in the Twin Territories, she knew. Her delight in staking her claim dimmed as she realized she was taking land the government authorities had told the Cheyenne would be theirs until the end of time.

When Sol spoke to Red Hawk in their native language, his cousin nodded, then strode up the path to where Rooster and Outlaw were grazing. Josie continued to admire the scenery in the secluded paradise, with its steep rock walls, while Sol peeled off a chunk of meat and handed it to her.

She moaned in delight when she tasted the juicy rabbit. "If you can cook as well as your cousin, I think I'll keep you. Judge Parker can find another deputy marshal to replace you."

"You mean as long as I can discourage unwanted

suitors from trailing after you, or lead you to the best tract of land for a homestead, or spring you from jail and prepare meals? Right?"

Josie felt ashamed, even though she had spoken in jest. "I formally apologize," she said softly, sincerely. "I have been a shrew. I've been overly suspicious and terribly unfair to you. I have thought the worst about you since we first met. I wished you to hell when I saw you outside the Oasis, receiving money from Bradley."

"I never set foot inside the brothel," Sol told her.

"I'm greatly relieved to hear it. Nevertheless, I was disappointed beyond words when I saw the two of you slink off together after our wedding ceremony yesterday."

"Understandable," he said, then bit into the delicious meat. "I shouldn't have confided my identity to you at all, because you must keep the secret. And I shouldn't have forced Muriel to keep secrets from you, either."

Suddenly, the sound of a howling coyote echoed around the canyon walls. Sol bounded to his feet. "That's Red Hawk's signal for trouble. If Bradley sends more men to steal your claim today, maybe this investigation will be over sooner than I expected."

When Josie tried to rise, Sol placed his hand on her shoulder, urging her back down. "Stay here and stay alert. If anyone besides a Cheyenne or Arapaho shows up, hold him at gunpoint until I return. If he doesn't cooperate, shoot him."

"Oh, good, I have your permission," she said, and

snickered. "There are all sorts of advantages to being married to a lawman."

Sol smiled faintly and repeated the warning to pay attention to her surroundings. Then he darted up the steep, winding path to rejoin his cousin. To be on the safe side, Josie retrieved her pistol from her waistband and scanned the surroundings. She could understand why the Cheyenne had chosen this remarkable box canyon as part of an allotment. She didn't know what the rest of the tract looked like, but the protected canyon and clear springs made the area prized property.

Good thing Bradley hadn't scouted out this place, she thought resentfully. White Eagle and his family might end up dead and buried, because the Texan would covet this land.

Damn him, she muttered to herself. She wished Bradley would swagger from the bushes—now that Sol had given her permission to blast away at unwanted intruders.

"This isn't your battle," Sol told his cousin as he studied the six approaching riders.

Red Hawk scoffed as he took his place beside Sol, his rifle at the ready. "And miss all the fun of shooting a few white claim jumpers? No chance, cuz. I've been itching to take out my frustration over this land run on a few palefaces. The brigade of hoodlums bearing down on us is the perfect place to start."

"I can guarantee the odds won't be in our favor," Sol warned.

"When were the odds ever in our favor? Story of our

lives…" His voice trailed off when the riders pulled their winded horses to a halt.

"Put on your badge," Sol requested. "I'll show mine only if necessary. I'd rather word didn't get back to Bradley until I'm damn good and ready for him to know I'm a federal officer."

Red Hawk fished the badge from his pocket and pinned it on his doe-hide shirt as Sol studied the leader of these saddle tramps Bradley had hired to stake claims for his ranch. According to the information Sol had gleaned, Elliot Morgan was Bradley's right-hand man. Sol had seen the hombre only once before, standing outside the saloon with the other gunmen.

Morgan appeared to be a few years older than Sol. He was a burly, muscular, rough-looking character with chips of blue ice for eyes. Long, thick brown hair scraped his shirt collar. Sol glanced past the leader, recognizing several men he'd met over drinks in the Saddle Burr Saloon the previous night. He'd pried plenty of information from the drunken saddle tramps, but this was his first confrontation with their leader.

Morgan disengaged himself from the ragtag brigade to ride closer. His frigid glare landed on Sol, then flicked to Red Hawk, noting the official badge indicating he was chief of the Cheyenne Lighthorse Police.

Morgan scowled, then glowered at Sol. "You must be Tremain, the horse trader," he said in a gravelly voice.

"I must be," Sol replied flippantly, not the least bit intimidated by the burly gunslinger, who sat atop his bay gelding, staring him down.

"This is Red Hawk, and you are trespassing on a staked claim. So ride off, Morgan."

Bushy brows rose over those chilly eyes. "So you know me by reputation. Good, that makes things easier."

"I know a lot of hombres by reputation," Sol remarked with a careless shrug. "I've squared off against your kind before. Most of them are dead and gone to hell."

Morgan glanced sideways. "Where are the three men that came here earlier?"

"One is dead and the other two are on their way to the stockade," Sol reported. "Of course, I've reloaded my pistols since then. Plus Red Hawk showed up to provide reinforcement. He prefers a rifle, and I guarantee you don't want to be on the wrong end of it."

Morgan snorted. "You think you can go up against six heavily armed men? Do yourself a favor, horse trader. Sign over this claim so you'll live to see tomorrow."

Sol scrutinized the five hungover riders behind Morgan. Then he tossed Red Hawk a quick glance. "Let's take down the bossman first. We'll see how many of his brigade want to stay and fight, and how many want to hightail it out of here."

A hint of apprehension claimed Morgan's leathery features before he composed himself. That's what Sol had been looking for—a crack in the gunslinger's veneer. He wasn't as confident of his reinforcements as he would have Sol believe.

"Hey, I signed on to stake a claim and that's all," a young, curly-haired rider mumbled uneasily. "I ain't getting paid to have a shootout."

"Silence!" Morgan snapped, without a backward glance.

"Why should he draw down in a fight if he isn't collecting gunfighter wages?" Sol challenged, then glanced from one somber-faced man to the next, watching them squirm uneasily in their saddles. "Any of you who don't think it's a good day to die should leave now. And keep in mind that the three men who were here earlier won't receive any pay at all. You could end up just like them."

Morgan growled in annoyance when all five riders reined their mounts around and galloped away.

"You came here to deal with me, so deal, Morgan," Sol invited. "But I'm not leaving this claim. All arrangements with Bradley are off because he tried to doublecross me.... Did he send *you* to kill Harlan Kane and set up Miz Malloy?" he asked abruptly.

Morgan's eyes flickered, and Sol bared his teeth for effect. "You pounded her on the head and set her up for murder, didn't you?"

"I don't know what the hell you're talking about, Tremain," he growled.

"Sure you do. Kane was drawing too much unwanted attention, I expect, mindless drunk that he was. The man was a loose cannon, too difficult to control, and Bradley didn't want any more to do with him. Since your boss held a grudge against Miz Malloy, he decided to torment her as much as possible and get rid of Kane in one fell swoop. I think Bradley acts the blowhard bully, but he uses *you* to do his dirty work, doesn't he?"

"You talk too much, horse trader." Morgan smirked. "You don't know as much as you think you do, either. Now get rid of your sidekick and—"

"I'm not leaving!" Red Hawk interrupted, leveling his rifle on Morgan. "I've been looking for an excuse all day to kill palefaces for overrunning my stomping ground. You are my one sure chance." He smiled slyly. "We didn't blink at two-to-six odds in *your* favor. How do you feel about two-to-one odds against *you,* paleface?"

Morgan's blue eyes narrowed into thin slits as his palm hovered over his ivory-handled pistol. Sol watched and waited, wishing for information he could use to bring murder charges in the Kane case—if Morgan had killed Kane under Bradley's orders.

"Did Kane know why he'd been sent into the alley?" Sol demanded, anxious to draw out a confession. "Did he receive a note, same as Miz Malloy?"

"You seem to know more about the incident than I do," Morgan replied.

"I'll bet," Sol said, and snorted. "I'm getting impatient. Decide whether you're leaving or staying. I've already killed one man and wounded two others today. Makes no difference to me if you leave here upright in the saddle or jackknifed over it."

Sol knew he was effectively working on the hired gun's nerves. Morgan kept darting glances from Sol to Red Hawk, whose dark eyes promised to deliver death if necessary.

"You should have wiped your tracks from the alley, hombre," Sol said grimly. "But you were sloppy. I also found the wadded-up note sent to Miz Malloy…. I suspect those were *your* boot prints in the dirt. Next time Bradley contracts a hit he should look elsewhere, for someone who pays closer attention to details." Sol smiled tauntingly. "When the smoke clears here today, and you're lying in a pool of your own blood, I'll compare your prints. Besides, you won't need boots where you're going, anyway."

"Who the hell *are* you?" Morgan demanded bluntly. "Certainly not one of the seedy characters Bradley has been collecting since we rode into town." He stared Sol down and said, "I did not kill Kane."

Sol wasn't sure he believed the gunslinger. After all, how much was a hired assassin's word worth? "Then who did? Bradley or one of his other men?" he questioned harshly.

Morgan studied him contemplatively, obviously not sure what to make of Sol. "Your guess is as good as mine, Tremain. I don't follow Bradley around night and day to see what he's doing."

"Maybe you should," Sol remarked. "If I were you, I'd find another employer and take up another line of work. Bradley is a sinking ship and you'll go down with him and the rest of the rats if you don't watch out."

"Can we dispense with the chatter and just shoot him?" Red Hawk snapped impatiently. "I have rounds to make to ensure other whites aren't encroaching on Cheyenne allotments."

"Two bullets in his broad chest should do it. He's a wide target," Sol noted.

"All right, damn it!" Morgan muttered sourly. "I'm backing off. But if you think you're done with Bradley, think again. He's not finished with you or that sassy female he's become obsessed with. You need to know that he means to have her. He's more determined than ever because you double-crossed him by marrying her yourself, Tremain. She's all the bargaining power the man needs to control you, so watch out."

Morgan backed up his horse ten yards, whirled around and spurred the animal into a gallop, heading in the direction of El Reno. A coil of dread gathered in the pit of Sol's belly. Morgan's words rang in his ears like a frightening premonition. Swearing, he wheeled and re-traced his steps to the clump of cedar trees. Another bad feeling slithered down his spine as he hurried to the canyon.

"What's wrong?" Red Hawk demanded as he jogged after him.

"I need to check on Josie." And damn it! She had better be exactly where he'd left her. If Bradley or one of his henchman had taken advantage of the distraction, while Morgan and company arrived to deal with Sol…

The unnerving thought sent another wave of panic rolling through him. He knew Bradley wanted Josie and this prime property. There was no telling what that obsessive Texan would do to get what he wanted.

Sol took off like a shot, his worst fears hounding him every step of the way.

* * *

During Sol's absence, Josie—with pistol in hand in case trouble came calling—ambled around the magnificent canyon, following the stream across the lush pasture. This secluded retreat was breathtaking. She could see why one of the tribe members had laid claim to this canyon, the grassy meadows and the rugged mesas beyond.

She halted when she heard a faint rustling above the sound of rippling water. Thus far, no gunshots had erupted in the distance. Josie took it as a good sign. Things were beginning to fall into place, she mused as she stared across the breathtaking valley, dotted with horses, clumps of cedar, blue sage and thick grasses.

She made a mental note to bring Muriel here to enjoy the sights. Her friend was scheduled to return before dark with food and supplies for their first evening on their homesteads. *If* Holbrook didn't forbid his new wife from camping out on her property without him.

Josie chuckled, wondering how that conversation would go. Not well for Holbrook, she predicted. Muriel was as adamant about her dream of becoming a woman of property as Josie was....

Another rustling sound erupted in the underbrush, putting her on high alert. She pivoted to point her pistol at the source of the noise. "Come out with your hands up—"

Too late, she realized the intruder had tossed a rock in the opposite direction to distract her. Her voice transformed into a pained yelp when someone tackled her around the knees from behind, knocking her toward the stream, sending her pistol flying sideways. She stumbled off balance and groaned in pain when her kneecap slammed onto rocks that lined the creek. Her attacker grabbed the back of her head and forced her face underwater, then held her down.

Panic assailed her when she couldn't catch a breath before being ruthlessly forced down a second time. The instant before she feared her lungs would burst, her attacker jerked her head up. Josie winced at the painful grip on her hair, but dragged in a huge breath before being shoved under again. She struggled for a half minute, then went limp, hoping to convince her assailant that she was drowning.

The moment he jerked her head up again, using a hank of her hair like a rope, she sprang into action. She kicked out with one leg, catching her attacker in the chest. His breath gushed out with a grunt and his grasp slacked off. Josie took advantage by launching herself across the stream, splashing through the shallow water to the far side.

She didn't bother scraping her wet hair out of her eyes to see who was after her, just clawed her way up the canyon wall—until her assailant grabbed her by the leg and dragged her down, so forcefully that she skinned her elbows and chin as she bounced over the protruding edges of the rock. Refusing to surrender, she elbowed her captor in the chest, provoking an enraged snarl.

When he shoved her cheek against the sharp-edged stones, she whimpered, then tried to shout for help.

But he slipped a noose around her neck and snapped it tightly into place, cutting off her air supply and forcing her to gasp for what little breath she could drag in.

When he tried to tow her backward, she gritted her teeth and pushed away from the vertical wall, slamming into him with enough momentum to knock him off balance.

Josie tried to wheel to face her mysterious attacker, but he landed a blow to her head before she could identify him. Vaguely, she wondered what there was about her that motivated people to hammer her skull. Unfortunately, she couldn't puzzle it out, because stars revolved in front of her eyes and nausea rolled in her stomach.

Battling to keep her wits about her, she tried to gain her feet. The second blow buckled her knees. Josie crumpled to the ground, faintly aware of sharp pebbles cutting into her face.

A second later, she passed out.

Chapter Thirteen

Sol huffed and puffed as he zigzagged through the dense cedars to reach the canyon rim. "Josie!" he called out anxiously.

He heard nothing. Only the chatter of birds in the surrounding trees. "Hell and damnation," he muttered.

Behind him, Red Hawk skidded to a halt. "Do you see her?" he panted.

Sol scanned the area, then swore foully. "No. I told her to stay put."

"Does she usually obey your orders?" Red Hawk asked as he came to stand beside Sol and survey the canyon below.

"No," he mumbled grudgingly. "But something is wrong. I can sense it."

Red Hawk nodded in agreement, then took the lead down the winding footpath to reach the small campfire, where a thin column of smoke still drifted upward. The tin plates remained undisturbed.

Sol shouldered past his cousin, searching for telltale

prints. His heart stalled in his chest when he noticed displaced rocks near the edge of the stream. Nearby stones had been splattered with water, indicating someone had dashed through the creek. Sol was certain a struggle had taken place, and he anxiously searched for signs of blood. He sagged in relief when he didn't find any.

"There." Red Hawk pointed toward a spot on the vertical rock wall. It looked as if someone—Josie maybe?—had tried to scale the rough surface in desperation.

Sol leaped over the rapids in the creek to survey the spot at close range. Cold fury hammered at him when he noticed other signs of struggle that had dislodged more stones. He could imagine Josie giving her attacker fits while he tried to subdue her. She was bursting with spirit and sass—which wouldn't work in her favor if her kidnapper became vindictive.

Josie did nothing halfway, Sol reminded himself. She would fight to the bitter end to prevent capture. The thought made him flinch, and he had to drag in a calming breath, hoping to get himself back under control.

Grimly, he sank down on his haunches to study the impressions left in the powdery dirt and gravel at the foot of the wall. He could visualize Josie sprawled here, unconscious or dead.…

He sucked in much-needed air and told himself to remain focused and emotionally detached. But it was damn hard when that blue-eyed hellion who was his wife had become a victim in his ongoing investigation. Sol pulled himself together, but it wasn't easy. Then he forgot to breathe when Red Hawk directed his attention to the deeply indented boot prints that eventually disappeared among the rocks.

"These prints match the boots with a run-down heel on the left foot," Sol hissed in raw fury. "I saw them in the alley where Josie was set up for murder." If Bradley or one of his thugs had captured her and knocked her unconscious again, there was no telling what that obsessive, egotistical Texan had in mind for her next.

But you know what Bradley ultimately wants from her, don't you? Sol asked himself as he surged to his feet, snarling like a grizzly.

"Where do we go from here?" Red Hawk asked, concern in his voice.

"I wish I knew," Sol growled, wanting to search in every direction at once.

His cousin whirled around, bounded over the narrow channel of the creek and took off at a run toward the path leading to the canyon rim. Sol heard him switch back and forth between English and the Cheyenne dialect. Sol's ripe oaths mingled with Red Hawk's when he realized all three horses—Outlaw, Rooster and the big, muscular pinto that Red Hawk called Paintbrush—were gone.

"At least tracking the horses will be easy," Red Hawk said, striving for a positive tone and only half succeeding. "Do you know where this Bradley character staked his claim?"

Sol pointed north. "But he knows that's the first place

I'll look. Worse, it will be dark in a few hours, making tracking difficult...."

His voice dried up when he heard the rumble of hooves in the distance. Sol sagged in relief when he recognized Muriel, Holbrook and the two soldiers that had accompanied her and Josie to town for lunch at the Land Run Café earlier that week. Sol remembered how strikingly lovely Josie had looked in her trim-fitting blue gown. He recalled in vivid detail how she had captivated him that day. How she had mystified him while he'd held himself above her during their passionate rendezvous that night at the river, when he had made love to her as if there were no tomorrow....

If there was no tomorrow for her, Sol wouldn't survive the crushing blow. That firebrand had touched off a myriad of emotions inside him and filled all the empty spaces he had sealed up years earlier in order to do his job effectively. How could he exist if Josie wasn't out here on her homestead, living her dream and building the ranch she wanted so much? How could he endure it if she wasn't *somewhere* in this world...?

The disheartening thought threatened to paralyze him, but he gritted his teeth and marshaled his resolve. He wasn't giving up on finding Josie. She wasn't a quitter and neither was he. Sol refused to abandon his search for that obsessive bastard who'd likely ordered her capture, until Sol knew Josie's fate—for better or worse.

His expression must have given away his grave concern. Before he could utter a word, Muriel stared down at him from atop her dapple-gray mare and frowned worriedly. "Where's Josie?"

"Gone," he told her bleakly.

"Gone?" she cried in dismay. "What do you mean, gone? As in she isn't *here* or she doesn't *exist* anymore? She wouldn't leave this precious homestead unless someone dragged her kicking and—" Her throat closed convulsively as her wild-eyed gaze settled on Sol. "He was here, wasn't he? Or he sent one of his men to capture her, didn't he?"

"*Who* was here?" Holbrook demanded.

"Bradley," Sol and Muriel said in unison.

"Where is he holding her hostage?" Holbrook looked every which way. "Where's his claim, Tremain?"

"That would be the first place I'd look, and he knows it. Plus that sly bastard ordered our horses stolen, so we couldn't follow immediately." Sol hitched his thumb toward his cousin. "Red Hawk, this is Muriel, Josie's good friend and Holbrook's wife. Of course, you already know the captain."

The men nodded in greeting, then Holbrook glanced back at the two young soldiers. "Ride north to see if you can locate Bradley, just in case." He gave them a quick description and sent them racing away.

Sol looked up when he heard Muriel's muffled sniff and saw the tears clouding her eyes. "If that scoundrel or his men harm one hair on her head—"

"Then they'll answer to me," Sol finished in a harsh growl. "I need to borrow your horse, Muriel." He grabbed the mare's reins. "You can ride double with Holbrook until Red Hawk and I return with new mounts."

Holbrook reached over to hook his arm around his wife's waist and transfer her to a spot in front of him on the saddle. "We'll scout the trees to see if—"

"No," Sol cut in quickly as he bounded onto the mare. "Don't risk Muriel. Take her back to the fort and keep a close lookout during the jaunt. Maybe we'll get lucky and you'll spot Bradley's men at a distance. Red Hawk and I will catch up after we commandeer two horses grazing in the canyon to the west."

Sol extended his arm to swing Red Hawk up behind him. The mare shifted beneath the extra weight, but obediently trotted off when Sol nudged her in the flanks.

While the Holbrooks headed east, Sol and Red Hawk skirted the canyon to retrieve horses grazing in the pasture. With nothing more than improvised halters made from willow branches and the fringe on Red Hawk's shirt, they secured two mounts and rode off bareback, leading Muriel's horse behind them.

Cold fury iced Sol's veins as he thundered across the prairie on his skewbald paint gelding. He tried to tell himself that he had to control his anger if he hoped to maintain an edge if…*when* he caught up with Bradley's men. No doubt Bradley—that two-legged sidewinder—would use Josie to his advantage. But Sol knew he couldn't take this confrontation personally and allow himself to play into the man's hands.

How could he not take this personally? Josie was his

wife. He planned to have only one in his lifetime and she was it. Hell, he'd never even planned *that,* come to think of it. But he'd be damned if he let Bradley take Josie away from him.

Think, man, Sol lectured himself fiercely. Where would Bradley hide Josie while she was his hostage?

"How do you plan to handle the bastard?" Red Hawk questioned over the sound of their horses' pounding hooves.

"I'm not sure. What would you do?"

Red Hawk tossed him a bitter smile. "If that hellion was my wife and Bradley gave orders to hurt her, I'd scalp him and his men. But first we have to find them."

Sol stared skyward, watching the sun make its final arc in the western sky. It was near sundown. He had no idea where his wife was.

The distressing thought made him snarl viciously. A man should always know where his wife was in case she needed him. Josie definitely needed him now, and he couldn't live with himself if he failed her.

"Scalping's good," he muttered belatedly. "We should stick with the old ways of our people. Afterward, I'll boil them all in oil."

Sol kicked the paint pony, urging him into his fastest gait, and racked his brain, trying to figure out where Bradley would have his henchman stash Josie before he showed up to do his worst.

Josie grimaced when she awoke to the pounding pain of a horrendous headache. *Not again,* she thought groggily. When she tried to roll onto her side, she realized she had been restrained. She pried one eye open to see a blur of red. Blood? No, that didn't seem right.

She tried to stare through the fuzzy haze that distorted her vision, but it demanded too much effort. Sighing heavily, she awarded herself more time for blessed sleep.

An hour later—or maybe half a century—Josie opened both eyes. Darkness enveloped her and she still couldn't move. It felt as if someone had strapped anchors to her arms and legs.... She gasped when a shadow loomed over her to dribble water on her face.

"Time to wake up," said a gruff, demanding voice that she remembered all too well.

Bradley, damn him. She wondered if he was the one who'd sneaked up on her while she was lollygagging in the canyon. So where was she now? She blinked the water from her eyes and looked around. Though her vision was still blurry, she noticed moonlight peeking between red velvet drapes to spear across a red floral carpet. She turned her head to note that Bradley was standing over her, while she lay on a bed, strapped to the posts like a human sacrifice.

"A brothel?" she croaked.

Bradley was holding her hostage in the Oasis? Of course, it was his second home. She wondered if Sol would figure that out when he realized she was gone. Or would he bother to come looking for her?

Sure he would, she convinced herself. Sol wanted this greedy criminal locked away for cheating settlers out of homesteads and spearheading the gang of gunslingers and thieves that preyed on this area.

"A brothel is the perfect place for you," he sneered. "You could have reigned beside me as the queen of my cattle kingdom. One that will dwarf my father's ranch. Now you'll be my whore and my slave instead."

Josie ignored his rant. She narrowed her eyes and acted on a hunch. "You're the one who clubbed me over the head in the alley behind the church, too, aren't you?" she accused. "I'd like to return the favor."

He smiled craftily, with a strange glimmer in his gray eyes. "Yes, that was my handiwork—to throw blame on you when I had to dispose of Kane, that stupid fool."

"What do you want now?" Josie demanded, refusing to show an ounce of fear and hoping to draw more information for Sol's case—if she lived long enough to convey it to him.

"Other than having you beneath me as many times as I want?" he said in that arrogant tone she despised. "I've decided I also want the deed to that canyon property where I found you. You are going to sign it over to me."

"No, I'm not," Josie countered, wishing she could reach the dagger she had placed in her boot this morning as a backup weapon against poachers. Fat lot of good that knife was doing her now. "I was wandering around on a Cheyenne allotment that sits besides my claim. You try to steal that land from its tribal owner and the federal troops protecting the Cheyenne will be all over you like a pack of vicious wolves."

Her vision cleared enough for her to notice the full force of Bradley's evil smile. She would have preferred to go all evening without seeing it.

"The redskin will give up his canyon to save your hide," he insisted confidently.

"No, he won't. I don't even know who or where he is, because we haven't met yet," she announced tartly.

Bradley towered over her, trying to intimidate her. Josie was too angry and defiant to kowtow to this crazed bastard. When he cupped her skinned chin in his callused hand, jerking her face up, she matched him glare for glare.

"Turn me loose before my husband tracks you down and blows you to smithereens. I saw him shoot all three of your hired guns this afternoon and he'll do the same to you."

Bradley smirked sarcastically. "You think he gives a damn about you? Ha! He and I both understand that women exist to serve a man's purpose and his pleasure. I learned my lesson all too well when a faithless bitch betrayed me to be with my father."

Once again, Bradley's wickedness boiled down to his hatred for his father and his former lover.

"I paid Tremain to break off your engagement, but after you begged him to get you out of jail and make the run as your husband, he knuckled under and returned my money. But you are the least of his concerns, honey. I sent six more of my men to rough him up and force him into submission so he'll do my bidding."

Josie refused to react to the insulting remarks. She

also told herself that Sol's pretended indifference was because he was trying to lure this unstable rascal into a trap and build a solid case of fraud, robbery and murder against him.

Yet she wasn't sure enough of herself or of Sol's feelings to know if he would discard her when he lost interest in her. True, she hadn't done much to endear herself to him. She was too cynical about the ulterior motives of men in general, and suspicious of Sol's activities in particular. But still…

"Nothing to say to that, smart mouth?" Bradley taunted.

"I'm betting my homestead that Tremain likes me better than he likes you, and that he can handle your thugs," she retorted.

A slow, deceitful grin thinned his lips, reminding her once again of a frog. That was how she would choose to remember him—if she bothered to think of him at all.

"I'm counting on Tremain to care just enough about you to see that you stay alive. Of course, I doubt he'll want you after I'm finished with you."

Josie didn't like the sound of that. Nor did she like the unnatural glitter in the Texan's tombstone-colored eyes. He looked a little crazy to her.

"Now what are you planning?" she asked warily.

"Tremain is going to file the claim in his name at the land office first thing in the morning, *if* he wants you to survive. Then he is going to turn the property over to me and ride off, so I can claim the forfeited land in six months. Then I *might* let you go. Or not. I haven't decided yet."

"A quarter section of land won't do you much good if you plan to bring in a massive cattle herd," she reminded him. "You lost three would-be claims this morning from men who tangled with Tremain. You think he isn't scaring off the rest of the saddle tramps you promised money to in exchange for deeds to adjoining land? What you want most, he won't let you have, Bradley." She hoped.

"And you'll have nothing for yourself," he jeered as he scooped up the blank deed he had brought along with him. "Sign it and I'll send it to Tremain, so he can add his signature and deliver it to the land office...*if* he can still walk after my men get through with him."

Josie waited breathlessly for Bradley to free her right hand so she could sign the document. The moment he did, she reached up to claw his face with her nails. He yelped, recoiled, then tried to backhand her, but she blocked the blow with her elbow. Then she struck out quickly, planting a fist in his crotch and jabbing him where he could be hurt the worst.

To her supreme satisfaction, he howled like a dying coyote, clutched himself and dropped to his knees. When his scowling face was level with her arm, she backhanded him.

While he gasped for breath and fell to the floor, Josie hurried to untie her left hand. Her wrist slipped loose a mere half second before Bradley recovered enough to surge toward her, seeking retaliation.

He went for her throat, and she went for his crotch with both fists doubled. His vicious grip on her neck slacked off when she punched him three times as hard as she could. He roared in pain while she gasped and coughed to catch her breath.

Desperate, she curled upward to retrieve the dagger in her boot. Heart pounding ninety miles a minute, Josie thrust the point of the knife into his thigh muscle. She retracted it while he shrieked furiously, then she took advantage of his distraction to slash the rope that held her right leg to the bedpost.

"You malicious bitch!" he hissed as he clamped his hand over his thigh to stop the bleeding. Snarling, he reached for his pistol. "See how *you* like hobbling around on one leg!"

Josie's heart ceased beating for that one awful second while Bradley aimed at her left leg and she sliced at the rope with her knife. She managed to cut herself free while he cocked the trigger of his six-shooter. With no time to spare, she rolled off the bed and sprawled on the floor, an instant before the bullet plowed through the mattress where her leg had been a split second earlier.

The shot slammed into the cheval glass beside the dresser. The mirror shattered to a million pieces that rained down on her head.

Cries of alarm and footsteps sounded on the other side of the door, distracting Bradley—who had taken another giant leap toward insanity after she had thwarted his grand plans and stabbed him in the leg.

"What's going on in there?" a woman shouted, and

then rattled the doorknob. "There is no gunplay allowed in my house. Come out this instant!"

Bradley swore foully when the door burst open and several men and women—all in various states of undress—rushed forward.

"Get out of here, all of you!" the Texan shouted in a shrill voice as he turned his weapon on the onlookers that crowded around the open doorway.

Josie took advantage of his diversion, for however long it might last. She bounded to her feet and threw herself at Bradley's blind side, knocking the pistol loose and sending it cartwheeling across the red carpet.

She used his body as a springboard to launch herself toward the exit. Wide-eyed, the bystanders backed up in synchronized rhythm, making room for her in the hall. Josie slammed the door shut and gestured for everyone to duck, just in case bullets started flying again.

Sure enough, they did. Bradley had retrieved his weapon and fired off two shots that blasted waist-high holes in the hallway wall. Josie took off running as fast as her legs could carry her. She bounded down the steps two at a time to escape the maniac who was cursing her at the top of his lungs.

He promised all manner of grisly revenge when he caught up with her. Josie vowed not to let that happen.

She burst out the front door of the bordello and sprinted down the street. She was home free, she thought. Surely the men in the brothel had subdued that raving lunatic and disarmed him. She could breathe easily now....

Josie yelped in surprise when a man's arm shot out of a shadowed alleyway to grab her around the waist and slam her against his muscular torso. Damnation, she had run into another of Bradley's hired guns. What rotten luck!

"Easy, honey," rasped a gravelly voice close to her ear. "You come along peaceably and you won't get hurt—ouch!"

Her abductor shook his hand in pain after she bit his fingers. Unfortunately, he dodged her flying elbow and came up with a pistol. The gun barrel gouged the underside of her jaw, warning her to hold still—or else.

"That's better," he told her as he clamped his arm diagonally across her chest. "Relax, I'm not planning to hurt you, firebrand."

"You're not? Then let me go." She turned her head slightly to get her first look at her captor after he removed the gun barrel from her jaw.

The rugged-looking gunman had icy blue eyes and long brown hair. Even the dim light didn't conceal the hard lines of his face. Josie had seen this man around town a few times before, but she didn't know him by name. She had noticed his gaze following her while she walked down the street on several occasions, though he had never approached her.

She suspected he was one of Bradley's men. Why else would he have latched on to her when she made a mad dash to safety?

"What do you want?" she demanded boldly. "Bradley is in the brothel, nursing a knife wound."

"Your handiwork, I presume," the man replied, his voice less gruff than before.

"Yes. He's loco, you know. If I were you, I'd find a new employer," she advised.

"Tremain said the same." The gunman stepped away, then inclined his head slightly.

Josie rearranged the blouse he had twisted when he'd grabbed hold of her. "So…you aren't taking me back to that maniac?" she asked hopefully.

He shook his head. "No, I am a contract gunslinger, but I draw the line at abusing women." His face puckered in a scowl. "I came looking for you to make sure the same thing that happened to my kid sister didn't happen to you. You're my good deed for the year."

His voice wobbled slightly, assuring her that his untold tale hadn't had a happy ending. Josie stared into the gunslinger's hard face, noting that his cold eyes had melted slightly. She wondered if his dangerous lifestyle, like Tremain's, had nearly wrung all the goodness and humanity out of him. Thankfully, Sol had softened up slightly over time. She wondered if this man ever would.

It was obvious the gunfighter carried around the torment of his sister's ordeal. Something about Josie's predicament had triggered his concern. Despite his past, he had attempted to rescue her, and she was grateful for that—

Josie yelped when a shadow came to life and pounced, knocking the gunfighter sideways and tossing her off balance. A steely hand shot out of the darkness to steady her before she could trip off the boardwalk and land in the dirt.

"You made another mistake, Morgan," Sol snarled as he reared back to deliver a punishing blow to the man's jaw.

"No, he didn't!" Josie grabbed Sol's fist before he could plant it in Morgan's face. "He was on his way to rescue me from Bradley, not abduct me."

"But this is Elliot Morgan, Bradley's main accomplice." Sol swiveled his head around to stare at the burly gunslinger. "What's your angle, Morgan?" he asked cynically. "Did you decide to hold Josephine for ransom for your own greedy purposes?"

"No, I was planning to deliver her to *you,* Tremain," he replied as he shoved away the hand that was clamped around his throat.

"I'm his good deed of the year…or so he says," Josie interjected, studying the man speculatively.

Sol gave a caustic snort. "Sure you are."

"Believe it or not, Tremain," Morgan said with a careless shrug. "At first I mistook you for a swindler, because you were mixed up with Bradley. I figured you deserved to be roughed up and manipulated. But Josie damn sure didn't deserve to be caught in the middle." He stared grimly at Sol. "I told you earlier that Bradley was obsessed with this wildcat. I've been looking for him, to ensure that he didn't hurt her."

Sol studied Morgan critically for a long moment. It baffled him that Josie was willing to take the gunslinger at his word, while she had been suspicious of everything *Sol* had said and done since they met. He wondered what Morgan had said to sway her opinion.

Sol shook his head and reminded himself that he didn't understand this complicated female. He probably never would, even if he devoted the next fifty years to trying to figure her out.

Finally, he nodded in acceptance. "Okay, so now you *aren't* on Bradley's side, right?"

Morgan inclined his shaggy head. "Never really was. His father hired me to keep an eye on him after their falling-out a few months back. The man has become more unstable with each passing day. Right now he's holed up in the brothel, and I'm going in after him. You coming, Tremain, or do you want to sit this one out?"

Sol wasn't completely convinced he could trust the gunslinger but he decided to give the hard-edged man the benefit of the doubt. Josie didn't trust most men's motives. She had sensed that Sol wasn't being truthful with her since the first day they met. Yet something about Morgan reassured her. Sol had to respect her instincts because she was usually dead on.

"I'll be right behind you, Morgan. Don't approach Bradley until I get there." He stared at Morgan good and hard. "And if this is a ruse to make your getaway, I'll track you down. Count on it."

"Damn if you don't sound as bossy as some of the lawmen I know. Why is that, Tremain?" Casting him a speculative glance, Morgan eased past Josie to stride down the boardwalk toward the bordello.

"You okay? Truly?" Sol asked as he gathered her in

the protective circle of his arms and thanked the deities—both Indian and white—that she had survived.

She nuzzled against him and expelled a ragged sigh. "Am I *okay?* Compared to what, Tremain? Being dead? Bradley tried to kill me a couple of times in the brothel. He nearly succeeded. It's a wonder I don't have a permanent part in my hair!"

"Damn good thing you have the nine lives of a cat, Josephine." Sol kissed her hard, hungrily. "Sorry it took me so long to figure out where he decided to stash you.... Red Hawk is positioned at the back of the bordello," he said in the next breath. "If Morgan wants Bradley in custody, the three of us should be able to capture him, unless he refuses to be captured and decides to take the short way down through a window, leaving him in a broken heap. If that's the way he wants it, I'll gladly open the window and help him out of it, the crazy bastard."

"Give him a push for me," she said, hugging Sol fiercely while she nuzzled her cheek against his shoulder.

Sol reluctantly pried her away from him. "I'll be back as soon as I can. And *stay put* this time, wife. It unnerves me when I keep losing track of you. Better yet," he added hastily, "go fetch Marshal Colby while I check on Morgan. We might need extra firepower if that lunatic Texan decides to hold everyone in the brothel hostage."

When Josie darted across the street to fetch the marshal, who had apparently heard the gunshots and was on his way to investigate, Sol took off running toward the front door of the Oasis. He muttered under his breath as he turned his thoughts to Bradley. Sol hadn't been able to see Josie clearly in the dim lamplight, but he saw her well enough to note the scratches on her face. Bradley would pay dearly for roughing her up, he vowed as he barreled through the door that led to the parlor.

When he caught up to Morgan, Sol crouched down beside him, in case gunfire broke out. None did, thank goodness. Sol could hear loud voices upstairs. Then he heard Bradley's demented roar of rage. Sol sent Red Hawk the signal to storm the back door, while he took the main steps three at a time, with Morgan at his side.

Gunfire exploded in the air, followed by Bradley's vow to shoot everyone in sight. Sol tried to peer around a corner in the hallway, but when he craned his neck to locate Bradley's position, a bullet whistled past his shoulder and plugged into the wall.

"What do you want, Bradley?" Sol called out in the most nonthreatening voice he could muster.

This was *not* the time to antagonize a madman.

"For starters, I want that hellcat on a leash!" he bellowed furiously. "She *stabbed* me!"

Good for her, thought Sol.

"Nobody attacks me and lives to brag about it! Nobody!" Bradley roared. "Especially not a damn woman!"

"I'll arrange to exchange your hostages for Josie," Sol lied convincingly. "But you have to promise to let everyone go unharmed—"

When Sol heard a door burst open somewhere nearby,

he knew Red Hawk had taken advantage of the distraction. Shouts and screams erupted after someone—Bradley, most likely—fired off another shot.

Sol dashed around the corner to see three women and three men, all of them half-dressed, sprawled facedown on the floor. Red Hawk and his rifle blocked the escape route down the back steps. Sol and his pearl-handled peacemakers, plus Morgan's six-shooter, blocked the front entrance, giving Bradley no options other than to surrender or be shot at from two sides at once. His choice.

"Better put down the gun," Sol ordered calmly. "Josie is the one you want, not these folks. They have nothing to do with your personal feud with the hellion."

Wild-eyed, Bradley's gaze bounced back and forth from Red Hawk to Sol and then landed on Morgan. "Traitor!" he screeched at his former right-hand man.

"You stepped over the line, Bradley, so I quit," Morgan told him gruffly. "I was only here because your father *paid* me to keep you out of trouble, but that proved impossible."

"You were spying on me and reporting back to him? Damn you!" Bradley's face turned a putrid shade of red and he puffed up so much that Sol swore the man was about to blow steam out his ears. "You tell that sorry son of a bitch that he can go to hell and stay there! This is *his* fault. He married her. She was mine and he *bought* her for himself, and sent me away with nothing!"

Sol muttered when he saw Josie step up next to Morgan, with the marshal at her side. Damn it, didn't that woman ever follow orders? Apparently not the ones Sol gave her.

"You're right," Josie told Bradley. "The man is a bastard of the highest caliber if he truly did betray you the way you say he did. My own father turned his back on me to enjoy social prominence. I hope they both get what they deserve. Same goes for the woman who chose money over you."

Bradley's gaze shot past Sol's right shoulder to where Josie stood between the marshal and Morgan. Her comments took the fight out of him. The knife wound in his thigh was taking its toll, too.

Although Sol knew his daring wife was responsible for Bradley's puncture wound, he wasn't sure he was in the right frame of mind to hear the nerve-racking details of her captivity and nightmarish battle to escape.

He had learned to control his own fear in the line of duty, but the thought of Josie's near-death experiences rattled him to the extreme. He had suffered hellish torment while he frantically tried to track her down, afraid he would arrive too late to save her....

His thoughts fizzled out when Bradley tried to put his gun to his own head. Then his arm dropped heavily to his side, his eyes rolled back and he slid down the wall to collapse in the hall. His pistol clanked against the door frame, then bounced on the floor.

Sol swooped down to retrieve the discarded weapon when Bradley passed out from loss of blood. Then he compared Bradley's boots to the prints he had seen in the alley behind the church.

Meanwhile, the rattled hostages scrambled to their feet and dashed into their respective rooms to retrieve their clothes.

"This is the man who shot Kane and set up my wife for murder," Sol informed the marshal, while Morgan nodded in agreement. "The worn heel of his boot matches the prints we found at the murder scene yesterday."

"Didn't think I'd ever solve that case with such an influx of settlers milling around, then scattering to take part in the run." Colby veered around Josie to slap handcuffs on his prisoner. "I could use help lugging him to Doc Walker's office."

Sol and Red Hawk toted Bradley downstairs and out the door. Once outside, Sol glanced back at Josie, noting that Morgan remained beside her protectively. Sol wasn't particularly thrilled with the fond attachment Morgan had developed for Josie, but the man was ready and willing to defend her, so he couldn't be all bad.

"Josie, rent us a room at the Boulanger Hotel and treat your scrapes and bruises," he suggested. "I'll be there after I give statements. You can give yours in the morning, since you've had a rough night."

"Yes, dear. Whatever you say."

Sol did a double take, wondering if someone had taken possession of his wife's mind and body. Nope, same woman. She was smiling at him—*really* smiling, without the usual trace of wariness and cynicism. She must've gone a little crazy herself during her terrifying ordeal, he decided as he watched her pivot on her heel and walk away.

"I'll make sure she arrives safely. She reminds me of my kid sister, who found herself in a similar predicament that turned out badly," Morgan said, falling into step beside her.

"Huh," Red Hawk grunted, studying Josie as she disappeared into the shadows. "Her encounter with Bradley must have flustered her more than I believed possible. And hell, Morgan seems as protective of her as you are. I guess a woman can do that to a man sometimes, can't she?" He stared pointedly at Sol.

Sol experienced another twinge of jealousy, wondering if Morgan had developed his own obsession for the spirited beauty. Hopefully, Morgan was just showing brotherly concern. But he reminded himself that Josie had good instincts. If she felt safe with Morgan, then he shouldn't be so suspicious.

Bradley stirred, then muttered a curse about a woman named Tessa, and Sol wondered if the crazed maniac had transferred his hatred for his faithless lover to Josie. He also wondered if Bradley's new stepmother was an attractive blonde, too.

Sol hoped beyond hope that Bradley hadn't molested Josie in his delusional rage. Being knocked around and knocked down was bad enough.

Which was why it had scared him senseless when he'd finally puzzled out where Bradley might have taken her for safekeeping—to his second home. The Oasis brothel was where he spent most of his time. Also, Sol had remembered the Texan referring to Josie as his whore—like the woman that had forsaken him and married his father for wealth and position. Given Bradley's warped brain, he probably thought it was an appropriate place to stash Josie.

Sol inwardly shuddered at the prospect of what Josie had endured. *I should have been there to protect her,* he scolded himself harshly. All her pain, terror and suffering was his fault! He vowed to find a way to compensate for every ounce of her misery…just as soon as he wrapped up this case.

On second thought… Sol wheeled around to make sure that Josie had been safely escorted to the hotel. Relieved to see Morgan standing guard outside the door after the attendants trooped downstairs with the empty buckets they'd used to fill her tub, Sol let his shoulders slump.

Morgan grinned perceptively. "I told you I would see that your wife is safe. She really is my good deed for the year. I occasionally hire myself out as a bodyguard. But no charge for you, Tremain." His expression sobered. "I meant what I said about watching out for her. You can depend on it."

Sol studied him for a long moment. There was something about Morgan that eased his concerns. They were two of a kind, he realized. Despite their hardscrabble lives, they both had a protective spot for Josie.

"I'll be back as soon as I can," Sol muttered.

"I'll be standing guard until then," Morgan vowed solemnly before Sol hurried on his way.

Chapter Fourteen

Josie sank into the warm bath that Morgan had requested the young male attendants prepare for her in the hotel room. Once he left her alone, she sighed appreciatively—and then burst into tears. Honestly, she didn't know what was wrong with her. She had held up reasonably well during her hellish ordeal and she had endured the past two days—the whole week, really—without coming apart at the seams. Suddenly the world came crashing down around her, ripping loose emotions she had tried so hard to hold in check.

She even understood how that rat Bradley had felt when he'd realized his vision of outdoing his father, and the woman who had betrayed him for wealth, power and position, had shattered. He had fallen apart, right along with it.

Josie still had her dream-come-true. She had staked her homestead. Yet that wasn't enough to sustain her against the onslaught of emotional turmoil her life had become. Was it only yesterday that she had been hauled to jail for murder and attended her own marriage ceremony—in her cell, of all places!—to a man she couldn't trust not to betray her?

Then she had spent a sleepless wedding night *alone,* wondering if Sol had sought out another woman, plus made plans with Bradley to steal her homestead—if Josie managed to stake one before someone beat her to it. She had fretted when Sol arrived late for the race. She had wanted him where she could see him, in case he was up to something sneaky. Then she had made the wild dash across the prairie to find her dream claim.

Not to mention that she had shot a man to protect Sol.

Then, to her stunned amazement, she had discovered her new husband was much more than he'd let on. He was a deputy U.S. marshal, for heaven's sake!

As if her emotions hadn't been run through the proverbial wringer already, Bradley had sneaked up to hammer her over her head—again. Josie had regained consciousness to find herself strapped to a bed in a brothel—to become Bradley's personal harlot and slave, a substitute for the woman who'd broken his heart, humiliated him and transformed him into a ruthless, scheming scoundrel who wanted to outdo his father.

Josie had fought for her life and dignity. She had stabbed Bradley, he had shot at her and she'd barely escaped before running headlong into Elliot Morgan. Thankfully, he had been on his way to rescue her because she reminded him of his younger sister and he was determined to make sure she was safe.

Throughout the emotional ordeals, Josie had hoped

and prayed Sol would show up to save her from disaster, as he had so many times since she'd met him. Yet she had kept her wits about her and made her own escape from Bradley, though Sol had been on his way to rescue her. He had always been there, solid as a rock, capably handling whatever catastrophe befell her, she reminded herself.

She wondered how he dealt with such intense situations on a daily basis. Obviously, he wasn't reduced to a yowling baby, the way she was right now.

Knowing he would leave her to her precious dream and her property, she wailed harder, loudly enough to wake the dead. Because she *still* wasn't satisfied, ungrateful shrew that she was.

Emotions came pouring out like rainwater gushing from a gutter pipe. Josie sank down in her bath, telling herself that she couldn't cry underwater without drowning, so she'd better stop it. But she couldn't seem to, and had to burst to the surface, gasping for breath and blubbering like a witless fool.

And there stood Sol, witnessing her complete collapse. His sea-green eyes were riveted on her. He looked as worried as she had ever seen him. Ordinarily, he was a master at expressions that masked his feelings, except when she made him mad and he glared at her.

"Are you all right?" He hovered near the bed, as if uncertain about what to do next. "Did Bradley molest you?"

"No, but I'm still not all right." She breathed raggedly, then hiccuped. "I'm falling apart. How is it possible that I held it together through one horrendous ordeal after another? And suddenly—"

She broke down again, embarrassing herself in front of Sol, the person whose opinion of her mattered most.

"I don't even have clean clothes to wear after my bath," she blathered.

Sol grinned as he plunked down on the end of the bed. "Is that all that's bothering you?" he asked as he watched her wipe away the stream of tears that mingled with the water dribbling from her hair. "I have no objection if you walk around naked."

"You're just saying that to make me feel better, but I'm not the least bit appealing with all my bruises and scrapes," she wailed, humiliating herself all over again.

Sol grabbed the towel draped over the commode, then stepped forward to gently help her to her feet.

"Bruises and scrapes don't matter," he murmured as he wrapped her in the towel, then lifted her out of the tub and into his arms. "You're safe and of reasonably sound mind. Better than Bradley. That's what really counts, Josephine."

He was being so sweet and comforting that she broke down again. Laying her head on his sturdy shoulder, she cried her eyes out.

"Shh," he murmured against the crown of her head. "This is a natural reaction. You've been through hell and you held up amazingly well, sweetheart. No one could have done it better."

Sweetheart? He'd never uttered sincere endearments—ever. Probably because she had been so distrustful and hostile toward him that he didn't like her much. Now he was trying to comfort her because he felt sorry for her. She didn't want sympathy. She wanted the wild, breathless passion she had discovered in his arms. She had secretly wanted it on her wedding night as well, but he had been too busy loosening tongues with liquor at the saloon in order to build his case.

Duty first with Sol. The unwanted wife second.

The thought made her howl with guilt for feeling resentful when she knew he served a higher, noble purpose—to protect people like her from greedy, conniving rascals like Bradley and his men.

"Now what's wrong?" Sol whispered as he carried her to the bed.

"I'm a terrible, selfish person," she said, and sniffed as he gently settled her beneath the sheet.

And damn it, he wasn't even looking at her as if he desired her, but was staring at the air over her soggy head....

Her life was a mixed-up mess of conflicting priorities. She desperately wanted her homestead and she wanted Sol to want her, too. But she couldn't have him. Not forever, at least. She had discovered that she *did* want forever with him but knew she'd never have it— and that upset her all over again.

Sol smiled indulgently while Josie grabbed a pillow and held it over her face to cry some more. He wondered what she'd say if she knew it demanded all the self-restraint he had spent thirty-two years perfecting not to toss aside that towel and cover her luscious body with his. He wanted her so badly that he ached from eyebrows to ankles.

Nevertheless, she needed consoling, so he had to ignore *his* hungry desire to provide what she needed. Otherwise, he would be taking advantage of her vulnerability, and he couldn't respect himself if he did that.

"Take a deep breath and try to get some rest while I soak off a few layers of dust," he suggested softly.

"You don't even have clean bathwater," she blubbered through her tears. "I'm sorry—"

He leaned over her to pull the pillow away from her face, and she said, "Go ahead and smother me and let's be done with it. That will finish off the horrendous day I'm having."

He stared at her puffy eyes, red nose and flushed cheeks. Bruises and scrapes marred her creamy complexion. She looked so adorably discombobulated that he impulsively lowered his head to kiss her quivering lips.

"The Josephine I know doesn't let little things like showdowns, kidnapping and life-and-death encounters get to her. She defies it all. So what have you done with my wife?"

"She's turned into a crybaby," Josie said, then hiccuped.

Sol dropped another kiss on her lush mouth, then peeled off his shirt. He unfastened his double holsters and set them on the small drop-leaf table beside the window. He was pleased to note Josie watched his every move. Those forget-me-not eyes roamed over his chest in feminine appreciation. He would be only too happy to strip for her if it would make her stop crying, because damn if her tears didn't hit him right where he lived.

Facing down bloodthirsty outlaws, against lopsided odds, he could handle. Watching his spirited, strong-willed wife decompose before his eyes tormented him no end. He wanted the feisty, independent firebrand back.

Sol toed off his boots, pulled off his socks, then hooked his thumbs in the waistband of his breeches, inching them down to pool around his ankles. His drawers came off next. He watched Josie's eyes widen when she realized he was aroused.

He grinned wryly as he walked naked to the tub. "That's one good thing about used bathwater. It's usually cold."

He eased down into it, then grabbed the soap to lather himself. He watched her watch him—and wondered if even this cold bath could ease his fierce arousal. So far, it wasn't helping. Not when she kept staring at him the way she did. Not when she propped herself up on her elbows and didn't clutch the sheet when it dropped away, exposing her full breasts.

"I didn't even get a wedding night, you know," she murmured, her gaze following the bar of soap that he skimmed over his arms and chest.

"Neither did I. Try handing out drinks to a bunch of sweaty saddle tramps to gain information from them. You think I wouldn't have traded all of them for a night with you?"

"Would you?" she asked as she settled back against the headboard, allowing the sheet to dip lower, draping all too seductively over her hips.

Sol swallowed hard while desire thrummed heavily inside him. *Is this an invitation?* he asked himself cautiously. And did she want him for who he was, or because she wanted to lose herself in reckless passion to forget the unnerving ordeals she had endured lately?

Before Josie exploded into his life, it wouldn't have mattered, he reminded himself. Passion for passion's sake was reason enough for casual sexual encounters. Sol had walked away from them without looking back. But this sassy blonde wasn't just an occasional scratching of an itch.

"How long are you planning to soak in the tub?" she asked, striking such a provocative pose that he nearly howled.

Sol was up and out of his bath in the blink of an eye. "That better be an invitation," he growled as he snuffed the lantern on his way to the bed.

"I thought you'd never get here," she whispered, moving suggestively against him when he crawled in beside her.

The fear and concern that had pelted Sol while he desperately tried to track down Josie tonight instantly switched to impatient need. The moment her soft lips opened beneath his, he savored and devoured them. Sol struggled to draw breath when her hand skimmed his chest. Then she circled his navel with her forefinger.

"Have I thanked you properly for all the times you

have rescued me from disaster when I didn't think I needed someone to back me up?" she murmured as her moist lips glided down the side of his throat.

"You're welcome…" His voice fizzled out when her adventurous hand slid over his thigh muscles. Her thumb brushed lightly against his pulsating erection, and need hammered him relentlessly.

Sol heard someone moan. He decided it was him. Then he tried to draw much-needed air into his collapsed lungs, and couldn't. When her damp hair drifted over his belly in a provocative caress, and her warm lips whispered up and down the length of his rigid shaft, he groaned in unholy torment.

Oh, damn, thought Sol, as intense pleasure bombarded him from every direction at once. So much for his legendary self-control. He was falling apart, burning beneath the erotic feel of her tongue flicking playfully at him. He shuddered uncontrollably when the edge of her teeth skimmed over his sensitive flesh. She took him to the crumbling edge of sanity and left him desperately grasping for restraint—and failing.

"If this is your idea of gratitude, that isn't what I want from you," he wheezed, then gasped when she took him into her mouth to suckle him.

"That isn't what this is, husband," she whispered against his aroused flesh. "Gratitude is a hug or a handshake. Is that what this feels like to you?"

He could hear the teasing humor in her voice, and his barricade of self-control burst wide open. Sol realized he was shaking with inexpressible need for her.

He had kept a steady hand and cool head during all the showdowns and the frantic search for Josie—for the most part, at least. Now here he was, a quivering mass of shameless desire—barely surviving from one tantalizing caress to the next, wondering if he would make it through the night when intense pleasure threatened to swallow him alive.

Someone would have to complete the assignment and bring formal charges of fraud, murder and robbery before the court. Not Sol. He would die from these incredible sensations long before the break of dawn.

"Have mercy!" he croaked when her intimate kisses and caresses assailed him again, leaving him burning with a scalding fever that promised no relief.

"You can't have mercy," she teased as her tongue measured him from base to tip. "You get me instead."

"I can't handle much more, Josie," he panted, tensing in hopes of controlling the bubbling caldron of passion that threatened to turn his mind and body into steamy oblivion.

"Yes, you can, Mr. Deputy U.S. Marshal," she insisted playfully, then encircled him with her fingers. "Nothing fazes you. Not harrowing land runs, blazing showdowns or crazed criminals on the loose."

"*You* do," he admitted huskily. "You defeat me as nothing else can."

The honest but humbling admission gushed from his lips as he reached down to bring Josie's bewitching face back to his. Then he kissed her, so hungrily that he feared he would frighten her with the intensity of the need pounding through him.

"Truly? Then I can have my way with you anytime I please?" she questioned when he rolled her to her back.

She grinned impishly up at him, her blue eyes sparkling like sapphires, and his heart caved in, right there and then. Sol lowered his head to savor her sensual mouth, and inhaled the unique fragrance that surrounded her. She shifted to accommodate him when he settled suggestively above her. He wanted to become the living, breathing flame inside her, to possess her as she possessed him, until they were one body and soul, soaring in ecstasy.

"I need you more than I need my next breath," he confided as he reached between them to stroke her, delighting in the knowledge that her body was moist, welcoming and waiting for him. "Always have. Probably always will."

"I want you even more," she whispered, looping her arms around his shoulders and arching toward him. "From the very first time until the last, Solomon."

He drove into her and Josie hooked her legs around his waist, giving herself up to the radiating pleasure that escalated with each penetrating stroke. Being with Sol, feeling his thundering heart pounding in perfect rhythm with hers, soothed away all fear and dried every tear that had overwhelmed her in the aftermath of the emotional firestorm.

Solomon Tremain was the safe, secure, whimsical haven where she needed to be if she had any hope of regenerating her spirit and replenishing her energy. She drew from his powerful strength. His indescribable passion inflamed her soul, saturated her senses and seared her body.

Of course, she knew she was just another part of the endless assignments he had handled over the years. She suspected there were other women who had fallen apart in his arms and savored the immeasurable pleasure and passion he provided.

But for tonight—her belated wedding night—this was a special, unique and unforgettable moment she would remember forevermore.

He would leave her behind, but she would treasure the memories of his touch, his dimpled smile and his kisses, and tuck them away in her soul. Then she would devote all her time to building her ranch, and dream of him every night for as long as she lived....

Her thoughts spun out of control as the crescendo of rapturous sensations converged within her. Every wild, electrifying feeling intensified, and she cried out as spasms of unrestrained pleasure bombarded her.

Josie ached to tell him that she loved him deeply, desperately. But she wasn't sure that was what a man who would be gone tomorrow wanted to hear. There would be other women waiting in his future, she knew.

The discouraging thought left her clinging frantically to him as he shuddered above her. She had to let him go with a casual fare-thee-well and a thank-you-very-much for handing her a dream. She had no right to expect more from a deputy U.S. marshal who was only doing his job to right the wrongs of the world.

A tear dribbled from the corner of her eye when he pressed a tender kiss to her forehead, then eased down beside her. She muffled a sniff when he wrapped her protectively in his arms. She lay awake for the longest time, thinking she would trade her homestead for a lifetime with Sol, no matter where his assignments took them. She wondered what he'd say if she blurted out that she wanted to go with him when he left—after he finished laughing at her absurd request.

Eventually, Josie fell asleep with Sol's powerful body pressed familiarly to hers. She snuggled as close as she could get, wishing the night would last forever.

Josie came awake the next morning with a start. She glanced sideways to see a note on Sol's pillow. A simple calico gown and pantaloons, which he had thoughtfully provided after she'd whined about not having clean clothes, awaited her. But that green-eyed, raven-haired lawman wasn't here beside her. She could feel the emptiness swelling to fill every corner of her aching heart as she read his note.

> *I'm taking my prisoners to the capital at Guthrie to bring formal charges and testify at the trial. Morgan is riding with me. I asked Red Hawk to supply you and Muriel with sturdy shelters until you can hire a carpenter to construct a cabin. Enjoy your dream, Josephine.*
> *Sincerely, your husband.*

"'Sincerely'?" she bleated, fighting the onrush of more tears—and failing miserably. Josie had assumed she'd cried herself dry last night. Apparently, she held more water than she'd thought.

Blotting her tears with the crumpled sheet, she inhaled several restorative breaths and tried to pull herself together—somewhat at least. She dressed, rolled up her soiled clothing, then exited the hotel. The massive crowds of would-be settlers that had overrun the town were long gone.

Josie was surprised to see her eye-catching sorrel stallion tethered to the hitching post near the marshal's office. Obviously, Sol had found Rooster and left him waiting for her before he and Morgan rode away with the prisoners.

After entering the jailhouse and giving her statement to Colby, she came back outside. Absently, she petted Rooster's muscled neck before she climbed aboard.

She detoured to the lumberyard to order supplies, so she could build fences and sheds on her new property. Then she sent a message, asking her brother to bring her small herds of horses and cattle from his farm east of town.

She used the jaunt to her new homestead to give herself silent pep talks. She had corrals to build, after all. She didn't have time to wallow in self-pity. She had what she wanted…didn't she?

Her confused thoughts scattered when she gazed across the rolling prairie grass to see two teepees standing side by side in the distance. A bubble of laughter burst from her lips. She was delighted with the choice of housing, compliments of Red Hawk's labor. It made her feel closer to Sol in some odd, unexplainable way.

She had hoped Muriel would be on hand to distract her, but evidently, her friend had yet to leave the garrison. Josie sighed heavily as she dismounted. She was alone in the middle of nowhere. She had dry wood to gather for campfires, and she needed to mark off the location of future livestock pens and sheds.

"This is your life, Josephine," she lectured herself, unaware that she had used the version of her name Sol preferred. "Now make something special of this place. You have what you wanted."

Resolved to make progress, Josie hiked off toward the tree-lined creek. Visions of Sol danced in her head, keeping her company while she went about her chores— and missed him like crazy.

Two weeks later, Josie had completed one of her corrals. Earlier in the day she had staked out the horses delivered from Noah and Celia's farm. The cattle were wandering across the pasture, and Josie herded them back to her campsite to bed down in the corral for the night.

She was alone—as she had been quite often, since Grant sent a military escort to fetch Muriel every evening. Red Hawk had stopped by twice to give her a few pointers, help with heavy fence posts and check on her.

Nonetheless, loneliness was her constant companion—and she was growing tired of its monotonous presence. Worse, she was afraid to fall asleep at night, because Sol was always there to greet her in her dreams—like an impossible fantasy that could never come true.

When her horses jerked up their heads and glanced east, Josie grabbed her pistol. She was constantly on guard against possible claim jumpers, and now waited with her weapon pointed and feet planted, daring intruders to take what was hers.

She gaped in disbelief when Sol, straddling his powerful buckskin stallion, appeared over the rise. Josie stood there, her pistol dangling uselessly from her fingertips, as she watched him approach. The moment he dismounted, she took five running steps toward him, then forced herself to halt abruptly, unsure how he would react if she leaped into his arms and smothered him with kisses.

He took two long strides, then pulled up short to stare at her across the gaping space that separated them.

"What are you doing here?" she squeaked, savoring the unexpected sight of him.

He shifted uneasily, then glanced at the teepees. "I was wondering if you might have missed me."

"Missed you?" she repeated, like a mindless parrot.

"I thought I might spend the night here, since I am in the neighborhood."

"Neighborhood?" she echoed, as she glanced at the wide-open spaces surrounding them. "Our address is Middle of Nowhere, Oklahoma Territory. We don't *have* a neighborhood."

"You need to know that I deposited my expense reimbursement, fees and the rewards I've collected the past ten years in our joint account at the bank in town."

She blinked in surprise at the news, then squared her shoulders and thrust out her chin. "I'm not spending your money. As it stands, I can never repay you for all you've done for me."

He surveyed the corral full of cattle and noticed the string of tethered horses. "So you need nothing more from me? Is that what you're saying, Josephine?"

All the loneliness that had crowded in on her for a fortnight caved in like an unstable mine shaft. Pride be damned! The new life she had made for herself meant nothing without sharing it with Sol. He was the vital part missing from her days and nights.

She reminded herself that if she hadn't taken one risk after another to make the run and stake her homestead, she wouldn't have her own ranch now. Furthermore, she would never know if she could keep Sol as her husband unless she worked up the courage to tell him she loved him—even if he saw her only as a convenient and occasional lover.

It would sting her pride like nothing else could, but she would be with him every once in a while, at least.

Before she realized it, her feet were carrying her across the yawning abyss that separated them. Josie flew shamelessly into his arms and hugged the stuffing out of him.

"Take me with you, Solomon. I'll become a camp follower if that's what it takes to be with you," she pleaded as she buried her head against his shoulder, inhaled his musky scent and held on to him for dear life.

He chuckled when she hooked her legs around his waist and linked her arms around his neck. "You'd leave all this behind? Not to mention the money I deposited in our account to help construct the cabin?" He tipped her head back to kiss her, quenching a maddening thirst that for the past two weeks had driven him as close to crazy as he ever wanted to come. "By the way, law officers don't have camp followers. At least this one doesn't."

Josie's declaration that she wanted to be with him gave him hope that she wouldn't shoot him down—figuratively speaking—when he offered her a proposition.

"I testified against Bradley, his hired guns and several of his saddle tramps in Guthrie," Sol informed her. "Morgan got all spruced up for his court appearance and provided more evidence in the case, though his testimony sent Bradley into a maddened rage. He had to be restrained when he tried to go for Morgan's throat.... Morgan sends his regards, by the way."

Josie smiled in satisfaction, then kissed Sol. "Good. I like Elliot Morgan. He sort of reminds me of you."

Sol lifted a brow and stared at her.

"I'm glad Bradley exhibited his madness for the judge to see," she added.

"Bradley and his men will be spending several years in the territorial penitentiary," Sol told her. "After the trial, I sent a telegram to Judge Parker, requesting a new assignment."

"Oh." Her lovely face fell. He hoped that meant she was disappointed that he might be leaving again soon.

"I'm joining the Legion of Guardians in charge of law enforcement throughout this new territory created by the run. Morgan decided to put his gun skills to better use, and he also applied for an open position. I recommended him and he was hired, too."

Her slow, dazzling smile tugged at Sol's heartstrings. "So you'll be home often at night? Sharing my teepee?"

He stared straight into her eyes, anxious to view her reaction. "Only if you want to be with me, Josephine. I can stay in the canyon to the west if you prefer."

She frowned. "I'd much rather have you here. Besides, you would need permission to camp over there, White Eagle might not want you squatting on his allotment, whether he is there or not."

"He won't mind," Sol insisted.

"You better track him down and ask him," she advised. "Don't wanna put our neighbor on the warpath, do we?"

"I can speak for him, because I *am* him, Josephine. White Eagle is my Cheyenne name. The canyon and the pastures are part of my allotment and the horses grazing there belong to me. Red Hawk's land has a similar canyon and bubbling springs, and it sits west of mine. He's been overseeing my property."

Josie leaned back in his arms, her mouth open. It took a long moment for her to compose herself. "*You* own that marvelous retreat where I sneak in to bathe in the creek every chance I get?"

He nodded.

"And I can wander over there anytime I please because we're married…and I love you so much that being without you has been killing me, and my dream of a ranch is empty and unsatisfying when you aren't here with me," she said, all in the same breath.

Her thick lashes swept down and her face turned pink. Sol curled his forefinger beneath her chin to lift it, so he could stare into those hypnotic blue eyes. "The two weeks I've spent without you were nearly intolerable. I don't want to have to do that ever again…. I'm in love with you, too, Josephine." Confessing the words unlocked the vault of emotion he had concealed from himself and the world for years on end. "I want to be with you every chance I get."

"Truly?" Her stunning smile affected every bewitching feature of her face.

Sol's legs nearly buckled beneath him. He'd never seen her smile quite like that before. He felt like shouting to the heavens when she framed his face with her hands and kissed him until his eyes crossed and his legs did collapse, dumping them both on the ground in a tangled heap…. Sort of like the first time they'd tumbled downhill, and he'd fallen madly, completely in love with her.

He hadn't been able to help himself. No matter how hard he tried not to, and no matter how many times he denied it, his blustering had no effect whatsoever on his reckless heart.

"Have you ever made love in a teepee, wife?" he questioned huskily.

"Ask me that in about an hour, husband," she replied with an impish grin, then rubbed provocatively against him.

He raised his eyebrows as he hoisted her to her feet, then headed toward their temporary home. "You think I'll last an hour, after I've been so hungry and aching for you that the past two weeks felt like hell without you?"

"Twice in an hour then," she negotiated, as he ducked beneath the flap of the teepee, towing her behind. "Not counting later tonight, of course."

"I'll make a deal with you," he said huskily as he helped her out of her customary attire of breeches and a shirt—and she made quick work of divesting him of his clothing. "You can have whatever you want from me, for as long and as often as you want it."

She rose on tiptoe to kiss him softly, invitingly. "We have a bargain, horse trader."

"Best deal I ever made," he murmured as he took her down to the pallet. He propped himself on his elbow to memorize every feature of her face, comparing the sight of her to the image that had haunted his dreams for two endless weeks—a lifetime of loneliness and misery without her, to be specific.

"Love me forever and ever," she whispered. "This homestead is nothing without you. I want you with me always, Solomon."

When she bared her heart and soul to him, assuring him that he meant more to her than her long-held dream, he knew he had finally found the only woman he would ever want, the only woman he would ever need to make his life complete. He longed to experience all the tender emotions he'd never expected to feel in life.

"There is no place I'd rather be than with you, Josephine," he assured her as he stared at her adoringly. He loved her so deeply and devotedly that nothing seemed as crucial as being with her.

At last Sol had returned to his native land, and to his bewitching wife—the one and only love of his life. He came to her then, giving all that he was, and knowing that he had finally discovered what had been missing from his lonely existence.

Flesh to flesh and heart to heart, Sol and Josie soared as one, sharing the most cherished dream of all dreams…from that day forward and throughout eternity….

* * * * *

REQUEST YOUR FREE BOOKS!

 HARLEQUIN® HISTORICAL:
Where love is timeless

2 FREE NOVELS PLUS 2 **FREE GIFTS!**

YES! Please send me 2 FREE Harlequin® Historical novels and my 2 FREE gifts (gifts are worth about $10). After receiving them, if I don't wish to receive any more books, I can return the shipping statement marked "cancel." If I don't cancel, I will receive 6 brand-new novels every month and be billed just $5.19 per book in the U.S. or $5.74 per book in Canada. That's a savings of at least 17% off the cover price! It's quite a bargain! Shipping and handling is just 50¢ per book in the U.S. and 75¢ per book in Canada.* I understand that accepting the 2 free books and gifts places me under no obligation to buy anything. I can always return a shipment and cancel at any time. Even if I never buy another book, the two free books and gifts are mine to keep forever.

246/349 HDN FEQQ

Name _____ (PLEASE PRINT) _____

Address _____ Apt. #

City _____ State/Prov. _____ Zip/Postal Code

Signature (if under 18, a parent or guardian must sign)

Mail to the **Reader Service:**
IN U.S.A.: P.O. Box 1867, Buffalo, NY 14240-1867
IN CANADA: P.O. Box 609, Fort Erie, Ontario L2A 5X3

Not valid for current subscribers to Harlequin Historical books.

**Want to try two free books from another line?
Call 1-800-873-8635 or visit www.ReaderService.com.**

* Terms and prices subject to change without notice. Prices do not include applicable taxes. Sales tax applicable in N.Y. Canadian residents will be charged applicable taxes. Offer not valid in Quebec. This offer is limited to one order per household. All orders subject to credit approval. Credit or debit balances in a customer's account(s) may be offset by any other outstanding balance owed by or to the customer. Please allow 4 to 6 weeks for delivery. Offer available while quantities last.

Your Privacy—The Reader Service is committed to protecting your privacy. Our Privacy Policy is available online at www.ReaderService.com or upon request from the Reader Service.

We make a portion of our mailing list available to reputable third parties that offer products we believe may interest you. If you prefer that we not exchange your name with third parties, or if you wish to clarify or modify your communication preferences, please visit us at www.ReaderService.com/consumerschoice or write to us at Reader Service Preference Service, P.O. Box 9062, Buffalo, NY 14269. Include your complete name and address.

HHI1B

Are you ready for a thrilling adventure in the Wild West?

Read on for a sneak peek of
REBEL WITH A CAUSE by Carol Arens,
available December 18, 2012, from Harlequin® Historical.

The woman's petticoat caught in the wind and whipped up to slap her chin. She struggled with it and tried to keep hold of the horse at the same time. Zane figured he must have dust in his eyes. It looked like a piece of her undergarment had come loose and begun to whip and whirl about the horse's hooves all on its own accord.

Wage, not one for missing an opportunity, took that instant to give the horse a hard kick. The pony lurched forward then galloped double-time toward the west.

With massive clouds dimming the light, Zane nearly missed seeing the woman's mouth form a perfectly pink circle of surprise when his horse, Ace, galloped past her.

Guilt squirmed in his conscience for hightailing on by like that. It couldn't be noble to leave a lady stranded so far from town in her underwear, not with one hell of a storm ready to strike the earth like a hammer.

Setting his sights on Wage again, he noted the outlaw was still a good distance in the lead, but losing some ground to Ace.

One fat, chilly raindrop smacked him on the cheek. It wouldn't be long until this whole area turned into a mud puddle. He could likely reach Wage before that happened.

He sighed hard. Heat skimmed his lips. He sat up slow and leaned back in the saddle. Understanding the unspoken command, his horse slowed to an impatient trot.

"Hold up, boy."

Zane watched Wage disappear over the next hill. His

whole body and soul itched to be on the run after the outlaw. With a sour lump in his gut, he turned to look once more at the stranded woman.

Missy's mouth hung open in disbelief. It was surely an unbecoming gesture that her mother would reprimand her for if she could see it.

The hooves of his huge horse pummeled the ground. Clumps of sod, ripped from the soil, flew about. The earth trembled, bringing her hero closer.

In her whole sheltered Eastern life she'd never seen a man like this. The West rode wild in his smoky brown eyes. Black eyebrows slashed across his forehead like fired bullets. This was a man of adventure!

Dive into adventure with Missy and her rugged cowboy!

Look for
REBEL WITH A CAUSE
by Carol Arens.

Available December 18, 2012, from Harlequin® Historical.

HARLEQUIN® HISTORICAL:
Where love is timeless

TO OBEY HIS DUTY
IS TO DENY HIS HEART

LOUISE ALLEN

brings readers a tantalizing tale of royal temptation
and forbidden love.

Anusha Laurens is in danger. The daughter of an Indian
princess and an English peer, she's the perfect pawn in the
opulent courts of Rajasthan. Even so, she will not return
to the father who rejected her.

Arrogant *angrezi* Major Nicholas Herriard is charged with
bringing the alluring princess safely to her new life in
Calcutta. Nick's mission is to protect, to serve—but under
the searing Indian sun an initial attraction unfurls
into a forbidden temptation.

Forbidden Jewel of India

**Available from Harlequin® Historical
December 18, 2012 wherever books are sold!**